DECOMPOSE

LAYNE DEEMER

For Angela
*You loved this book before I ever wrote a word and I couldn't have
written it without you.*

Chapter One

A PLACE FOR EVERYTHING AND EVERYTHING IN ITS PLACE

THE FRONT DOOR OPENS WITH A LOW CREAK. "MOM? I'M HOME!"

"I'm in here, sweetheart," I call from the kitchen.

A few seconds later, my seventeen-year-old daughter appears in the doorway, leaning her slender body against the molding. Gertrude May Singleton—Gertie, for short—is my first-born. I pause my frantic dicing of celery and smile up at her. "How was your day?"

"It was really good." She grins and lets out a contented sigh.

I give her a knowing look. "Uh-oh, what's his name?" My girl has grown into quite a beautiful young lady, so it's no surprise that she's caught the eye of yet another boy.

"How do you do that?"

I purse my lips. "It's a mother's job to know everything there is to know about her children, sometimes even before they know it themselves."

"Well, if you must know—"

"I must." I wink at her.

She chuckles. "His name is Reed. He's new, and he's in my AP History class."

"He's new? The school year is nearly over. It's odd to start so late in the year."

"It is, but he just moved to the area."

I nod. "That must be rough, picking up and moving to a new school at the end of your junior year."

She shrugs. "If it is, you'd never know it by looking at him. He seems to have adapted well." A wistful look fills her face. "He's brilliant, actually. Shy and smart and perfect."

"Well, he sounds nice and you sound smitten." I tap her on the nose.

Gertie smiles. "You'd love him, Mom."

"If you do, then I'm sure I will, too. As long as he treats you with respect, then he'll pass my test." I resume my chopping, but continue to glance up at her.

She nods earnestly. "Of course."

She grabs a lock of hair and begins twirling it absentmindedly. There's more that she isn't telling me. "So what's your question," I prod.

"Uh, my question?" She looks down at the parquet floor. I set down my knife and turn so that my whole body is facing hers. Her eyes lift to mine, and I watch as her throat bobs. I give her a nod of encouragement, and she smiles shyly. "It's just, well, we've gotten to talking and I get the feeling he's gearing up to ask me out. I guess I'd just like your permission to say yes, if he does. I know how you and Dad feel about me dating someone you don't know, but I was wondering if maybe you might reconsider. That is, if you can trust my judgment?"

I smile proudly. "My sweet girl, I can see how hard it was for you to ask that question and I admire your tenacity. I don't think you've ever given us a reason to doubt you. I think it's fine if you want to go out with him."

Her hands cup her mouth, but her excitement bubbles out in a delighted squeal. "Really? Wow! Thank you so much!" She scrunches up her nose. "But, what about Dad?"

I hold up my hands. "Don't worry about him. Just like I trust you, your dad trusts me. I'll talk to him."

"I appreciate that, Mom."

"Now come over here and give your old mom a hug."

She skips across the floor and into my waiting arms. When I'm holding her like this, I can pretend for a moment that she's still the same tiny little girl with pigtails and red ribbons in her hair who used to climb into my lap. I press my nose to the top of her head and inhale the sweet scent of strawberries. I know it's from her conditioner, but I close my eyes and imagine we were just outside picking berries in the warm sun. She pulls back and smiles at me. "There's one for the money."

I grip her shoulder, giving it a light squeeze. "Two for the show." We both laugh. For as long as I can remember, we always repeated that rhyme to each other whenever we hugged.

The entire exchange lasts less than a minute, but it's just enough. It's like inhaling fresh air after holding your breath for hours. Sometimes that's how it feels when my family is gone all day. Like I'm holding my breath.

"Who died?"

Gertie and I startle at the intrusion. My son glares at the two of us as though we're locked in some conspiracy. Wyatt John is all of fifteen years old, but he was born with a questioning soul. The problem is, he's never content with the answers he finds, and so he's forever searching for new ones. A small amount of distrust is healthy, but lately I've felt his discontent radiating off of him in endless waves. I'd be lying if I said it didn't worry me.

"Hi, Wyatt. How was your day?"

He shrugs. "It was a day." These are the answers we get. He just rearranges the words in our questions and fires them right back at us. We never glean anything from what he tells us. I remind myself that he's a teenager and this is par for the course, but it's hard when all I have to compare him to is a sister who never behaved this way. But it isn't fair to compare them. They're not the same person. They're two separate individuals who merely bear the same origin.

Wyatt ambles over to the refrigerator and pulls out the orange juice. He twists off the cap and puts the opening against his mouth, drinking directly from the carton. Gertie grimaces and lets out a groan.

I shake my head. "Wyatt, how many times have I told you, *please* use a glass?"

He pops the cap back on the carton and slides it onto the shelf, closing the fridge door with his hip. He sidles out of the kitchen, calling over his shoulder, "I saved you the trouble of washing one. You're welcome."

Gertie's mouth rounds with shock. "I don't think there's any hope for him. I weep for the future," she says dramatically.

"He's not hopeless. He's just a fifteen-year-old boy. They grow out of it, or so I hope."

We giggle, but I instantly feel guilty. My son isn't a joke, and I should never make him one. And I most definitely should not be encouraging Gertie to laugh at her brother.

I sigh. "That's not fair of me. Your brother deserves our compassion." I pat her arm. "Why don't you go freshen up for dinner. Your father will be home soon."

With my kitchen to myself, I get back to work, chopping vegetables and checking on the roast in the oven. The radio on the counter is tuned to a station that plays calming instrumental music. As I finish preparing dinner, I ponder a few topics I could bring up to encourage a lively discussion at the table.

Gertie is easy. All you need to do is ask her about any of the clubs she's involved in, and she's off. She can speak on that subject for hours. Frank isn't so tough, either. A simple question about the latest medication to hit the shelves will have him pontificating on side effects and the dangers of mixing drugs. Wyatt, on the other hand, well, he's a different story. It's hard to get him to sit at the table, much less join in a conversation.

Normally, when I want to speak to someone, I'm looking for their heart. I want to find what moves them. What is it that makes them tick? What motivates them? But with Wyatt, none of that applies. It makes me sad to admit it, but my son doesn't seem to be motivated by anything, save for his video games. I knew that Xbox was a bad idea, but Frank assured me it wouldn't be an issue. I can still hear his patronizing voice. "Listen, Jeanette, a boy his age needs a healthy way to blow off steam. You wouldn't understand." Mm-hmm, and now look where that got us. I'll tell you what I don't understand. I don't understand how anyone could sit in a room for seven hours straight wearing tight fitted headphones and screaming at a screen. How is that, in any way, relaxing, much less "healthy"?

My thoughts are interrupted by the *beep beep* of the automatic door lock on Frank's car. A few minutes later, he enters the kitchen, gliding over to me and placing a chaste kiss on my cheek. "Mmm, something sure smells good, honey."

I grin, feeling my tank fill up with his approval. "It should. It's your favorite. Meatloaf, mashed potatoes, and seasoned mixed vegetables. Oh, and there's also chocolate cake for dessert."

"Jeanette, you spoil me." He peers down at me, cupping my face. "Never stop." His lips find mine, and I let myself give in for just a moment. But I can tell he'd like to push for more, and today is not the day.

I pull back and cock my head. "Now, Frank, last time I checked, it's only Monday. Try that on Tuesday, Thursday, or Saturday and you might just get the reaction you're looking for."

He groans. "I know, but maybe we should reconsider the schedule just this once—"

"Uh-uh," I chide, placing my finger on his mouth. "Sorry, dear. Schedules exist for a reason. They hold us accountable for the day's events. We cannot go around ignoring the rules at random. It would only bring about chaos, leading to a complete breakdown of our household." He nods, but doesn't seem convinced.

"What was it you told Wyatt the other day when he complained about the size of the TV?" I cock my head.

"If it ain't broke, don't fix it."

"Exactly." I bat my eyelashes at him and he chuckles softly.

I step away from him and brush my hands together. "Now, why don't I finish up in here and you go tell the kids that dinner is nearly ready?"

"Sure thing, love." He sighs.

This schedule was an idea I had early on in our marriage. My parents never had sex, and I don't mean that in the way that kids are certain their parents never do it because…gross. I know it didn't happen because my mother told me. It was one of the rare occasions when she was feeling slightly maternal. I was watching a movie and she came into the room and sat beside me. A delivery room scene was playing and when the doctor handed the mom her baby, my mother said, "That's the only good thing that can come from letting a man touch you, Jeanette. And once you have it, you don't ever have to let them touch you again." She said those words like a child was a gift, but she certainly never behaved that way.

When I met Frank, I was bound and determined to never let what we have turn sour. So, a sex schedule may seem a bit ridiculous, but really, I think it was one of the best ideas I've ever had.

I reach for the dishes out of the cabinet, counting out four matching plates. My blue Italian bone china sparkles in my hands. It was a wedding gift from my aunt. "Every good wife needs a set of fine china," the handwritten note said. She was right. Over the years, my collection has tripled, making it possible for me to use the good china for every occasion. When a table is adorned with only the best, it sets the tone for the meal. Family dinner is a sacred ritual. It should never be taken for granted.

I retrieve the meatloaf from the oven and arrange it on a serving platter. Leafy greens surround the succulent meat, which I've sliced into perfect portions. Holding either side of the dish, I make my way toward the bi-swing door that separates the dining room from the kitchen. I had Frank install it the week we moved in. The space was previously wide open, but I much prefer the grandiose entrance you can make when the door is pushed open and then automatically swings closed behind you. I give it a nudge with my toe and ta-da my way into the dining room, presenting my handiwork on a literal silver platter.

My family sits around the table before me. Gertie is to my left, looking posh with her hair out of her face and properly secured by a satin pink scrunchie. Wyatt occupies the chair on my right. His eyes are cast down at his lap where I can see his —not so concealed—phone. I clear my throat, and his hands still on the screen. He doesn't look up, but I still register it as a win. Finally, my eyes land on Frank. He's seated at his spot at the head of the table, eyeing me like I'm the meal. I give him my "behave yourself" look, but he just smirks.

I place the platter in front of Frank, and he begins serving himself. The side dishes are next as we take our portions and pass the food on to the next person. When it's my turn to hand the tray of meat to Wyatt, I pause until he tilts his head. His hair is in need of a trim. A dark fringe of bangs hangs low on his forehead, obscuring his eyes. I nod at him, and he reaches for the platter, muttering a tight "thank you" under his breath. It isn't much, but I'll take it.

I'm sitting opposite Frank, at the *other* head of the table. Head of the household isn't just a job for one. It's a dual role. It requires someone on the outside and someone on the inside. I make sure everything runs seamlessly within our home, which affords us all the ability to live unencumbered by worry, and Frank brings home the means to ensure I'm able to complete my job. We're a well-oiled machine.

I survey the table, feeling content. Everything I've ever wanted is here with me. And I'll stop at nothing to protect them from the evil of the world.

"GIRLY? WHERE YOU AT?" Henry Tadinger's voice slices through the dark.

"Please try not to speak so loudly. My family is asleep," I scold.

"Pshh, still don't know why the hell I had to come all the way over here so late," he grumbles.

"I already told you. The humming sound only happens at night." I shake my head. For someone who fixes cars and is skilled in electricity, he's not so bright.

"And why'd you tell me I had to walk over? I'm no spring chicken, you know? You said your street was all ripped up, but there ain't no construction happening here." He crosses his arms.

I flap my hand dismissively. "It was supposed to start this afternoon, but I guess it was delayed."

"Fine," he huffs. "Just show me where the problem is so I can go home and sleep like a normal person." He glares at me.

"That's what I've been trying to do." I take a deep calming breath and point toward the door of my shed. "It's right in here. Follow me."

Once we're inside, I let the door swing shut behind us. "I can't see a damn thing in here," Henry complains.

I flick on the light switch, bathing the entire room in a warm yellow glow.

"What the hell is that?" He points at the steel compost bin in the corner.

"We'll get to that, but first…" I push past him and tug open the circuit breaker box. I step back and motion for him to look inside. "The hum is coming from there. I'm not sure what the problem is, but I can't imagine it's good."

Henry trudges across the small space and peers into the open box. "Who did this wiring? Was it that doctor husband of yours?"

I roll my eyes behind his back. "He's a pharmacist and no. We hired someone we found online."

"Well, there's your problem. You can't trust that Internet. It's a web, all right. A web of lies." He leans in with his face inches away from the breakers. The lenses on his glasses are like Coke bottles, but they don't seem to be doing the trick. "Now, let's see here…" He presses a few buttons and I take a tentative step toward him. My hand drops into the pocket of my dress and my fingers fumble around until they make contact with the syringe I stashed inside. Henry's bony back is hunched over as he mumbles to himself about shoddy electrical work. I take another step and wrap my hand around the needle, pulling it out into the open. The light gleams off of the tip as I hold it out in front of me. One more step and I'm almost touching Henry. He hasn't even noticed. He's so engrossed in my circuit breaker box, I think he may have forgotten I'm even here. He's almost making this too easy. I raise my hand and jab the needle into the pulse on the side of his neck, plunging enough phenobarbital into his body to kill a two-hundred-seventy-five-pound man. I doubt Henry weighs that much, but I didn't want to take a chance.

The look on his face is one I've seen before—a mixture of

shock and confusion, followed by a brief flash of realization before the drug kicks in. The legs give out first and then the body collapses. Unconsciousness sets in quickly while the medication effectively shuts down the heart and brain within two minutes. It's painless and, although that might not be what someone like Henry deserves, it's the swiftness that appeals to me. It's over before he even knew it began. There's no resistance and no mess. Well, provided I act quickly. A body can sometimes release unwanted secretions, but that shouldn't happen until I'm finished.

Henry lies at my feet. His lifeless gaze is fixed on the ceiling. "Henry, Henry, Henry," I chide. "You only have yourself to blame, you know? The residents of this neighborhood trusted you with their cars *and* their children. You could've lived out your retirement in perfect harmony here, doing odd handyman jobs, fixing cars in your garage, and employing teenagers—teaching them valuable life skills. It was a win-win, but you couldn't keep your disgusting hands to yourself, could you?" I sneer as I walk around his body. "I know what you did to Jason Myers, so don't even try to deny it. Oh, that's right, you can't, can you?" I chuckle. "I saw the pictures, Henry. The ones you thought you had hidden in your tool chest." I shake my head. "You didn't even bother to lock it. It's almost as if you wanted to get caught."

I kneel down and begin undressing the old man. As I undo the buttons on his flannel shirt, my eyes roam over his face. I stop what I'm doing and slide his glasses off, glaring into his murky eyes. "Jason wasn't the only one, was he? How many others were there, Henry? He's only thirteen, you know? How could you do that to him? What's wrong with you?" I sigh. "Well, I guess that doesn't matter anymore, does it? And to think, Wyatt was going to start working with you this summer. Would you have tried this with him?" I shiver. "This isn't my fault. You brought this on yourself and you made it personal when you brought it into my home. It's my one rule, Henry, and you broke it. And now I've made it so that you can't hurt anyone else. I did what I had to do. I was just protecting my family."

I continue undressing him in silence. My slow even breaths are the only sound. Once Henry is naked, I wheel out my hydraulic lift cart and slide his body onto it. With a few pumps of the foot pedal, he's level with the opening of my compost bin. It takes a bit of finesse to move him from the cart into the bin, but after a few minutes, I have him safely secured inside. With a spin of the door handle, the bin is closed.

I give the metal container a hearty pat. "Nighty night, dear Henry. In your next life, you get to be food for my garden. I think you'll be more useful that way. I'll see you in thirty days."

Chapter Two

LETTING THE CAT OUT OF THE BAG

WHEN I WAS AROUND SIX OR SEVEN YEARS OLD, MY MOM WAS outside working in the garden. She was always out there, tending to her plants the way I wished she would to me. She even referred to them as her "children." Nurturing them with water and soothing words. I felt like I was always outside looking in, wilting right in front of her. It wasn't that I was blatantly ignored. It was more that I was forgotten. I was on par with the spare change you might find buried under a sofa cushion. You didn't even realize it was there, but for the few minutes that you did, you'd delight in its presence. Turning it around a few times to admire it and then stuffing it into your pocket where it would, once again, be forgotten. Where my mother was concerned, this was devastating. I just wanted her to notice me. But with my father, it was better that I blended in and went about unnoticed.

At a young age, I caught on pretty quickly that in order to survive this house, I needed to follow every rule and never ever break one. Still, on occasion, it happened. I was only human, and humans are inherently flawed. On this day, I had just gotten back from a trip to the library. I was holding in my hands a brand new copy of *The Polar Express*. I couldn't believe my luck. It had just released, and our library only had two copies. I managed to snag one and felt like I won a major prize. I burst into the house without a care in the world. My only desire was to curl up in my bed and read. I skipped down the hallway and flung open my bedroom door. I shoved it hard behind me without even thinking. The resounding *BANG* filled my room and bounced off of the walls. I stood still in the center of my room with my eyes closed, silently counting to ten. I only made it to four when I heard him. He was louder and more startling than any slammed door.

"Jeanette!" My father had the uncanny ability to make my skin erupt in goose bumps the instant I heard his voice. The boom of his footsteps came next as he stomped his way up from the basement and through the house. The closer the sound came, the more I started to shake. My body trembled with awful anticipation. I had broken a rule, and that never went unpunished. But this wasn't the first time I slammed a door and I knew my father's punishments grew harsher each time I broke the same rule.

My door flew open and the knob made a sickening crunch when it sunk into the plaster of my bedroom wall. I was too scared to turn around. My feet felt as though they were stuck in cement. I was sure I wouldn't be able to move, but my dad proved me wrong. He grabbed my shoulder and roughly spun me around. My eyes landed on his feet, but he fixed that, too, shoving a hand under my chin and pushing force-fully until I was looking right into his cold, dark eyes. "How many times have I told you not to slam your door?"

I felt tears prick the corners of my eyes, but I couldn't let them fall. It would be much worse if that happened. I swal-lowed hard and found the mole on the bridge of my father's nose. I always focused on that when I needed to face him. It gave the illusion that I was looking into his eyes while allowing me a bit of a reprieve. There was no fury in that mole. No hatred. "Too many times, sir." My voice was timid and meek, just the way he liked it.

He nodded with satisfaction. "And what do we say when rules are broken in this house?"

"Every action has a consequence," I parroted the words I knew by heart.

"Yes, it does, and I'm afraid the consequences were not severe enough last time. If they were, you wouldn't continue to be so careless, now would you?"

I lowered my head in agreement and made a quiet wish that this punishment wouldn't leave a mark. I was still nursing the wounds on my back from last week when I spilled water at the dinner table.

"Now, let's see." He tapped a finger on his chin. "For us to ensure this never happens again, perhaps you need to understand how brutal slamming a door can be."

My eyes widened with terror. He couldn't mean what I thought he meant, could he?

He seized my hand and tugged me forward. I was still holding *The Polar Express* in my other hand, and when he pulled me, it slipped from my grasp and landed face up on the tweed carpet. I kept my eyes on it as he yanked my body toward him. My feet tripped over each other as I struggled to keep my balance. When we were standing in front of the open door, he let go of my hand and gripped my wrist. He led my hand to the wood frame and splayed my fingers around it. I knew what was coming, but I told myself I could survive it. It was my own fault for slamming the door in the first place. My father walked around me until he was standing beside me. The door was in his hands and he called my name, commanding my attention. "This hurts me more than it hurts you. But when rules are broken, lessons must be learned."

I let my eyes fall from his. My gaze drifted, once again, to the book on the floor. The light on the front of the train was a warm yellow. I imagined diving headfirst into the brightness, bathing in its golden warmth. It lit the way, making it possible for that train to travel all the way to the North Pole. The place where magic lives. I kept my eyes trained on the cover with such intensity; I swore I could hear the chug-a-chug of the engine and the high pitch choo-choo! when the conductor pulled the whistle. I felt completely transported. Lifted out of this hell and placed in a world of possibilities. It was working. Until my father shoved the door with all of his might. The force of the slam broke every one of my fingers and reminded me that the fantasy world of my books wasn't real. There was no magic train that would steal me away from here in the middle of the night. I would have to stay here and endure this life until I was old enough to leave.

My father punished every broken rule, doling out consequences for every action that didn't fit his narrative. But the rules were more of a vessel for his anger and insecurities. He thrived on being feared, and in order to maintain that status, he created a guideline for me to conduct myself, making sure it was impossible for me to always succeed. My failures kept life interesting for him and a nightmare for me.

And throughout it all, my mother remained indifferent, turning a blind eye to everything my father did. I'm certain she heard my cries that day, but she kept right on working in her garden. She never asked if I was okay, never tried to console me. She was just…absent.

After a trip to the hospital, where I lied and told the doctor that I pinched my own hand in a car door, I picked the book up off of my carpet and walked it right back to the library. I pushed it into the return slot, never having read a page. When my kids were younger, a movie version of that book was released. Frank took them to the theater to see it while I feigned a headache and stayed home. To this day, I've never opened that book and I've never been able to watch the movie. Not because it holds such a dark memory, but because it was the day I realized my fantasies wouldn't save me. That day, I decided the only way to survive in life was to create rules of my own. Rules that I would eventually demand my father follow.

You might think after what I went through as a child, I would steer clear of rules. But actually, I've found a comfort in them. The difference between my father's rules and mine is at their core. His were created as a form of dominance and mine are rooted in love. The only similarity between the two is that they exist to maintain order.

At a young age, my father sat me down and told me, "Jeannie, rules aren't developed overnight. They take time and require much forethought. And once a rule is set, it's set. Breaking it is unthinkable. Understand?" I nodded immediately because listening to my father was the number one rule in our home. He governed our household like a king. His policies were ironclad, and he doled out swift punishment whenever he was crossed. Once I understood their importance, I obeyed all of his rules without question. The scars on my back still serve as a reminder.

Over the years, I've established many rules for myself. *Things that take less than a minute to do should be done immediately*, and *a calm voice is more effective than a raised one*, both ensure a tidy household and a peaceful home environment. While rules like, *never gossip, it's bad form* and *you can be a lady and still show strength*, help maintain proper etiquette and develop a strong moral code.

I have rules that are specific to each person in my life. Frank craves physical affection, so even if it's not one of our scheduled sessions, I still maintain a tactile connection with him, resting a hand on his shoulder or giving him a lingering hug when he comes home from work. Gertie thrives on positive affirmation. I try to give her daily praise, even if it's for something as trivial as shaving off a few minutes of her lengthy morning routine. And then there's Wyatt. I'm ashamed to admit that I'm not quite sure what he requires.

The only rule that currently applies to him is patience. If I wait long enough, I'm sure he'll come around. Eventually.

Some rules allow me to breeze through mundane chores, while others make the more difficult tasks much simpler. There are some rules that change over time, adapting to the current climate of life. And there are some that remain rigid.

All rules are sacred, but at the very top is one rule that is, without question, the most important. The cardinal rule, as I call it, is *those I care about must be protected at all costs*. It's ten words, but in that order, they are the ten most important words in my world. I created this rule to ensure that the people I love remain safe and happy, and if anyone should threaten that safety or happiness, then they must be disposed of by any means necessary.

And that's exactly what happened to Henry Tadinger.

I FLICK the oven light on and peer into the glass window. Rich rivers of golden au jus glide over the pot roast, marinating it as it cooks. I have no doubt it will taste divine. Over the years, I've worked hard to perfect my skills as a cook. The food I prepare provides nourishment for my family. It's one of my most important roles in life and I take it very seriously. Almost as seriously as I take my garden. Which reminds me…

I wanted to snip some parsley for my herbed potatoes. I pad over to the back door and slide out of my house slippers. Wiggling my toes, I step into my white Keds. They're nearly two years old and still the same brilliant white they were when I bought them. Soaking them in a one-to-three ratio of bleach and water every month is the secret. I lean over and tie my shoes, making bunny ears with my laces. My children are nearly grown, but it's a habit I've never been able to let go of. Once a mother, always a mother.

Stepping outside onto the concrete pad, I breathe in deeply. The fresh air fills my lungs and I close my eyes, reveling in the feeling. "Ahh." I exhale and gaze up at the crystal blue sky. What a lovely day in Whispering Woods. My family and I moved to this cozy little suburban neighborhood five years ago. It's nestled in a small town in Eastern Pennsylvania and is a little slice of paradise.

The sun warms my back as I bounce toward my pride and joy. My garden. Its beauty never ceases to amaze me. It occupies a fifteen-foot square patch of my backyard. A wooden fence affixed with metal wire surrounds the perimeter. The knots and wormholes in the wood give it a rustic charm, while the rich mahogany stain adds just the right amount of upscale touch. A small gate is latched with an intricate combination lock. My hands move effortlessly over the dials, and with a satisfying *click*, the gate is unlocked. I tug on the handle and carefully step onto the stone walkway inside.

A series of six raised beds arranged in neat rows stands before me. A path of cobbled stone weaves up the middle, branching out to envelop each side of the beds. Every section is labeled with wooden stakes that I crafted myself out of the off falls from the lumber we used for the beds. Each piece of wood has been stained the same mahogany color to create uniformity. Nothing is out of place. I know because I planned it that way.

I run my palm along the tops of my tomato plants. I recently transplanted them. They're less than a foot tall, still just babies. But when they're ready, they will be beautiful. My tomatoes are all an heirloom variety. The ripened fruits will be gorgeous shades of plum, orange, and auburn. I reach for a leaf and rub it between my fingers and then hold them up to my nose, inhaling the perfect scent. New life.

I only grow organic vegetables in my garden, which I start myself from seeds that I cultivated from the previous year's harvest. I waste nothing.

I survey the orderly layout in front of me. It's the beginning of May. There's almost two months left of spring, but I'm not sure Pennsylvania got the memo. It's just after four in the afternoon, and the heat is borderline oppressive. The conditions are perfect for my compost, and I feel an almost giddy glee as I size up the empty bed in the far left corner. It's almost time for my peppers to move to their final resting spot. Just a few more weeks.

My herbs occupy the first bed on the right. I glance at the placards, reading off the names aloud. "Basil, you're looking quite well today. And Dill, I have salad plans for you this week. Ah, Rosemary, there's a whole chicken in my fridge with your name on it. Now, let's see, where is Parsley hiding? Oh Parsley," I singsong. "Come out, come out, wherever you are." I turn my head this way and that in a pseudo game of hide and seek and then zero in on the leafy plant. "Aha! There you are. Your services are needed today, my friend. I have some potatoes in the oven that just won't be complete without you sprinkled on top." I reach into the pocket of my blue gingham dress and pull out my shears. I lean over and brush my hand along the plant in search of the perfect fronds, snipping them off and catching them in my cupped hand. "That'll be all today, children. As you were." I nod like a schoolmarm and turn on my heel.

"Ahoy there, Jeanette," a voice calls out as I exit the garden, locking the gate behind me.

"Bob. Well, that's just great," I say under my breath. I have nothing *against* him, but I suppose I have nothing *for* him either. Bob Stuart lives in the lilac split-level next door and is, for the most part, a good neighbor. He keeps his lawn mowed and his flower beds in order. There's no chipping paint anywhere on the exterior of his house. He lives alone save for his toy poodle pretending to be a dog, but even Rusty is relatively bark-less. And with the gleaming white synthetic fence between our properties, I barely ever see his dog unless he's holding him like he is right now. The lattice topper on the fence was my idea, but on days like this, when Bob can easily spy into our yard through the holes, I regret choosing design over practicality.

I raise my hand and feign a look of happiness. It isn't hard to do. I just picture something that brings me joy, and the smile comes naturally. Today I'm imagining my compost bin, which I was just about to visit. "Hello, Bob. Lovely day, isn't it?"

He nods. "Sure is! I was just admiring my azaleas out front. Have you seen them?"

Have I seen them? They are the most obnoxious shade of orange, and they clash horribly with the purple siding on his house. It's as though his home were preparing for Halloween five months early. They're an abomination, if I'm being blunt. But I just smile and think about warm compost. "Yes, sir. They are quite the sight to behold." I'm careful not to lie. That's not a rule that I intend to break.

Bob grins, seemingly satisfied with my response, and I make a beeline for my shed. Just as I reach the door, he bellows, "Terrible thing about Henry Tadinger, isn't it?"

I grit my teeth and pull in a breath through my nostrils. "Uh-huh. It's just awful. Have you heard anything new?" There's a beautiful lilac bush beside my shed that's in full bloom, and when I crane my neck to peer at Bob, the delicate flowers nearly touch my nose. I watch him through the branches, using them as a shield for whatever he's about to say.

He half shrugs. "Not much. In fact, word on the street is, it's a dead-end case."

I nod and bite at my lower lip to keep from smiling. We're far enough apart and with the bush in the way, I doubt he'd see, but I can't risk being careless at this point. "That's too bad. Well, if you'll excuse me. I need to get a move on if I want to have dinner ready by five!"

I don't wait for him to respond. I punch in the code on the screen to disarm the alarm system and then I unlock the door. It may seem like overkill—Frank sure thought so—but as I told him, all of my most prized artifacts are housed inside these walls. They must be protected at all costs. If someone tries to breach my lock, my alarm system will be activated, sending out an alert to all of my devices. There's way too much at stake for me to be willy-nilly about security.

This shed is my safe haven. Frank gifted it to me for our anniversary a few years ago. I had one at our old house, but it was nothing compared to this. I designed this shed to look like a small Cape Cod style cottage. It even has a little front porch with a small chiminea and a bench swing. We chose the same shade of pastel blue siding as our home with mahogany trim to match the garden. It's perfection.

My entire collection of SnapLid storage containers is housed in here. They're all arranged by shape and size on custom-built shelving that takes up the entire left wall. I have a little side business selling them door to door and—humble brag alert—it's been fairly lucrative for me. It's helped fund my garden supplies and given me a way to stay "in the know" with my neighbors. I keep other gardening tools in here, as well, but the pièce de résistance stands before me in all of its steely glory. My compost bin.

I had it custom-built by a welder I found on Facebook Marketplace. He was hard up for cash, so I made him an irresistible offer and he turned out this beauty within a week's time. Due to its size, it had to be installed on the shed's foundation before the walls went up. It's enormous, but experience has shown me that it has to be. Resting on a wooden frame made from that same mahogany stained wood, its steel body is roughly five feet in diameter and seven feet deep. I had it capped with a rounded steel door that doubles as a crank. When I place my hands on it and grip it like a steering wheel, I can turn it, effectively rotating the contents inside. I need to turn this compost every three days to ensure that the microbes and essential bacteria have enough time to grow and break down what's inside. This isn't your average everyday run-of-the-mill compost bin.

I give the wheel a turn. "How's it going in there, Henry?"

Chapter Three

HOME IS WHERE THE HEART IS

"OH, CRAP CRACKERS!" I CHASTISE MYSELF WHEN A DROP OF AU jus spills over the platter and onto the white tablecloth.

"Mom! What has gotten into you? I can't believe you used such crassness at the dinner table," Gertie mock exclaims, covering her mouth as a laugh bubbles out.

Frank pipes up from his end of the table. "She's right, you know? How do you think those poor crackers feel when you take their name in vain like that?"

Their ridicule even has Wyatt chuckling. I glance over at him with humor dancing in my eyes, but his laughter dies as soon as our eyes meet. I try not to take it personally. It's just a phase.

"Ha. Ha," I say with a roll of my eyes. "Laugh all you want, but this gravy stains and now I'm going to have to whip out my arsenal of products to get it out."

Frank smirks. "That's right, and you love every minute of it. It's a challenge and you never shy away from one of those."

He's right, and from the way he's beaming at me, he knows it. I chuckle and take my seat across from him. Clapping my hands, I start off the conversation. "So, who wants to tell me all about their day?" Twin groans come at me from either side as my children simultaneously shake their heads.

"You know why she does this, right?" Wyatt asks his sister.

"I sure do," she answers.

They both sit up straight with their hands folded neatly on the table. "Because it's important to me that you feel as important as you are," they recite in unison. They follow it up with a fit of laughter and I can only shake my head. I've been saying those words to them ever since the day they were born. I won't apologize for it no matter how ridiculous they think it is. The point is, I was nowhere close to being important to my parents and I never want either of my children to feel that way.

"All right, all right, apparently it's pick on Mom day and I missed the memo." I try to sound annoyed, but it falls flat. I can overlook the teasing if it means my kids are getting along. It never used to be an issue, but the older they've gotten, the more strained their relationship has become. It would be easy to pin it all on Wyatt, but Gertie could make more of an effort as well. In this case, even if they're laughing at me, at least they're laughing together.

"You know we're only kidding, Mom," Gertie reassures me.

"Speak for yourself." Wyatt's voice is barely above a whisper, but there's no missing what he said. I deflate a little.

"Ahem." Gertie clears her throat. "It's nice that you care so much about us and want to hear all about our day. I'll tell you what, I'll go first."

I smile at her. She's assumed the role of referee between me and her brother. It's not a fair position for her to be in, and it makes me feel partially to blame for the distance between the two of them. "Okay, sweetie, I'm listening."

"Well," she says, folding her hands in her lap. "It was a pretty humdrum day. Nothing all that exciting happened.

Let's see…the cafeteria served tacos at lunch, I got an A on my Physics paper, oh, and I found a dollar on the sidewalk in front of the school."

"An A on your Physics paper? Honey! That's incredible news!" I clap my hands rapidly.

"Yes, it sure is, Gertie. Good for you, kiddo," Frank adds.

Gertie's cheeks flush and she looks shyly at the table. "It was a bit of a surprise, if I'm being honest. Mr. Leonard is pretty tough."

I bat away her modesty with a flap of my hand. "Nonsense. You worked hard and it shows. I'm not saying you should gloat, but it's okay to feel a little pride in yourself. You earned it."

She looks up at me. "Thanks, Mom."

"Suck up!" Wyatt coughs the words, but we all heard him loud and clear.

I turn to face him. "And how about you, Wyatt? What sort of things transpired in your day?"

A Cheshire cat grin fills his face and I regret my question immediately. "My day? It was a banner one," he exclaims. "First, I robbed the Wawa on Third and Penn. It was a little disappointing, though, because the register only had eighty-nine dollars. Still, not too shabby. Then, I walked the rest of the way to school, but kept right on walking when I got there because why the hell would I ever want to waste such a beautiful day stuck in there? And I rounded out the afternoon by squatting in the old abandoned barn on Elmhurst, where I met some friends for a hearty game of beer pong. So," he splays out his hands, "as you can see, it was a pretty productive way to spend a Wednesday." He looks so proud of himself, and it makes me wonder where I went wrong. He used to love to tell me everything about his day. His *actual* day. Not some made up narrative that he's constructed just to get a rise out of me. Maybe it's my fault. Actually, I know it is. I'm the parent and somewhere along the way, I failed. And

Frank? Well, he's barely containing his laughter right now. He and Wyatt get along well, and although I might not approve of the behavior, at least they have a connection.

"Nice one, son." Frank snorts. When his eyes catch mine, he sobers up. "Um, but maybe you should back pedal a little on the details. That was a bit much." He shoots me an apologetic glance and I tip my head in thanks.

"Is any of that even true?" Gertie asks, wrinkling her nose.

Wyatt slides his eyes over to hers and shrugs. "Maybe. Maybe not."

"Okay!" From the surprised looks on their faces, I guess I said it much louder than I meant to, but I don't bother apologizing. That conversation needed to end. "So, Frank, were you able to fit in that lunchtime foursome you had hoped to?"

"I did!" His whole face lights up the way it always does when he's about to talk golf. It's a subject that the kids and I find terribly boring, but we indulge him. "Cliff and I met up with Jeff and Tom, those slimy bastards."

"Honey, I don't know why you and Cliff don't find a new duo to play with." I sigh.

"It's fine. They're tough to beat, so at least they bring a challenge to the game. I just wish they weren't so obnoxious. Just today, Tom was giving Cliff a load of shit for not finding Tadinger yet." Frank shakes his head.

My ears perk up at the mention of Henry's name. "You're not serious? Why is it Cliff's fault? He's just one officer. It's not fair to pin it all on him."

Frank met Officer Cliff Duran during a routine traffic violation two months after we moved here. A huge maple tree with wild branches concealed a stop sign and since we were new to the area, Frank had no idea it was even there. When Cliff pulled him over, he spotted the golf clubs in the back seat and the conversation quickly shifted from running a stop sign to planning a foursome later that week. Frank never even got a ticket. I'll admit, I wasn't too keen on this new friendship at first, but now I think it just might be one of the best things to happen since we moved here.

"I know and Cliff knows that, too," Frank continues, "but it still bugs him that they haven't located him."

"Hmm." I nod. "And did Cliff happen to mention if they have any more clues on his whereabouts?"

"Actually, he told me today that he thinks it's a cold case."

"Really?" I ask, masking my excitement as surprise.

"I'm afraid so. They aren't closing the case, but it's been three weeks and there haven't been any leads at all." Frank leans in, his voice dropping to a whisper. "There *was* a new development, though."

I feel pin pricks on the back of my neck and my forehead begins to bead with sweat. "What kind of development?" My voice betrays me with a slight crack at the end, but no one seems to notice.

"This stays in this room." Frank locks eyes with each of us and we nod in agreement. "It turns out old Henry Tadinger was a bit of a creep. A couple of officers were searching through his garage and they found a rusty tool box with pictures in it."

"Pictures of what?" Gertie asks, her forehead creasing.

"Well, I'd rather not say, but I'll tell you this, that man should never have been around young boys in this neighborhood and I hope that his disappearance means he's gone for good." Frank grits his teeth. I know exactly what he's talking about. Try as I might, I can't get the image of poor Jason out of my head. "They thought at first, the family of the boy might've had something to do with it. You know, like a revenge thing."

My heart rate begins to elevate. I don't want to get caught, but I also don't want Jason's family to take the blame. They've been through enough already. "You said, 'at first,' does that mean they no longer think that way?"

Frank shakes his head. "They questioned the parents and

that poor kid. Turns out they were vacationing in Florida the week Henry went missing. It's a solid alibi."

I exhale slowly, feeling immensely grateful. If the police had continued to suspect Jason's family, I wouldn't have confessed, but I would've had to plant some evidence to shift the case. I'm glad it won't come to that.

"I was supposed to start working in his garage this summer," Wyatt adds. "I guess it's a good thing that won't happen."

"You can say that again, son," Frank agrees.

Wyatt's face splits into a wide smile. "I guess it's a good thing that won't happen."

Leave it to my son to make a joke out of something so horrible, but we all join him in laughing because it's what we all need right now. As I sit here among the three most important people in my life, I think about Henry. My motives may have been to protect my son, but now that he's composting, he will never be able to hurt anyone again.

Chapter Four

KILLING TWO BIRDS WITH ONE STONE

IT'S ALWAYS AN EXCITING DAY WHEN A NEW SHIPMENT OF SnapLid containers arrives. The line is constantly expanding, and every three months, I get a box of new styles. I've been a rep for SnapLid for nearly four years. I know the business in and out, and I use the containers in my everyday life so I can speak to their durability and impeccable quality.

The growing trend these days is to host *online* parties. I have a few reps on my team who only sell that way and they have a lot of luck with it. I, on the other hand, am a firm believer in the power of door-to-door sales. It's a dying art, and that's a shame. The way I see it, the only way to truly make a personal connection with someone is by speaking with them face-to-face. Nothing quite compares to handing over a container so that a person can hold it in their own hands. I know a lot of people are content with buying something based solely off of a picture, but I much prefer doing it in person. And I believe that's why I've been the top salesperson in the Northeastern region for the past three years.

Today I'm showcasing the pie safe container and the medium round casserole. I load both into my denim duffel bag along with plenty of order forms. I also pack some freshly baked zucchini bread sliced and arranged in a small rectangle container—a gift for our new neighbors. They moved in a few weeks ago, and I've yet to give them a proper Whispering Woods welcome.

Once I have everything packed away, I breeze out the front door and begin my "visits," as I like to call them. This isn't only about peddling merchandise. Stopping by my neighbors' homes allows me the opportunity to check up on everyone. It's the most effective way to ensure that tranquility is thriving and the neighborhood remains safe.

That's how my first suspicions about Henry started. I was making my rounds, demonstrating our medium-sized container when I saw Jason leaving Henry's house. He started out briskly walking away from the garage, but as soon as his foot touched the sidewalk, he bolted, turning his head a few times to look behind him as if someone might be chasing him. It was such an odd exit; it stopped me in my tracks. I'm embarrassed to admit it now, but at first, I thought maybe Jason had stolen something from Henry. It sickens me now to think about it. How I felt concern for a monster like him.

I walked up the cracked driveway toward the garage and noticed the door was slightly ajar. I'm sure that was due to Jason's hasty exit, but it put me on high alert. Something told me not to go barging in. Instead, I peered in through the opening, careful not to make a sound. Henry was standing in the corner of the garage with his back to me. His pants were around his ankles and he was leaning over to reach for something on the ground. A Polaroid photo. I watched as he scooped it up, pulling up his pants as he stood. He set the photo onto a work bench next to a camera and then fastened his belt. When he turned to retrieve the picture, I ducked. Slowly, I craned my neck until I saw Henry pick up a toolbox that was stashed inside a cabinet. He was holding the Polaroid, and although I could only see his profile, there was no missing the intensity of his gaze before he dropped the picture inside the toolbox. A few days later, I waited until I knew Henry wasn't home and then I snuck inside his garage to look at the picture.

Henry Tadinger was a vile, disgusting man. Now he's three days short of becoming rich, organic topsoil for my garden. And that's thanks, in part, to door-to-door visits like the ones I'm embarking on today.

The first home in my circuit is Bob Stuart. I groan as I stumble up the front walkway toward his gaudy house. Rusty's incessant scratching on the other side of the door begins the instant my foot lands on the cement pad. I could skip Bob's home altogether. He never buys anything from me, but he's a busybody and people like him tend to know things that are of value to people like me. My hand is in a fist, poised to knock, but the door flings open before I ever make contact.

"Jeanette! How are you?" He looks me up and down, settling on the bag hanging off of my shoulder. His eyes narrow slightly. I almost put him out of his misery and cut right to the chase, but that's not the way this dance goes.

I grit my teeth and launch into my carefully rehearsed spiel. "Hello there, Bob. You're looking well today. I'm just stopping by to show you the latest additions to the SnapLid line. Tell me, are you a pie baker, by chance?"

His eyes flare with amusement and he shakes his head.

"Very well, then I'm guessing our new pie safe container is of no use to you, however, I'm certain our magnificent medium round casserole dish would be something you could put to good use. It's perfect for leftovers or when it's your turn to bring the spinach dip to a party." I chuckle and he gives me a tiny sympathetic laugh.

Once I hit all of my talking points, it's time for the demonstration. I take out the casserole dish, popping off the lid and handing the container to Bob. He flips it over and knocks a fist against the bottom. "I have to say, this does feel mighty sturdy. Is this as durable as the last thing you brought over or the thing before that?" I suppress a groan. At the very least, he could call the containers by name rather than "thing." He blathers on, "What happens when you drop it? Will it crack? Shatter? Explode into a million tiny pieces?" His beady eyes bore into mine. I've done drop tests before, but I think this is the first time Bob has ever asked for one.

I splay out my hands. "Let's find out." His brows lift in shock, and I goad him on. "Go ahead. Drop it."

He hesitates for only a second and then he opens his hands, letting the container fall to the concrete slab. I watch with confidence as it bounces a few times before coming to a standstill. I scoop it up and hand it back to him. He turns it over and over in his hands, assessing it from every angle. "Huh. Not even a scratch. Impressive."

I nod, filling with pride for the company I represent.

Bob leans in and holds his hand aside of his mouth. "Between you and me, I think our new neighbors could use a few of these in their kitchen." He snickers.

Here we go. This is what I came here for. "Excuse me? I'm sorry, I'm not sure I follow." I brace myself for whatever it is Bob is about to share with me.

"Well, last night, I was sitting out on my patio with a glass of wine, minding my own business"—*Uh-huh, sure you were* —"when lo and behold, I heard the most tremendous crash. Poor Rusty was so startled he fell right off my lap!"

My interest is piqued. "What kind of crash?"

"It sounded like breaking glass, but not just one glass. This sounded more like an entire box of dishes hit the floor."

"Really? Did you happen to find out if anyone was hurt?"

"Well, I went over to make sure everything was okay, but the kitchen window slammed shut and the blinds were drawn. Then I heard a repeated *thump thump* sound and I, uh, decided they probably didn't want my company, if you know what I mean?" He wags his eyebrows.

I know exactly what he's inferring, but the look on my

face must say otherwise because he decides to add on an unnecessary tidbit of information. "If you ask me, I'd say the new couple is into some kinky shit."

"Have you met them yet?" I ask with a desperate edge to my voice.

His eyes widen as he nods. "I've met her, but not him. She was on her deck one day last week and I stopped over to introduce myself. We got to talking and before I knew it, a whole hour had passed!" I'm not surprised. If I don't watch myself, the same could happen here. Once Bob gets his hooks into you, he isn't quick to let go. "She's nice. Pretty quiet. Come to think of it, I did most of the talking." *Imagine that.* "What about you? Have you been by their house yet?" He juts his chin at me.

I grin. "No time like the present! I'm heading over there next." I hand Bob an order form that I know he'll toss into the trash as soon as I'm gone. "Have a good rest of your day," I say as I turn on my heel.

"You, too, Jeanette! And, uh, I'd be careful with anything breakable if I were you," he calls.

Great advice, Bob. I roll my eyes. Despite his insistence that something disgusting is going on with our new neighbors, it seems more likely the sound he heard was an accident. Maybe a box of breakables was mistakenly dropped. They did just move in so it wouldn't be unheard of. And a cacophony of thumping? Well, that could've easily been the sounds of home improvement—or if it's what Bob thinks it was, then it's between consenting adults and it's none of our business.

I pause on the sidewalk and look at the pale orange Cape Cod next door to Bob. It once belonged to sweet little Angela Heart, an elderly woman in her eighties. She lived in that home her entire adult life. She and her husband, Stuart, raised their three daughters there and when Stuart passed away four years ago, Angela stayed on. She kept going about her life in that same home until last year when she decided it was too much for her and she moved in with her oldest daughter.

A few weeks ago, I watched a large moving truck pull up and spied a slight woman with shoulder-length dark hair and bangs scurry back and forth between the truck and the house. She was carrying boxes that could've easily weighed twice what she does, but she did it with ease. It impressed me. There was also a large muscular man with tattooed arms making similar trips. By the way they were standing close to one another, it was apparent they were intimately connected.

When I reach the bright blue front door, I pause for a moment to collect myself. A shiver of excitement runs down my spine. I love meeting new neighbors. I knock three times in quick succession. Less than a minute later, the door slowly creaks open and big round eyes peer out at me.

I give a friendly wave. "Hello, there! I'm Jeanette Singleton. My husband, Frank, and I live over in 102." I arc my thumb toward my home. "It's the pale blue one, right over there."

The door opens a little wider, but the woman still stands slightly behind it as though it were a shield. Even though she's partially obscured, I can tell it's the same petite brunette I saw hefting the moving boxes. She looks to be in her late twenties or early thirties. There's not a stitch of makeup on her face, but she doesn't need it. She has the sort of beauty that doesn't need to be enhanced. It's a little strange that she's not speaking, but maybe she's shy. "I'm here to welcome you to Whispering Woods," I exclaim. "It's a wonderful place to live. You'll love it here. We're such a close-knit community. Always watching out for each other's children." At the mention of that last word, I watch her eyes for any change. It's always struck me as odd when someone freely asks another person if they have kids. I've always viewed it as a delicate topic, and rather than blurt out the question, I toss the word out into the air to see where it lands. She stays still, hiding her tiny frame behind her door so that only her eyes are visible. The mere mention of kids seems to have no effect at all. If I had to guess, I'd say that while she doesn't have children of her own, the subject is not off-limits.

I lean in slightly. It's akin to approaching a frightened animal. "I have two teenagers, myself," I say, pressing my hand over my chest. "My daughter, Gertie, will be eighteen this summer and Wyatt, my son, will be sixteen in a few months. They go to Vernon High." I pause as the words overwhelm me. "Wow. When I say their ages out loud like that, it still catches me off guard sometimes." I chuckle. "Wyatt used to mow the lawn for Mrs. Heart when she lived here. Such a dear lady. She had the most adorable collection of miniature hens and chicks that she prominently displayed in her front window. She was always moving them around and switching up the scenes. Wyatt always got a kick out of checking out the chicks whenever she moved them. Even as he got older, I still caught him eyeing them up from time to time." I gaze fondly at the window and lose myself in the memory. After a few seconds, I glance back at my new neighbor, feeling embarrassed. "Oh my, listen to me going on and on. Where are my manners? I haven't even asked you your name!"

Her lips pull back into the tiniest smile, but then, just as quickly, they straighten out. It's as if she caught herself doing something that was forbidden. *Odd*. She clears her throat, and when she speaks, her voice is clear and sharp like a bell, surprising me. "Hello. I appreciate you stopping by. My name is Madison. Madison Munch."

"It's so nice to meet you, Madison." I reach into my bag and find the container I packed. "Here," I say, handing it over. "I baked some of my famous zucchini bread for you. The zucchini is from my garden. I harvested it last year and froze some, so I always have it on hand."

She sucks in her lips and nods, looking impressed. "I would love to have a garden here, but Paul—that's my husband—says that with my black thumb I couldn't keep anything alive." She lets out an empty laugh that's laced with sadness.

I wave my hand. "Oh, nonsense. It's a little overwhelming at first, but once you got the hang of it, you'd be fine. I'd be happy to help if you—"

"No, no, I couldn't ask you to do that."

"Really, it's not a problem at all. You'd actually be doing me a favor."

Her eyes narrow. "What do you mean?"

I smile warmly. "Working in the ground, running my hands through the soil, planting little seedlings, it's all very cathartic for me. And, sure, I have a garden of my own, but there's nothing quite like the thrill of starting fresh."

She grins, and this time, she lets it happen. "That would be wonderful. I just need to run it by Paul first, but…" Her smile falters, but she shakes her head and her mouth curves again. "I'm sure it won't be a problem."

"Excellent. Then it's settled," I say, feeling a sense of accomplishment. Madison started out as a tough nut to crack, but I think I'm beginning to see some splinters in her armor. And I definitely need to meet this husband of hers. "Would you and Paul like to come by tonight for cocktails on the deck? Frank and I often sit out there after dinner. Around six thirty? Sound good?"

Madison backs up just a bit. The movement is so slight, if I wasn't paying close attention, I would've missed it. "Um, well, I'm not sure."

"Please come. It would be nice to have the company. I adore my husband, but sometimes the conversation can get a little stale, if you know what I mean." I give her a conspiratorial wink, but she remains stone-faced.

"Thank you for the invite. It's just that Paul works long hours, and he's often pretty exhausted when he comes home. He usually just eats dinner and then falls asleep on the sofa with a beer in one hand and the television remote in the other." She laughs, but the humor is missing.

Hmm, so far, I'm not very impressed with Paul. "What does he do for a living, if you don't mind my asking?"

"He works for a roofing company."

"I imagine that workload is pretty grueling."

She nods. "Yes, it is. I'm just afraid he won't be much company tonight. Maybe some other time, though." She's just saying that to be polite. I get the feeling "some other time" is code for never.

I could press her to try to get her to cave, but the signals she's sending are loud and clear. "Of course. I understand. How about I come by on Friday morning and we can chat more about your new garden?"

She smiles. "That sounds wonderful. Thanks for coming by, Jeanette. And also for the bread. I'll get this back to you when you stop by on Friday," she says, holding up the container.

I wave my hands. "No, that's yours to keep."

"Are you sure?"

"Positive. That's a SnapLid classic rectangular container. I'm a rep for the brand and it's my favorite one they make. It's so versatile!"

"That's so generous of you, thank you! I'm sure I'll find lots of good uses for this."

"The best part about SnapLid containers is their durability. They're practically unbreakable. Not like the old glass ones! I can't tell you how many of those I shattered over the years before I discovered these. Broken glass is the pits to clean up. No matter how hard you try, you always miss a few shards and then you find them days later when you step on one with your bare foot."

"Huh. Good to know. Thanks." I may be imagining it, but I think her eyes might have widened a fraction at the mention of broken glass. After the story Bob told me, I couldn't help myself.

I fidget with the straps of my duffel bag, lifting them higher onto my shoulder. "Well, it was nice talking with you, Madison. I'm looking forward to our visit on Friday."

She exhales, looking almost relieved. It's in direct contradiction to the words that leave her mouth. "Oh, me too. See you then."

We smile at each other in that awkward stranger way, and then Madison closes the door, shutting herself back inside her house.

Chapter Five

IT TAKES ONE TO KNOW ONE

I POP OPEN THE DOOR TO MY COMPOST BIN AND AM GREETED BY the richest, darkest topsoil. It's truly remarkable how something as disgusting as Henry Tadinger could turn into something so incredibly useful.

I reach for my shovel and scoop out the compost, dropping it into my wheelbarrow. "Just think, Henry, you may have made a mockery of your life, but I've given you a do-over. This is your swan song." I'm positively gleeful as I stare down at the mound formally known as my repulsive neighbor. In this state, it's virtually undetectable as human remains. Not that it matters. No one suspects a thing. I've been careful. I cover my tracks well and before Henry was even a blip on my radar, I established myself as a pillar of goodwill in this community.

I started this garden the summer after we moved here and over the years, it's developed quite a reputation. Once the season is in full swing, I start loading up baskets of veggies and distribute them to my neighbors. The residents of Whispering Woods appreciate me and they welcome me into their homes with open arms.

When Jacob Millhouse lost his dog, Pepper, I was the first

one scouring the streets in search of him. When Octavia Wilkins woke up to find her home had been egged during the night, I was there scraping away all the dried-up residue from her siding. And when poor old Mr. Jeffrees passed away, I spearheaded the meal deliveries for his widow, Marissa.

I make it a point to know each and every one of my neighbors. I know their favorite color; how they take their coffee; what turns them on. In a way, I guess you could say I'm neighborhood royalty and I don't take my position lightly. With it, comes responsibility. I may have turned Henry into compost, but that wasn't a decision I made haphazardly. It required a lot of planning and forethought. I don't make a habit of going around offing people at random.

I don't consider myself a serial killer. I don't *have* to end lives. It's not an itch I can't help scratching. I see myself more as a protector of my family and a steward of this neighborhood.

There were two and a half others that came before Henry Tadinger. The first…well, I'm not ready to talk about that one, yet. I'll start with the "half" because I know that sounds confusing.

When I was eighteen, I left my small town bound for college life. I had already been out from under my father's control, but I never felt truly free until I pulled up to the university.

My life in college was typical. Cramming for tests all night long, going to parties every weekend, drinking myself into oblivion, and finding my first love.

Derek Short was the epitome of a classic college frat boy. He was tall with a larger than average build and he had an amazing head of sandy blond hair that I could run my fingers through for hours. We met in Psychology 101 and the attraction was instant. Every minute I wasn't in class, I spent with him. I was sure he was "the one." I was wrong.

Word started to travel that Derek was cheating on me. I

didn't believe it at first, but the rumors were so persistent I decided to follow him one night. I watched him breeze into Jessica Linderman's dorm. When he emerged two hours later, his shirt was wrinkled and untucked and his lips were red and raw. It was all the proof I needed. So, the next night, we made plans to hang out in my dorm. My roommate was home visiting her sick grandmother, so I knew there was no chance of her walking in on us. Before Derek arrived, I stopped by a drugstore and bought a box of Unisom and a thirty two-ounce bottle of cranberry juice. I played bartender that night, mixing up a continuous flow of vodka cranberry drinks. Only my first drink had vodka. I needed a little to take the edge off, but I also needed my wits about me for what I had planned to do. For Derek, I added a few crushed Unisom to each drink, steadily increasing the dose with every one. A few drinks in, Derek's speech started to slur. He thought it was funny and he laughed in slow motion. He said he was tired and was going to take a nap. Within seconds, he was out cold. At first, I felt elated. I couldn't believe I had gone through with it. I tugged my pillow out from under Derek's head and placed it over his face just like I had planned. I pressed on it for a few moments, but then my thoughts started to jumble. What was I doing? How was I going to explain this? I definitely couldn't sneak his body out of here myself. He must've weighed at least two hundred pounds. It would be impossible for me to lift him, and even more impossible for me to go unnoticed. I lifted the pillow off of his face and watched as his eyes danced beneath closed lids. But he cheated on me. I couldn't let him get away with that. I pushed the pillow back, intent on smothering him. And again, I had second thoughts. This went on for at least twenty minutes before I stopped for good. Derek was a cheating jerk, but death didn't feel right and yet, it didn't feel wrong, either. As I sat on the bed next to his sleeping body, I spent hours lost inside my own head. Something changed that night. I may not have killed him, but I'd proven to myself that I could and I would if ever there was a need.

I decided I needed a code. Something to follow so I would know with absolute certainty that death was the only logical response. At that point, I didn't have a family of my own yet, but I imagined if I ever did, I would stop at nothing to protect them. Which is why I didn't try it again until seventeen years later.

Gertie was twelve and had just finished reading *The Baby Sitters Club* series. She was so excited about the idea of starting her own babysitting business, but at the time, we lived on a quiet street in a tiny neighborhood where there weren't many children younger than her. I talked her into switching gears and start a dog walking service instead. There were several dogs with busy working owners living around us. It seemed like the perfect plan.

We made a few fliers, and before long, she had three steady clients. One, in particular, kept her very busy. Ty Westing lived on the street behind ours. He was a bachelor in his early thirties and his dog was a little Yorkshire Terrier named Lionel. After only a couple of weeks, Ty started paying Gertie to walk Lionel every day and then it quickly turned into twice a day. It seemed excessive for such a small dog, but he paid her weekly and she was happy so I didn't worry about it.

And then one spring afternoon, I was tending to my garden when I spied Gertie walking Lionel. Only she wasn't alone. Ty was walking with her. They were laughing and something about the way he looked down at her made me stop. I couldn't take my eyes off of them and when they turned the corner, dropping out of my sight, I jumped to my feet and took off running. When I reached them, I was out of breath. Gertie looked at me strangely and Ty backed away from her like he knew he was standing too close. I'm sure he hoped I didn't catch that, but I did. I made up some excuse about needing Gertie's help with something and she followed me back home. Later that night, I poked my head into her room and found her sitting in front of her vanity brushing her long blond hair.

"Hey, kiddo. How's it going?"

She smiled at my reflection. "Hi, Mama."

I took a seat on her bed behind her. Staring at her through the mirror, I started a conversation I will never forget. "So, you've been walking Lionel a lot lately, huh?"

"Mm-hmm, twice a day."

"That's a lot of walking for a little dog. Does he ever get tired?"

She stopped brushing her hair for a beat before answering me. "He does. Sometimes, Ty says she's too pooped to walk and so he and I walk instead."

The little hairs on my arms stood on end. "Honey, Mr. Westing is an adult. You shouldn't call him by his first name. It's bad manners."

She giggled. "Oh, it's okay. Ty told me that Mr. Westing was his dad's name. He says I should just call him Ty."

"Well, I don't care what Mr. Westing told you, Gertie, in this house we have rules. You will not refer to him as Ty anymore. Is that clear?"

She half shrugged. "Okay, if you say so."

I met her gaze in the mirror. "I do." I took a breath to calm my nerves, but it was no use. "Listen, Gertie, when you and Mr. Westing go for walks, what sort of things do you talk about?"

She tipped her head in thought. "All sorts of things. Like how we both love tacos and the color blue. Sometimes, Ty, um, I mean, Mr. Westing asks about my favorite clothes. He's so funny, too, because he always has to ask what color underwear I have on." She laughed. "Isn't that such a silly thing to ask?"

That son of a—.

"Oh, Mom, before I forget. Mr. Westing has been telling me all about his tropical fish tank in his house and he wants me to come by tomorrow after school so he can show it to me. He said I could see it before I walk Lionel. Is that okay?"

The rage that I thought I had over stupid Derek Short was multiplied by the thousands at the thought of this sick bastard even thinking of laying a hand on my little girl. I know what grooming looks like and this pervert was doing it to my daughter right under my nose. I shook my head. "I'm sorry, sweetie, but I don't think tomorrow is a good day. In fact, I need your help around the house after school so I'm afraid you won't be able to walk Lionel, either."

Her face fell, but she nodded and kept brushing her hair.

I knew this day would come, but this time, I was ready. After what Gertie told me, I never allowed her to go back over to Ty's. She'd been begging me for horseback riding lessons for months, so I signed her up for some and they helped fill her afternoons. I took my time, gathering bits and pieces of information about Ty Westing. I managed to run into him a few times while I was out walking the neighborhood. I learned that he worked from home doing freelance web design. The work was unfulfilling, but it paid the bills. He told me his dream was to move to Thailand someday. And the best part? He had a brother who knew that, too. It was the perfect "excuse" for his disappearance.

Luring him to my house was easy. I just told him I needed a sitter for Gertie and the disgusting piece of human filth jumped at the chance. What he didn't know was that weekend Frank took the kids on a camping trip, while I stayed behind. I had Ty meet me in the backyard and I convinced him to come inside my shed first so I could show him a few of my new gardening tools. He was fidgeting with the hem of his shirt and I knew he didn't care about my tools, but he was trying not to appear overeager to be alone with

Gertie. Once he was inside, I acted swiftly. With a lethal dose of phenobarbital, he was incapacitated in minutes.

Years ago, I came across an article about human composting. It's still a relatively new idea, but it was recently legalized in Washington state and it's starting to gain momentum. The article covered the intricate process in detail, and the cogs in my brain immediately started moving. Up until that point, I hadn't tried anything since the night with Derek, but I thought it was best to be prepared. When I was shopping for a compost bin, I picked the largest steel container I could find. It wasn't big enough. I'll spare the gruesome details, but in order to get Ty into the compost bin, I had to make a mess. Let me just say, Dexter was right about the plastic covered room. I shudder just thinking about it.

I made sure to swipe Ty's keys from his pocket and let Lionel out at a time when I knew Mrs. Myers, the elderly widow on the corner, would be outside watering her flowers. The scenario played out perfectly. She tried to take him back a few times, but, of course, Ty never answered so she kept him. And just as I had hoped, Ty's brother, Jeff, assumed he finally took off for Thailand. He moved in to his brother's house and never even filed a missing persons report, which definitely set off alarm bells with me. Not long after Ty finished composting, I convinced Frank we needed a bigger house with a bigger yard. We moved to Whispering Woods before the end of the summer.

In the case of Henry, the wound is still fresh, so to speak. No one has any real idea where he is, but word about his crime is starting to spread and people aren't as concerned that he's gone. They're only hoping he doesn't come back. Including his niece. She's his only living relative, which makes her his next of kin. Apparently she's waiting until the end of the summer for him to turn up and then she's planning to have the entire home, contents and all, put up for auction.

She just wants to wash her hands of the whole thing. I can't blame her for that.

These two men were the worst example of what it means to be a human being. We're all born with a mission, and it's our job to uncover what that is. Every one of us has a purpose, a way to make a difference. These three pathetic excuses ignored their destiny and contributed nothing worthwhile. It's no one's purpose to take advantage of young girls or cause irreparable harm to teenage boys. They threatened my family, so I did what I had to do. A serial killer takes lives like they're souvenirs. I take lives so they can no longer inflict harm on others. The difference is clear.

Chapter Six

ACTIONS SPEAK LOUDER THAN WORDS

It's the last Thursday of the month, which in our house can only mean one thing. Lasagna night. I look forward to this dinner all month long.

I meander down the cobblestone path toward my herb bed. "Well, hello there, Basil. You gorgeous little devil. It's your time to shine." I select the perfect little bunch, pinching the plant right above a leaf pair. It breaks off easily and I bring it to my nose, inhaling the heady aroma. "Ahh," I exhale. "You will be the perfect finishing touch on the master-piece of a lasagna that's baking in my oven."

I carefully place the basil into my small collection basket and weave my way around the garden. The few veggies that I've planted are thriving thanks to Henry Tadinger. I can't help the grin that overtakes my face when I think about how well I've rehabilitated that man. I gather a few greens for a small salad and then I make my way back to the house.

I glance at my watch. It's nearly time for my children to come home from school. Thursdays always feel like a treat since Gertie doesn't have any after-school activities. Wyatt should be right home as well—at least, I hope he will be. He rarely shares any of his plans with me, but I know lasagna night is his favorite, so I'm feeling pretty confident that he won't dawdle with friends.

The kitchen smells incredible. I peek into the oven; I can't help myself. My mouth waters at the sight of bubbling cheese. It's nearly time to prepare my famous garlic bread, but first I dice up some of the vegetables and toss them together with a simple vinaigrette. I'm so busy working that I don't even hear Frank enter the room. He grabs me from behind, wrapping his arms around my waist. He croons a haphazard version of "Strangers in the Night" while swaying our joined bodies. I hum and allow my head to rest back against his collarbone.

"It's Thursday night, my love," he sings low in my ear.

"Mm-hmm, that it is."

"I've been thinking about it all day long. I keep picturing you in that lacy blue number of yours with your legs—"

I spin around, placing my finger over his lips. "Ah ah ah, now, Frank, you know the rules. That kind of talk is reserved for the bedroom and *only* the bedroom. Take a look around. Is that where we are right now?"

He laughs. "Jeanette, you slay me. You and your rules."

Frank loves to remind me that he thinks my schedule is ridiculous, but if he really thought about it, it takes all the guesswork out of the equation. I mean, how many other guys know, with absolute certainty, that their wives will reciprocate their sexual advances? Frank never has to question it. Every Tuesday, Thursday, and Saturday night, it's a sure thing. "Hmm, it would seem that me and my rules have had you feeling mighty fine all day. Dare I say, even more confident. Am I right?"

He nods. "You aren't wrong."

I grin with triumph. "Well, then, maybe it's best you remember that the next time you feel like criticizing my rules." I wink at him, and it sets him off.

He pulls me to him so that our bodies are flush. The effect he has on me is instantaneous, and it takes all of my willpower to press my palms against his chest and push away. "Listen, I keep forgetting to tell you, about a month ago, Gertie told me she was interested in a boy at school." Frank groans, but I put a finger on his lips. "Just a minute. I know this isn't your favorite topic—"

"You can say that again."

I shake my head. "I *may* have already told her it was okay to date him."

Frank raises an eyebrow.

I clear my throat. "She hasn't said any more about him since that day. I'm not even sure if he reciprocates her feelings. And I know this is usually the sort of thing we like to discuss, but honey, she's a good kid and has never let us down. She came to me and I know it took a lot of courage. I just wanted to give her the benefit of the doubt. What do you think?"

He huffs. "I don't have a choice in the matter, do I?"

"Oh, you have a choice, all right. It just better be the right one." I tip my chin, and he chuckles.

"Sweetheart, you know I'm always in favor of giving our kids more freedom to make their own decisions. Gertie will make good choices in life. We've raised her well. We've raised *both* of them well." He says that last sentence with a challenging gleam. I just roll my eyes. It would be pointless to argue with him. He has an entirely different relationship with Wyatt than I do. I'd rather not talk about it right now, so I change the subject.

"I do have an idea on how you can work off some of that pent-up energy of yours."

He cocks an eyebrow. "Do you now?"

"See that French bread over there?" I tip my head. "What do you say you slice it up for me?"

His shoulders slouch as he sighs. "Sure." His arms slide from my waist and he trudges over to the counter.

"I'll be right back. I just want to quickly check on the kids.

I haven't seen them yet." When I reach the door to the dining room, I turn and let my eyes roam over the back of my husband. His taut forearms ripple as he works the knife through the bread. He's not the only one who's been thinking about tonight. "Oh, and Frank?"

"Hmm," he answers without turning his head.

"Remember, I like them nice and *thick*." I watch as the knife stills. He looks back at me with heat in his eyes, and I give him a show as I saunter out of the room, swaying my hips like a pendulum bob.

GERTIE'S DOOR IS OPEN. She's lying on her bed, resting on her stomach with her legs bent up in the air. A book lies open in front of her. Her head is propped in her hands as she intently reads the words on the page. I hate to interrupt her concentration, but it's nearly time for dinner so I lightly rap on her door. She startles. "Oh! Hi, Mom."

"Hi, sweetie. I didn't hear you come in. I guess I was outside when you got home." I move closer to her. "What are you reading?"

"Hamlet." She flips up the book, showing me the cover. "Mr. Grant asked us to choose a quote from Shakespeare and relate it to our own lives."

"He's one of my favorites. Have you chosen your quote?"

She nods. "'To thine own self, be true.' I know, I know, how original of me," she says with a shake of her head.

I chuckle. "Ahh, that's a good one and there's a reason why it's so popular. Do you know what you'll write?" I take a seat on the bed next to her.

"Well, I think, first and foremost, it means you need to be true to yourself above all else. Find what's real and hold on to it. Everything else will fall into place, and if it doesn't, then it wasn't meant to be in the first place."

My chest fills with pride. This girl of mine is so smart. "I think that's a brilliant interpretation. You have a good head on your shoulders, kiddo." I rest my hand on the side of her face.

She smiles brightly. "What about you, Mom?"

My face scrunches. "Hmm?"

"You said Shakespeare was one of your favorites. Is there a quote you love?"

I think on it for a moment. The first one that comes to mind is a lesser known line from the Tempest—"Hell is empty and all the devils are here." It reminds me of Henry and Ty. It perfectly illustrates my life's purpose—to vanquish the devils among us. But I can't share that with my daughter. "I think, if I had to choose, I'd go with, 'We know what we are, but know not what we may be.'"

She smiles. "Ophelia."

"That's right, but when she says it, I think it takes on a more negative tone. I choose to read it as, we have so much potential in life and if we channel it properly, the future will have big things in store for us."

She hums. "I like that."

"But for right now," I say, rising from her bed. "The only thing the immediate future holds for you is dinner."

She rolls her eyes in mock annoyance. "Ha. Ha. Ha."

I pause at her door. "See you in the dining room in a few minutes?"

"It's lasagna night. I wouldn't miss it."

I drum my fingers against the doorframe as I leave her room. Padding down the hall to Wyatt's room, I notice his door is closed. It's always closed. Just like his life. He keeps everything wrapped up so tight. I think about how I found Gertie just now. In an open room with an open book. My children couldn't be any more opposite.

I knock on the door, but I know he'll never hear me. Chances are, he's wearing his headphones and glued to his gaming system. I wait the appropriate thirty seconds before turning the knob. When you're a minor living under your parents' roof, privacy is a privilege you have to earn. And, as far as I'm concerned, we're not there yet.

I find Wyatt lying just like Gertie, on his stomach, sprawled out on his bed. But that's where the similarities end. Just as I suspected, his headphones are plastered to his ears and a pro controller rests in his hands. A steady stream of profanities pours from his mouth as he attempts to gun down a pixelated opponent. There's so much wrong here. I don't even know where to begin.

"Wyatt John!" I have a rule about raising my voice, but in situations like this, it's a necessary evil.

He registers no surprise. It's as though he knew I was standing here all along. He was just choosing to ignore me. I feel incensed. His eyes slide to mine for a second. His fingers never stop moving, frantically pressing the buttons on his controller. "What's up?"

He doesn't wait for my answer. His gaze snaps back to the screen like a boomerang returning to its owner. I shake my head and stare up at the ceiling, quietly counting to ten. "Excuse me? Wyatt? I need your direct attention, please."

He huffs loudly, causing his shoulders to bounce up and down. My patience dwindles as I wait for him to stop his game. He lets the controller fall from his hands and rests his headphones around his neck. He tilts his head to face me and raises an eyebrow. "Did you need something?"

Did I *need* something? I narrow my eyes. How about some respect, for starters. This kid is unbelievable. And by that, I mean, I can't believe he came from me. I blame Frank's DNA. I clear my throat and try to find a smile. How did we get here? "I just wanted to see you. I miss you when you're away at school all day."

He groans. "I'm gone for what? Eight hours? And it's not like we spend much time together when I am home."

His words strike me like a fist to the gut. "No, I suppose we don't. But we could change that, you know?"

"Oh, yeah?" He tilts his head and looks at me, really looks at me. For the first time in as long as I can remember, he seems genuinely interested in what I'm about to say.

"Sure!" My head bobs enthusiastically, and I wonder if it's as much for my benefit as it is for his. The truth is, as much as I'd love to have a stronger relationship with my son, I wouldn't know where to begin and that terrifies me. What mother doesn't know how to *be* with her child?

He cocks his head. "Okay, then. What do you suggest?"

"Well, we could…" My eyes widen as my brain frantically tries to fill in the blank. What could we do? There must be some common ground between us. I snap my fingers. "I know! We could try baking a cake. Remember how much you used to love cracking eggs into the bowl?"

"I did love that." I nod, feeling pleased with my quick thinking, but then Wyatt finishes his thought. "When I was seven."

He levels me with a look of pure disappointment and tugs his headphones from his neck, tossing them on his bed. "I'm guessing it's time for dinner. That is why you came in here, isn't it?"

"Uh-huh." My voice is barely a whisper. This must be what it feels like to fail as a parent. Everything Wyatt says is always laced with sarcasm, but he threw me a bone and instead of picking it up, I threw it back and missed the mark by a mile.

He brushes past me as he leaves his room. "Good talk, Mom."

THE REST of the evening goes by in a blur. After my epic fail with Wyatt, I've been in a funk. Even lasagna night wasn't enough to save my mood. It didn't help matters that Wyatt never spoke during dinner, much less even looked up from his plate. We used to be so close when he was little. He was my buddy, my shadow. I don't know when or how it happened. It wasn't sudden, but gradual. As he started to get older, it felt like he was pulling away from me, but maybe I pulled away from him, too. Teenage girls I could relate to. Despite my disaster of a childhood, I was once a teenage girl myself. I understood how they thought. Teenage boys, on the other hand, are a whole different animal. I didn't know the first thing about what Wyatt was going through and he never seemed willing to let me in. Somewhere along the way, I stopped trying. It was easier to just ignore him and hope the distance was something we'd outgrow. Sure, I have moments where I try to breach the barrier he built around himself, but lately they're few and far between. I need to make it a priority to repair our disjointed relationship. I just wish I could figure out a way to connect with him.

I ponder a few ideas while I take myself through my nightly routine. It's arguably the most important part of my day. The saying, "you're only as old as you feel" is correct, but there's more to it than that. I believe the most important tool in anyone's arsenal is skin care. Age may be just a number, but it's also a guideline. I'm constantly adding to my regimen based on the common skin concerns of my demographic. And the wide array of vials on the counter in front of me are proof of that. I have serums and elixirs for every issue under the sun—including the sun, actually. You can never be too careful when it comes to damaging UV rays. And with the amount of time that I spend outside tending to my garden, it's important for me to be extra vigilant.

I reach for the rose hip seed oil and squeeze a few drops onto my fingers. Leaning in close to the mirror, I pat it onto my T-zone, spying Frank out of the corner of my eye as he sashays into the bathroom wearing nothing but a towel. I close my eyes for a moment and try to find my focus. I was looking forward to this earlier, but after my conversation with Wyatt, I'm not feeling quite as eager.

I watch Frank through the reflection. He smiles as me like I'm a rare gem he's just discovered and I'm sure my father never looked at my mother that way. I can only imagine how different life might've been if he had. I raise my eyebrows suggestively and Frank grins and drops the towel. Ready to go, as always.

He has incredible stamina. It's something I've always appreciated. The headboard of our four-poster bed slams rhythmically against the wall as he pounds into me. The *bang bang* echoes in the room and I wrap my legs around my husband giving in to his relentless thrusting. My eyes roll back as I feel him take me right to the edge. I hover there for a few seconds and finally tip over. He lets out a crescendo of grunts followed by a booming, "Fuck!" and then his body collapses onto mine in a sweaty heap. I giggle and shake my head. This is one of those times when cussing fits a situation, and Frank never misses the opportunity.

His breath is hot against my neck, and I feel his heart pound against my own. We stay like that for a few moments as we slowly come down from the high. As our breathing levels out and our heart rate slows, Frank chortles gruffly and lets out a low whistle. "Well, my goodness, that was pretty fucking incredible. Wouldn't you agree?" He lifts his head and gazes down at me.

"I can barely form any coherent thoughts at the moment. I think that's a pretty good sign." I wink and he laughs.

I lie still for a moment and my thoughts drift to our new neighbors. The little bit Madison has told me about Paul has my suspicions on overdrive. I only just met her, but I already feel strangely protective of her. She seems so meek and I hope she isn't being taken advantage of, or worse.

I push myself up to sitting and look down at my husband. His eyes are closed, but he's still awake. "Frank?"

"Hmm?"

"I'm getting a little low on my medicine. Think you could bring some more home for me?"

He cracks open his eyelids. "Sweetheart, are you sure you still need it? It seems like you've been sleeping really well lately."

I feel my frustration start to rise and I fight to keep the condescending tone out of my voice. "Darling, if I've been sleeping well, it's *because* of the phenobarbital."

"I haven't noticed you taking any, so I guess I just assumed you weren't."

I nod. "Yes, not every night, but often enough. I take it before I start my skincare routine." Frank thinks my night-time ritual is tedious, so he usually makes sure he's never in the bathroom with me during that time. He'd never know if I happened to take any medication. "But I only take the prescribed amount." I add that last part for his benefit. I know I'm technically lying, which is against my rules. But when it comes to protecting the people I care about, my purpose supersedes everything else. After all, this is not a lie for personal gain, it's a lie to benefit the greater good.

"Well, I'm glad to hear you're adhering to the label. I'm sure I don't have to remind you, that drug is extremely dangerous when taken in large doses."

Oh, you definitely don't have to remind me. "Uh-huh, don't worry, I remember."

He rests his hand on my knee, sliding his thumb back and forth. "We're getting a new shipment later this week. I'll grab some off the shelf when it gets there."

The night terrors started a few months after Gertie was born. I've never shared much of my past with Frank, but he knew I didn't grow up in a loving home. When my daughter was born, I was terrified of repeating the mistakes of my parents. The fear kept me awake at night and the anxiety led to "episodes." Once I'd fall asleep, I would flail and thrash about in bed, screaming at the top of my lungs. Poor Frank. He had to subdue me by throwing all of his weight on top of me. It scared him and he begged me to see a doctor. I drug my feet because I knew a doctor would want to know things. They'd want details about my past, and I never wanted to relive that. But the pain and fear that I saw in my husband's eyes was enough to convince me to put my own worries aside. I only saw her a few times, but Dr. Myers was extremely helpful. I told her a few stories from my past, and it didn't take her long to diagnose me with a form of post-traumatic stress disorder. Growing up the way I did was hard enough, but getting married and having a child triggered all sorts of trauma. Phenobarbital was prescribed to help calm my anxiety and help me sleep and it worked. I don't need it anymore; not for myself, anyway. And my prescription has long since expired, but that's where being married to a pharmacist comes in handy.

Chapter Seven

BITING OFF MORE THAN YOU CAN CHEW

Every weekday morning begins the same way. I'm always the first one up. I wake at dawn and after a brisk yoga practice, I hop in the shower and then I get ready for the day. I blow out my shoulder-length blond hair, giving the brush a curl at the ends so it flips under. Next, I apply a hint of makeup, always adhering to the rule that less is more. A light-coverage tinted moisturizer with a dusting of blush, a swipe of brow gel, and a coat of mascara are all I need to slightly perfect my face without masking it.

I wear a dress nearly every single day, except for the rare occasion when I opt for a sensible pair of skinny jeans. My closet contains a wide array of dresses in every color imaginable. I make my choice based on my mood, and today I'm feeling yellow. It's warm and welcoming and that's exactly the sort of air I want to give off when I visit Madison.

I stand in front of the full-length mirror on the bathroom door and smooth my hands along my waist. The A-line cut of this dress flatters my curves. I finish off the look with a delicate gold necklace. A dainty teardrop-shaped moonstone rests just above the swell of my breasts. I smile at my reflection.

Who said women are most beautiful at age thirty? From where I'm standing, forty is the new thirty.

I prepare a full breakfast for my family every day. You should never start your day on an empty stomach, and I take pride in filling theirs. Today's menu is scrambled eggs, bacon, toast, and sliced strawberries. Frank is the first to arrive in the kitchen. He's humming Frank Sinatra and shoots me a wink as he fills his plate to the brim. "Thank you, my love," he says as he takes a seat at the island.

I smile. "I'm happy to do it."

He pauses with his fork dangling in the air. "Oh, I appreciate the breakfast, but that's not why I thanked you." A sly grin overtakes his face.

I feel my cheeks heat as I recall last night. It's Friday, not the day to be discussing the activities of last evening, but I'll let him have his moment. He's earned the right to gloat.

Gertie skips into the room like a ray of sunshine. She beams at me, and I smile in return. She grabs a plate of food and sits on a stool next to Frank.

The room is blissfully quiet. The light scraping of forks along plates as they scoop up breakfast is the only sound. It's moments like these when I feel the most gratitude. My loved ones are cared for, my home is tidy, my garden is flourishing, and my neighborhood is safe. There's an abundance of things to be thankful for, but it's the small victories that often feel like the biggest triumphs. And right now, with my husband and daughter happily eating the food that I prepared, I feel fulfilled.

Several minutes later, Wyatt graces us with his presence and brings my gratitude trip to a screeching halt. His inky hair swoops down in front of his eyes, and every few seconds he does a Justin Bieber head shake, sweeping it to the side. I wish he'd let me take him for a trim, but I don't bother asking. It feels like an unspoken game between us. He'll keep growing it out just to annoy me, and I'll stay silent about it, refusing to give in. It's petty, and I'm the parent. I should speak up, but we're on tumultuous ground. I need to keep my eye on the prize. I intend to win the war, and this isn't a battle worth waging.

He's dressed in black jeans with holes in the knees and a chain that extends from a belt loop to the wallet in his back pocket. He's paired it with a gray T-shirt that says:

Intelligence Test
(Please read your answers out loud)
1. Say "EYE"
2. Spell "M-A-P"
3. Say "NESS"

I definitely didn't buy it for him. "No," I say at the exact time Frank says, "Yes!" He starts laughing and adds, "What a great shirt!" I roll my eyes up to the ceiling. I am surrounded by idiots.

Thankfully, Gertie looks appalled, and I feel slightly vindicated. I glare at my son. "Wyatt, that's not an appropriate shirt for school."

Frank huffs. "Lighten up, Jeanette. It's funny."

I let Wyatt go with a shake of my head, but I level Frank with a steely glare and watch as his Adam's apple bobs. We've always agreed to never disagree on parenting in front of the kids, and he just broke our rule. He knows I hold grudges, and if he wants the schedule to remain unchanged, he'll heed the warning in my eyes. He takes his plate to the sink and then scoops up his briefcase. After a chaste kiss on my cheek, he retreats to the garage with his tail between his legs.

Gertie clears her throat, and my eyes snap to hers. She smiles politely. "Thank you for breakfast, Mom. It was yummy!" She pats her stomach. "I should get going. I don't want to be late for school." She slides her backpack onto her shoulder and turns to Wyatt. "You coming?"

He keeps his eyes trained on me, never once glancing her way. "No. Gage is picking me up."

"Gage McNamera?" I ask.

"Yep," he answers, popping the *p*.

I take a deep breath, attempting to remain calm. Gage was suspended last month for pulling the fire alarm at school, and two months before that, he called Mr. Winslow, the algebra teacher, a "dick in the mud." Gage is not the influence I want for Wyatt and he knows that. He's testing me. He's always testing me. So I weigh my options. If I tell him no, he'll do it anyway and I'll be showing him my hand so he'll know he's gotten under my skin. But if I say nothing, he'll get in Gage's car, but with a little less spring in his step. And maybe, just maybe, hanging out with Gage will lose some of its appeal.

I keep my eyes on his, or at least his one eye that isn't obscured by his ridiculous hair. "Have a good day at school."

"Thanks, Mom," Gertie calls over her shoulder as she bounds out the front door.

"Yeah, thanks, Mom," Wyatt echoes, but his voice lacks the warmth that his sister's had. He snatches a piece of bacon off of the table and our eyes stay locked for one, two, three seconds, before he blinks in slow motion and walks away.

———

PINK and white rhododendrons frame the walkway leading up to Madison's front door. They're a little overgrown—something Angela Heart never would've allowed. They were her pride and joy, and she pruned and fussed over them every spring. Still, despite their unruly shape, they add a bit of charm to the house. They've always been one of my favorite flowers, a reminder that spring is here and summer isn't far behind. Prime garden season is nearly upon us.

I know I told her I was just coming over to chat about gardening, but I couldn't come emptyhanded. I don't have it in me. So I decided to bring a few mint starter plants. Herbs are fairly straightforward, and I hardly think her husband could have much to say about a few harmless plants.

This time, when Madison opens her door, she stands in full view. Not that it matters. I still can't really see her. She wears her clothing like a cloak. Her black pants are loose and long, covering up her feet, which I believe could be bare. It's just after 10:30 a.m. and the temperature is already seventy-five degrees, yet she's wearing a charcoal gray hooded sweat-shirt. Her russet hair is stick straight and parted in the middle with bangs shielding her forehead. It's as if she's hiding in plain sight.

"Good morning, Jeanette." There's a formalness in her tone when she greets me. I'll need to work on getting her to warm up to me if I want to get to know her and that myste-rious husband of hers.

"Hi there, Madison! It's so good to see you again. Are you ready to talk about all things gardening?"

She nods. "Yes, I am. What have you got there?" She juts her chin toward the herbs in my hands.

"Well, I thought it might be nice to start simple, so I brought you some mint plants."

Her face pales a bit. "Oh, um, I thought we were just *talking* about gardening today. I didn't realize we'd actually be planting anything."

I'm a little thrown, but I recover quickly. "It's not a big deal, really. It's just a few plants, and if you're not ready to put them in the ground, they can easily be planted in pots."

She gives me a small smile, but it doesn't quite reach her eyes. "Maybe we should start there. I haven't had a chance to talk to Paul about a garden yet, and I don't want to upset him."

Hmm, what a peculiar thing to worry about. I suppose

Paul may be one of those alpha-type guys who measures his manhood by the condition of his yard. He might find it irritating to have something to mow around. But after seeing the state of the shrubs out front, I have to say, it's a bit hard to imagine he's obsessive with the state of his yard. I file my curiosity away under *things I need to convince Madison to talk about*.

"Not a problem. Should we get started?"

"Sure. Did you want to come in through the house or should we just walk around and sit out back on the deck?"

I desperately want to get inside that house, but there is no tactful way to say that. "Whatever is easiest for you."

She thinks on it for a moment. "You can head back there, and I'll meet you in a minute. I just need to put on some shoes." Barefoot. I was right.

Darn. I was hoping she'd invite me in, but I won't let it deter me. I'll just have to think of another way to get inside.

Madison's deck has seen better days. The teak colored stain has faded and is chipped in a few spots, and a few of the boards look like they could use replacing. I remember seeing Angela's son-in-law stain it for her. Thinking back on it, that was about two years ago. It hasn't been that long, but Pennsylvania winters can be harsh.

A small round metal table sits in the left corner of the deck. Another relic that Angela left behind. I imagine when it was new, it was a bronze color, but now time has turned it a pale patina. I set the mint on the floor beside me and take a seat on one of the metal chairs. The glass door that leads to the kitchen slides open, and Madison tiptoes outside. From the slight tapping I hear as she cautiously steps toward me, I assume she put shoes on, but I can't say what they look like. The legs of her pants balloon around her and brush the ground as she walks. They remind me of bell bottoms you might see at Woodstock.

She sits across from me, looking down at her hands. She's

absentmindedly spinning the rings on her fingers. She hasn't said a word. Nervous energy radiates off of her in waves. I decide on a joke to ease the tension. "What do you say to a fancy cactus?"

Her brow furrows. "Uh, I'm not sure."

"You look sharp!" I cackle. She doesn't. In fact, she barely cracks a smile. Tough crowd.

I clear my throat. "So, what sort of plants did you want to grow in your garden?"

She shakes her head. "I haven't really given it that much thought."

Somehow I doubt that. "Okay, well, as I mentioned earlier, herbs are a good place to start. Think of it as dipping your toes in the water. It'll give you a taste of what it's like before you submerge yourself in a full garden." I lean over and grab one of the plants, placing it on the table. "Mint is super hardy and pretty hard to kill."

Madison takes a break from fidgeting with her rings. Her hand hovers above the leaves. It's clear she wants to touch it, but she's waging an internal battle. "It's okay. You won't hurt it. Trust me, this plant actually thrives with a bit of abuse." She flinches and sucks in a breath. Her entire body closes up tight. It's such a strange visceral reaction.

"I have an idea. Let's survey your space and see where you might envision a garden." I stand, striding over to the railing. Her yard is about the same size as mine, but it appears even bigger without the garden and shed. I look back over my shoulder as Madison slowly rises out of her seat. Every move she makes is timid. She's like a turtle peeking its head out of its shell, only to pull it right back in at the slightest hint of danger.

She stands beside me and looks out over her yard. I have a few ideas on where a good garden spot might be, but I keep it to myself for now, hoping she'll speak up first. She's quiet for a beat. I peek at her out of the corner of my eye and watch as she transforms in front of me. Her posture changes first. She was hunched over, but now she stands straighter. Her eyes seem to glisten as the fog clears from them. And a small smile plays on her lips in the same way that a child's might as they stare out at a playground. "There," she says, extending her arm and pointing toward the upper right corner. I follow her finger and nod with approval.

"That's a perfect spot. See? You're a natural." I turn to face her and that's when I see it. The sleeve of her sweatshirt has inched up her arm, and there on her forearm are four circular bruises. About the same size and shape as fingertips. My eyes zero in on the purple and blue hues as I consider how those bruises came to be. In an instant, she pulls her sleeve down to her wrist and once again curls into herself. Her smile is gone and so is the light behind her eyes.

I rub my hand back and forth on the railing, and my palm snags on a chipped piece of wood. I gasp as I lift my palm and survey the damage. A splinter. Great. Madison takes my hand in hers. "Oh no, this old deck is such a mess. I'm so sorry."

"It's fine. I can see the edge peeking out of my skin. If you have tweezers, I'll have it out in no time."

She lifts her head and when her eyes find mine, I see a glimpse of uncertainty, but it passes quickly. "I have some in the bathroom. Follow me." She's still holding my injured hand as she leads me in through the sliding glass doors. We pass through her kitchen and into the hallway. She's moving so quickly, I hardly have time to focus on anything.

We stand toe to toe in her bathroom. "Does it hurt?" Her teeth clench with empathy. She's no stranger to pain.

"Not too bad," I reassure her.

She tugs open the medicine cabinet, revealing a neat row of medication bottles inside. Her movements are jerky, and I can tell the situation makes her uncomfortable. Her hand rifles around on the bottom shelf. "Got it," she exclaims, holding up the tweezers. She wastes no time shoving the cabinet door closed in the same way you might hastily slam a laptop shut to hide the screen from curious eyes. Unfortunately for her, I've already seen enough to know I need to see more.

The splinter pulls out with ease. I survey the damage, but I can't even see where it was. "Much better. Thank you, Madison." I smile at her.

Her smile is shy with a hint of embarrassment. "It's no problem. I'm just sorry it happened in the first place. As soon as we moved in, I wanted to hire someone to refinish the deck, but Paul said he would take care of it." Her gaze shifts down and settles on the sink, as though she might find an answer there. I haven't met Paul yet, but I can already tell he's the type of guy who insists on "taking care" of everything himself. And, in the end, he takes care of nothing.

I pat her arm, and she shakes away whatever dark thoughts were starting to consume her. "Now that I'm in here, I realize I need to use the restroom. Is that okay?"

Her eyes crinkle at the corners as she smiles kindly. "Of course. Take your time. I'll be in the kitchen getting us some lemonade."

"That sounds perfect."

With Madison gone, I'm anxious to crack open the medicine cabinet. But before I can do that, I wait an appropriate amount of time and then I flush the toilet and turn on the faucet. The sound of running water paired with the residual flushing provides the perfect buffer to conceal the creak of the cabinet door. The bottles are all turned so the labels are facing forward. It's as if Madison wants me to read them. There are a few over the counter varieties—Advil, Motrin, Tylenol, Aleve, but it's the prescription bottles that catch my eye. They're all prescribed to her. With Frank's job as a pharmacist, I recognize all the names on the bottles. Celebrex, Toradol, and Daypro. These medications are all used to manage pain. I could understand having a few of the common brands on hand, but why would anyone need this much pain medication, especially the stronger prescriptions? I push the door closed and turn off the water. I've garnered some important information today, but I think the next step is to meet Paul. I'll have to figure out the best way to make that happen.

I open the door to the bathroom and walk directly into a wall of hardened muscle. Two calloused hands grip my wrists. Tilting my head up, I see a chiseled jaw with the beginnings of a five o'clock shadow. Steely eyes regard me with an unreadable expression.

I pull my lips into a smile, but he doesn't return it. "You must be Paul. I'm Jeanette Singleton. I live a few houses down from you." Without the use of my hands, I angle my chin in the direction of my home.

He grunts and turns his head toward the kitchen where Madison has just roughly closed a cabinet door. I swear I hear him mutter, "Interesting."

"What is?"

His eyes snap back to mine and his brow pulls down. "Huh?"

"You said the word 'interesting,' and I was just wondering what you meant." He's still holding onto my wrists, though his grip is so light, I could easily pull out of it. I'm not sure why I haven't.

He doesn't answer my question, making me wonder if I heard him correctly. He lets go of one of my wrists, but keeps the other one in his grasp, using it to tug me through the house. What is it with these people and yanking me around like a dog on a leash?

We stop short when we reach the kitchen. "Maddie?" Paul's voice has a slight edge to it. There's a question and an accusation hidden in the way he says her name.

Madison stands with her back against the counter. She's holding on to a dish towel like it's a life raft. She's in danger of floating away and it's the only thing keeping her grounded.

"H-Hi, Paul," she stammers. "You're home early."

"Forgot my thermos." His eyebrow lifts and there's a strange gleam in his eyes.

Madison's head nods in a continuous robotic motion. I wait for her to speak, but she stays quiet.

There's an odd tension in the room, but it's one I can't quite place. Madison seems very calm, almost in a Stepford Wife sort of way.

She chuckles, but it doesn't sound right. The little hairs on my arms stand on end. "Oh, where are my manners? Paul, this is our neighbor, Jeanette. She just came over to welcome us to the neighborhood. She got a splinter in her hand from the deck and I had to help her remove it." She's twisting the towel in her hands, wringing it until it resembles a makeshift garrote. I'm certain she doesn't even realize she's doing it, but somewhere deep inside the confines of her mind, she's dreaming of strangling Paul with that mangled up towel. It's at that moment, I wish it were possible to communicate tele-pathically. I'd reassure her that I'm getting the message loud and clear.

Chapter Eight

TURNING LEMONS INTO LEMONADE

My feet shuffle along the sidewalk as I stumble back to my house. My body moves slowly as though I just finished running a marathon, but my mind is sharp and ripe with plans. After those tense minutes in the kitchen at Madison's, I'm certain there's something very wrong in that house. I suspect that Paul is hurting his wife, maybe both mentally and physically. But I need more proof.

After Madison explained why I was there, Paul finally released my arm. I fought the urge to rub a hand over the spot where he held me. I glance down at it now and find a neat row of pale pink circles similar to the ones on Madison's arm. He wasn't pressing hard, but it was still constant enough to leave a mark. Bruising will probably follow, and after a week the marks will disappear altogether, but the memory never will. I wonder how many memories Madison has had to live with.

It was interesting to watch Paul's behavior change once he realized who I was and why I was in his house. I imagine it's not unlike watching a chameleon change colors to adjust to its surroundings. It was odd because I had already told him my name and that I lived nearby, but it wasn't until Madison explained it to him, that he actually spoke. He grasped my hand and shook it. His hand tightened slightly around mine, but he tried to keep his arms soft. I could tell it was a hard battle for him. The fire behind his eyes told me he'd like to clamp my hand in his and send me crashing through the glass door with a swing of his massive arm. I could hear the gritting of his teeth in his gravelly voice when he spoke. "Pleasure to meet you, Jeanette. You'll forgive me for my behavior. You can never be too careful. I'm sure you understand."

That's how he spoke. As though holding my wrist and dragging me through the house was justifiable behavior. Please. I hardly look imposing enough to be any kind of viable threat. I matched his determined glare with one of my own. His eyebrows lifted slightly. I'm the sort of woman who sees through the bullsh—well, whatever you want to call it, I see through it. And I could tell that a woman with a backbone was not something he was used to. The corners of my lips tugged into a sly smile. "No worries. You're new to the neighborhood so you wouldn't know, but we look out for each other here. And if that's how you greet a stranger, I can't help but wonder how you'd react to an enemy." I laughed, and he joined in. Out of the corner of my eye, I could see Madison's head twitch as her gaze bounced between us. No doubt she was wondering what she was witnessing. I'm not even sure of it, myself.

And then there's that word. *Interesting*. Sure, I could've misheard him, but I really don't think I did. It was such a strange thing to say. What did he find so interesting? Was it that Madison invited me into her house or that she left me alone? Either way, if it turns out he is hurting his wife, I think it'll be even more interesting when he realizes how much he underestimated me.

I think my biggest advantage in all of this is the element of surprise. To look at me, you'd never guess what I do in my spare time. I'm sure all of my neighbors assume I spend my days tooling about in my garden, tidying up my home, and slaving away in the kitchen. And, of course, they'd be right, but I also take out the garbage, so to speak.

Which brings me back to Paul. I need to observe him in action, but despite his brusque manner a few minutes ago, I get the feeling he reins in his temper as much as he can when he has an audience. What I need is to see how he is when he's alone with Madison. Short of peeking in their window at night, I'm not sure what the solution is.

I need an idea, and some of the best ones have come to me while I'm baking. I look through my pantry and decide on a simple double crust apple pie for tonight's dessert. I grab some apples out of the fridge and begin the prep work, peeling and coring them, followed by slicing each one into thin slivers. As I shake some cinnamon and sugar over the apple slices, it hits me.

Wyatt. A few years ago, he went through a spy phase. For Christmas that year, we bought him an electronic espionage set. It came with a pen that had a tiny microphone concealed inside that connected to wireless Bluetooth headphones. There was also a miniature camera about the size of a peanut that could easily attach to practically any surface using a suction cup. I know it seems pretty advanced for a toy, but we expected the audio to be garbled and the video quality to be grainy, at best. We were wrong.

It didn't take long for us to realize if you give a thirteen-year-old boy a tiny camera and a microphone, he's going to use them to spy on his older sister and her friends. When Gertie's friend, Jen, came to our house for a sleepover, Wyatt planted the pen microphone in his sister's room and secured the camera to the side of her desk. We found him hiding under his covers. A giggling little pubescent boy wearing headphones. I can still see his face when we pulled back the comforter. A wide-eyed look of surprise morphed into a cheeky grin. He knew what he was doing, and he knew he shouldn't be doing it. He also didn't care.

We confiscated both the pen and camera, and later that night, we pulled the video off of the device. We were shocked to find a nearly crystal-clear image of Gertie and Jess sitting cross-legged on the carpet painting their nails. A test of the microphone also revealed static free sound quality. We unknowingly bought our thirteen-year-old son an actual working spy set. A spy set that is still in a shoebox on the top shelf of our closet.

I rinse my hands, washing off the grit of cinnamon and sugar, and then I march up the stairs to my bedroom. I glide open the bi-fold doors and walk into my closet. As far as walk-in closets go, it's a modest one. There's a small aisle with his and hers shelving and closet rods on either side. My clothing occupies the right side. All of my dresses are organized by style and then by color, and my shoes are stacked neatly into cubbies along the wall. A few drawers containing tops and pants line the bottom just above the hardwood floor. At the top, a shelf extends across the length of my side. Frank's side isn't quite as neat, but I let it slide. I know he's a bit challenged when it comes to organization. The built-in storage helps a little, but he still manages to allow T-shirts to peek out of drawers that aren't quite shut all the way. I spy a worn navy blue sleeve of one of his polo shirts sticking out of the drawer near the wall, and I can't help myself. I stroll over and slide open the drawer, plucking the shirt from inside. If it was once folded, it definitely wasn't done correctly. The shirt is a wrinkled mess. It's no wonder it was poking out. I refold it and smooth it into place on top of the pile of shirts, resisting the urge to pull out the rest and refold them as well. Nope. I'm not here for that.

My gaze lifts to the shelf above my dresses. From this vantage point, I easily catch sight of the Bass shoe box where we stashed Wyatt's spy gear. I grab a stool from my bedroom and balance on it while reaching for the box. When I have it in my grasp, I sit down on the stool and rest the box on my lap. I swipe my hand along the top, ridding it of an inch worth of dust. Lifting the lid, I find everything just as we left it. The pen and camera are on top, and underneath are the instructions. Now all I need is a plan for how to get this into Madison's house. A shrewd smile curls on my face. I know just what to do.

PAUL MENTIONED that he only returned home for his thermos, and a quick glance outside confirms that his candy red pickup truck is no longer parked in the driveway. I waste no time skipping over to Madison's house and ringing her doorbell.

She answers with a confused look. "Jeanette? I wasn't expecting you back so soon."

I smile. "Sorry to bother you, Madison, but I seem to have misplaced my wedding ring."

She gasps. "Oh, no! That's terrible!"

I nod. "Yes, yes, it certainly is. I'm retracing my steps and that's what brought me here. It may have fallen off when I was in your bathroom. Do you mind if I take a quick peek?"

Her eyes shift to the empty driveway and then to the watch on her wrist. "Um, yeah, sure. I don't see why not."

She opens the door wide and beckons me in with a flick of her wrist.

"I'll just be a minute."

I walk toward the bathroom, but Madison starts to follow me down the hallway. That won't work. I can't hide the pen and camera with her in the room. I spin around to face her, and she jolts to a stop. "Sorry." I giggle. "It's just, you had offered lemonade when I was here earlier, and I've been craving it ever since. Would it be rude of me to ask if I could take you up on that glass after I've looked for my ring?"

She smiles. "No, that wouldn't be rude at all. In fact, it was rude of me not to give it to you earlier, but well, with Paul home…"

I rest my hand on her shoulder and give it a squeeze. "It's okay. Now is as good a time as any to share a glass of lemonade with a friend." I feel some of the tension leave Madison's body as her shoulders sag with relief. Paul has her wound so tight. I wasn't planning on sticking around after I planted the microphone and camera, but I can tell she needs a friend and I feel drawn to her in a way that I can't quite explain.

I remove my hand and point down the hall toward the bathroom. "I'll just be a few minutes. Fingers crossed I find it!"

"I hope you do," she calls to me as she retreats to the kitchen.

I take my time walking to the bathroom and once I reach it, I give a cursory glance over my shoulder. Madison is gone. Time to act fast. I shove my hand into my pocket, retrieving my ring. I slide it onto my finger and keep moving past the bathroom to the next door on the left. Her house is set up similarly to Josephine Barrett's who lives down the street. So, if memory serves, this should be the main bedroom. I turn the knob with care so it doesn't squeak, grateful when it opens easily and with no sound. I was right. Just like Josephine's home, this is Madison and Paul's bedroom. I take notice of the queen-size bed with a white comforter and white sheets. The bed is adorned with white pillows in an array of sizes. The walls are also white, and nothing hangs on them. The room is sterile and cold, and I instantly feel an unease settle in my bones. What kind of life is poor Madison living? There's no warmth here. No love. I shake those thoughts away. That's why I'm here. I'm going to fix this for her. I just need a little more proof.

There are dark brown nightstands on either side of the bed. The one closest to the door is barren with only a simple digital alarm clock and wrought iron lamp. The other one has a matching lamp, but it also has a white lace doily covering the surface. My eyes catch a glimmer of something. I move in close to inspect it and find a gold necklace with a pearl pendant on the doily. This must be Madison's side of the bed. I tug open the drawer of the cabinet and find a blank notepad inside with a few pens scattered around it. This is almost too easy. I grab the pen microphone in the pocket of my dress and drop it inside. It's so ordinary looking; it's impossible to tell the difference between it and the other pens.

Now I need to hide the camera. It needs to be concealed enough that it won't be discovered, but not so much that it doesn't catch anything. I survey the room and notice a dresser along the wall that faces the bed. It's the perfect spot to stash the camera. I suction it to the underside lip of the counter and angle it so it captures enough of the room. It's motion activated, so if any activity happens in here, it'll turn on and start recording.

"Any luck?" I hear Madison call from the kitchen. I scurry out of the room, closing the door carefully behind me. Just as I reach the bathroom door, she rounds the corner. Her eyes follow my hand, which I instinctively rested on the doorknob, making it seem as though I just closed the bathroom door.

"Found it!" I hold up my left hand so the front of it is facing her. The light filtering in from the kitchen windows spills down the hall and is enough to catch on the facets of the diamonds that line my wedding band, making it sparkle.

Madison smiles wide. "Oh, good! Where was it? You know, I was in there just before you came over and I never noticed it." Her eyebrows stitch together like she's working out a puzzle.

"Well, I'm not surprised. It wasn't easy to spot. I had just about given up hope when I decided to lift up the rug in front of the sink. I never thought I'd find it, but lo and behold, there it was! It must have somehow slipped underneath." I say it so convincingly, I almost believe it myself.

I see Madison's trust in me all over her face. It's in the light behind her eyes and in the curve of her smile. She doesn't doubt my story for a second.

I walk toward her. "I have an idea. Think we could take that lemonade to go?"

She rubs at her chin, looking befuddled. "Why would we need to do that?"

"I would love to show you my garden. The season is just getting started so nothing is really at peak bloom yet, but still, it would make me happy for you to see what's possible with a small space. So, what do you say?"

She tugs at her lip for a moment. Giving a quick glance at the door, she looks back at me and nods. "Sure, I would like that."

I beam. "Great!"

"IT'S JUST RIGHT THROUGH HERE," I say as I lift open the latch to the gate on the side of our house. Madison breezes into my backyard, leaving behind any of the trepidation she usually carries. She hustles past me toward the garden. There's a childlike wonder in her eyes as she marvels at the structure before her.

"Did you do all of this?" she asks, sliding her hand along the wooden posts surrounding the garden.

"I did. With a little bit of Frank's help, of course." I wink at her. "I had the vision and he had the brute strength." I chuckle, and she joins me. It strikes me that it's the first time I've heard her laugh in a genuine way. It's nice. I hope that pretty soon, she's laughing like that all the time. "Here," I say as I maneuver my hand over the lock and tug it open. "Go ahead in and take a look around."

She smiles, taking a tentative step onto the cobblestone path. She weaves around each bed, slowly taking in all the plants. Her hands gently caress the tops of a few of the taller plants, and I watch as she brings her fingers up to her nose to inhale. She's a natural and she doesn't even know it.

"So? What do you think?"

"What do I think? I feel like Charlie with a golden ticket. This is the most wonderful place in the whole world." She spins in a circle like a belle at a ball.

It's so freeing to watch her dance among the plants. Her joy is contagious. I almost want to join her.

Madison cranes her neck and studies my shed behind the garden. "What a cute little cottage."

I smile. "That's my she shed, otherwise known as the place where I store my favorite things."

Her eyes gleam. "Can I see?" Her legs begin moving as though there's a magnetic force pulling her body to the shed.

I hesitate. Is it wise to let her go inside? My compost bin is far from ordinary. What if it strikes her as peculiar, or worse— she starts to become wary of me? But why would she suspect me of any wrongdoing when no one else has? I'm over-thinking this. "Sure, follow me." But she's already ahead of me. There's a spring in her step that I've never seen. She looks…free.

When we reach the door, my intricate security system piques her curiosity. "Wow, you must really love the things inside. I've never seen such high tech means of keeping people out." She studies my face like she might find the reason for such extreme protective measures there, but she won't. Not the real reason, anyway.

I nod stoically. "My entire SnapLid inventory is housed inside these walls. Whispering Woods is a safe neighborhood, but I'd rather not take chances with something so important."

I pull open the door and wave my hand inside. Madison steps carefully onto the cement floor. There are no windows in my shed. The space is a void of darkness. I flip the switch at the door, and the room fills with light. Madison's head tick-tocks back and forth as though she can't decide where to look first. She settles on the shelves where my containers are orga-nized. Moving in closer, she lifts one—the small oval snack container. She turns it over in her hands and then places it back. Her head tilts up, taking in the vast inventory. "You weren't kidding. You must have every shape and size in here."

I nod, proudly. "I do. More than one of most of them and a few discontinued styles."

Her head bobs as she surveys the rest of the space. Finally, her eyes land on the metal beast in the corner. She floats across the floor until she's right up against the bin. Her hands land on it, and she slowly taps each of her fingertips on the surface. "So this is…interesting." There's that word again. Something tells me when Paul and Madison say it, it holds more weight. It's a simple word with a much more compli-cated definition. "This must weigh a ton. How'd you get it in here?"

I don't miss the fact that she didn't ask what it's used for. She moved right into asking how it got here. "It was built on the platform first and then the rest of the structure was erected around it."

She turns to face me, leaving her left hand still pressed against the cold metal. "I've seen something like this before." Her eyes narrow to pinpricks as she rifles through the contents of her mind trying to find the source. I hold my breath. A bin like this was featured in an article about human composting, but it was in an obscure science magazine and never made headline news. She couldn't have read it. Could she?

Madison snaps her fingers. "That's right! I was reading an article at the dentist's office a few months ago. It was in Better Homes and Gardens." I exhale the breath I'd been holding. There's no way a magazine centered on fluff pieces about ground covering and the difference between annuals and perennials featured a story about composting human remains.

She doesn't notice my relief. "There was this story about a small community college," she continues, "and they were known for their agricultural department. They taught a course that was held completely outdoors, and they needed an extra-large compost bin. That's what this is, right?" She pats the side, and her ring makes a ting sound on the metal.

"Yes, that's my compost bin. The place where trash turns to treasure with a few cranks of the handle."

A look of pure amazement fills her face. "It sounds like magic."

"That's exactly what it is."

Chapter Nine

ALWAYS KNOW WHICH WAY THE WIND IS BLOWING

WHEN THE KIDS WERE LITTLE, A FEW OF THE OTHER PRESCHOOL moms would often refer to Fridays as their "day off." They'd say housework is so tedious and draining. They needed a break. I'd bite my tongue when they would complain and nod politely when they would say Friday nights were made for pizza.

Tonight is the first time I feel a bit of solidarity with them. My evening is booked. I have a potential tyrant to spy on, a garden to tend to, and a family to look after. It's a lot to focus on, so it's easy to see the appeal of takeout. It'll surprise my family, but it's not entirely out of character. In the past, we've had pizza delivered when our schedules are packed or if I'm not feeling well. Sure, I could probably count the number of times on my hands, but I also don't think Frank or the kids will be suspicious enough to press the issue. They'll be far too occupied shoving greasy dough piled high with cheese down their throats. I cringe and remind myself to pop a few antacids before indulging in a piece.

Even though I'm taking a shortcut tonight, I can't let myself off the hook completely. I may be relaxing my duties slightly, but there's no such thing as a day off. So, I dash out to the garden and collect some leafy greens for a salad. They seem to be thriving—thanks, in part, to Henry's contribution.

For a moment, I allow myself to imagine what I might do if it turns out that Paul is abusing his wife. Madison isn't family, but my rule extends to include people I care about, and I already find myself caring deeply about her well-being. My lips arch into a grin as I imagine Paul turning over and over in my compost bin. A man his size would surely provide a mountain of black gold for my garden. Enough to last most of the summer.

Madison was so impressed with my compost bin. She talked nonstop about saving banana peels and watermelon rinds once she starts her own. Her enthusiasm was infectious, but as soon as her feet landed on the sidewalk and her eyes shifted toward her house, her carefree attitude disappeared and was replaced, once again, with a meek and sullen demeanor. If Paul is the poison in her life, it's going to be hard not to snuff him out.

I put the finishing touches on the salad and take the apple pie out of the oven, setting it on a rack to cool. In a few minutes, the doorbell will ring and the pizzas will arrive. I've timed it all perfectly. Gertie and Wyatt stroll in just as I'm setting the table.

"Hi, Mom!" Gertie singsongs, smiling wide at me.

"Hi, you two! You're just in time."

Wyatt asks the only question he seems to be capable of asking. "What's for dinner?"

Ding-Dong!

I tip my head toward the door. "Pizza."

"Pizza?" they echo in unison.

I nod as I breeze past them.

"I swear, we're the only family who eats pizza off of fine china. It wouldn't be *proper* otherwise." Wyatt's voice is low, but loud enough for me to hear. He's made sure of that. I stop walking. My back is facing him, but I can feel his eyes on me.

If I were to turn around now, I have no doubt I'd see a grin of satisfaction as wide as the ocean, merciless and without end. I breathe deep and fight the urge to chastise him. It's what he wants. I know I need to deal with this, but now is not the time. I shake my head and keep pushing forward.

I stride through the entryway to the front door. Jeffrey Catanacci stands on the other side. He's a year older than Wyatt. They used to play baseball together, but from the way things look now, that feels like a hundred years ago. Wyatt is tall and lanky and sullen. Jeffrey is short and round and happy. His hair is neatly trimmed, and his clothing is bright and unmarred by tasteless words. I imagine when he comes home after school, he gives his mom a hug and maybe even a kiss on the cheek. My shoulders sag with remorse when I catch myself comparing my son to this boy in front of me. Things aren't always what they seem; I should know. It's possible that when you peel back the layers, Jeffrey is really just a snide little twit. The thought does little to make me feel better, though. I'm a good judge of character, and I'm pretty sure my first impression was spot on. "Hi, Jeffrey. It's good to see you!"

"Hi, Mrs. S. I have your pies. Two pepperoni and one mushroom, right?"

Jeffrey's parents own Mama C's pizzeria. On the rare occasion that we order out, I always like to support our community and steer clear of the chains. Truth be told, Mama C's is mediocre, at best, but aside from Domino's and Little Caesar's, it's our only option for pizza here.

I take the boxes from Jeffrey, shuffling them onto the small table I keep by the door. Frank thought it was a silly waste of furniture, but once I insisted it live here, he stopped putting up a fight. I can't tell you the amount of times it's come in handy in moments just like this one. He doesn't complain about it anymore, but I suspect it's not because he sees its value. It's probably more that he knows he has no chance of winning the argument.

"How much do I owe you?"

"Well, it's normally twelve dollars a pie with an extra dollar for toppings, but on Fridays, we run a buy two get one deal!" He grins, and I see the pride he has in his job written all over his rosy cheeks. My instincts were right. This sweet-natured kid is the real deal.

"I guess it's my lucky night," I say as I sift through the money in my wallet. I pluck two twenty-dollar bills and hand them to him. "It's yours, too. You can keep the change."

He cradles the money in his hands the same way a child might hold a firefly, with wonder and a sense of accomplishment. "Thanks so much, Mrs. S. I really appreciate it!"

"Sure thing, Jeffrey. Please say hello to your parents for me."

He nods. "I will. Bye."

"Drive safe," I say as I push the door closed.

"Pizza, huh? What's the occasion?" Frank's voice bounces off the cathedral ceiling, making me jump. His shoes click on the travertine tile as he strides over to me. He grips my shoulders and presses his body against my back. "Sorry, hun. Didn't mean to startle you." He's trying to sound seductive, but his voice is like a fly buzzing in my ear. It's not his fault. I'm so preoccupied with the neighbors down the street. I don't have time to indulge his advances right now, but I don't want to hurt him, either.

I turn around and run my hands along the lapels of his sport coat, smoothing out the wrinkles. "Save it for tomorrow, dear. Now, come eat some pizza while it's hot." I sidle past him, looking back with a grin.

He arcs an eyebrow and adjusts himself, sighing audibly. Then he follows in step behind me.

NO ONE TALKS DURING DINNER. I'm usually the one to initiate conversation, but I'm only here in body. My mind is two houses down. It's just after 5:30 p.m. and I know Paul is home from work. I spied his truck in the driveway when I feigned a trip to the kitchen for a glass of water.

Wyatt sits on my right. He pushes the sides of his pizza together like a taco. We took the kids to New York City seven years ago and stopped at Joe's for an authentic New York slice. For Gertie, it was just another pizza joint, but Wyatt watched with rapt attention as city residents took their slices to go, folding them in half and eating as they walked. He's been eating pizza that way ever since. I know he wants me to believe that he's just trying to find his own way, but Wyatt is the type of kid who is as impressionable as a fresh lump of clay. It's why I worry about him, but it's also why I still have hope.

He cocks his head, studying me like I'm a new species that he's seeing for the first time. "What's with the weird smile, Mom?"

I lift my hand to my lips and sure enough, they're curved. I didn't even realize I was smiling. I let the memory of that little boy seep into my heart and it's written all over my face. I shake my head. "Jeffrey Catanacci delivered the pizza. Do you ever see him in school?"

Wyatt lifts his shoulder in a half shrug. "I guess."

"You guess? Why would you have to guess? I would think you'd know if you have."

He looks at me like I'm a splinter under his skin. "Sure, Mom, I've seen him. Happy?"

"Do you ever talk to him?"

He drops his pizza onto his plate, splattering grease onto the tablecloth. I make a mental note to stain treat it immediately after dinner. "Jesus Christ, Mom, what's with the third degree?"

"Language," I scold.

"Watch your tone with your mother," Frank pipes up from his end of the table. I lift my gaze to him, and he nods at me. I smile in thanks, and his eyes fall down to his plate with satisfaction. He's added his two cents and now he's left the conversation.

I glance back at Wyatt. He's no longer looking my way, but from the way he's shoving the pizza into his mouth, I can tell he's planning to make his escape. "You're not on trial here, Wyatt. I was just making conversation. I hadn't seen Jeffrey in a while and the two of you used to be so close."

"We were kids. A lot can change in five years."

"Oh, believe me, I know." My eyes catch on his T-shirt. I bite at my lip, holding my words back. Nothing else I want to say right now will help.

Wyatt watches me with narrowed eyes.

Gertie clears her throat. "Salad's good, Mom."

Her words wash over me. My daughter always seems to know the exact moment I need to be reassured. I may be floundering a little, but she helps me remember I haven't completely failed. And there's still time to save Wyatt.

———

"I'M GOING OUT FOR A WALK," I call to Frank. He's sprawled out on his recliner in the living room, watching a rerun of *The Office*. His baritone laughter grates on my last nerve.

"Be careful, hun."

"It isn't me who needs to be careful," I say under my breath. I pat my pocket and feel my Bluetooth earbuds. I'll need to find a place where I can hear what's going on inside the Munch's house while also remaining concealed.

It's just after 8:45 p.m. and the sun is mostly gone. There's a faint haze of orange on the horizon, but it's dark enough for the streetlights to come on.

I shift my eyes to the right and left, canvassing the neighborhood for looky-loos. Maple Avenue is like a ghost town tonight aside from the Thorn's bulldog, Chester, across the street. He's sprawled out on the lawn with all four legs fanned out like a starfish. When I start walking toward the sidewalk, he doesn't even open an eye. He won't be a problem.

I desperately want to turn left and head straight for the Munch's, but I need to be cautious. Just because I don't see any of my neighbors outside doesn't mean they don't see me. Instead, I turn right. I'll walk around the block and when I approach their home, I'll pop in my earbuds and keep my eyes peeled for somewhere out of sight.

I try to pace myself, but it's nearly impossible. I don't stroll. No one in this neighborhood has ever seen me move slowly. If I'm out for a walk, it's a brisk one, and if anyone can see me now, I doubt they'd notice if I pick up my speed slightly.

As I round the corner heading toward Madison's house, I notice a cobblestone path between her home and the Nester's. I snap my fingers. That's right! With older children at home, I had completely forgotten about the playground. It's behind a row of trees that line the Munch's property making it the perfect location for me to hide out. It's close enough that the Bluetooth should reach without a problem.

The path has seen better days. It's a bit run down and overgrown. My Keds crunch on broken stones as I stride with purpose down the trail. When I reach the end, I find outdated playground equipment scattered around with tufts of knee-length grass and weeds surrounding it. The butt ends of cigarettes litter the ground. The space was once open and well maintained, but now it's a sad shell of its former glory. This area used to be filled with the delighted squeals of children, but a quick look around proves that it's become a refuge for teenage hooligans.

A few tree limbs hang over the top of the slide, obscuring

it from view. The bark of one has been chipped away and the words *Eat Shit* are spray painted in red. My eyes follow the slide to the end. When we moved here, Gertie was almost thirteen and Wyatt had just turned ten. They had mostly outgrown playgrounds by that point. But Wyatt used to humor me. He'd tag along on walks and we'd meander back here sometimes. It wasn't all that long ago that I was standing here, laughing at Wyatt as he tried to fit his growing body into a slide made for toddlers.

The merry-go-round used to be coated in shiny blue lacquer. Wyatt's face was a blur as I'd hook my hands on the iron rungs, making it spin faster. Now it's chipped and dented with a hole in the middle that some *creative* individual decided to turn into an anus. The wonders of graffiti art never cease to amaze me.

The swings were where we spent most of our time here. I would take the one on the right and Wyatt would hop on the swing in the middle. We would race to see who could touch the sky first. It would always end in a tie. The metal was once a steel gray that felt cool to the touch. Now it's rusted and worn. A lone swing still hangs in the center, but the others are long gone. Only a few bolts remain. I tug on the chains, testing their strength. Once I feel satisfied that I won't plummet to the ground, I take a seat and pull out my earbuds. I click them on and push them into my ears. I paired them with the microphone before I hid it in Madison's drawer, so they should still be connected. I turn up the volume and wait. The only sound I hear is the slight creak of the swing as it sways.

It stays silent for so long that I begin to worry. Maybe this was a bad idea. I should head home. Frank is used to my evening walks, but if too much time passes, he may go out looking for me.

I sigh. This spy set is almost three years old, and it's spent most of that time stashed away in my closet. It's possible it no longer works. I tug an earbud from my ear, and just as I'm about to remove the other one, I hear voices. They're quiet at first, more like a low murmur. I can pick out both a masculine and feminine voice, but not anything they're saying. I slide the other earbud back into place and close my eyes, trying to focus on the voices.

"You still didn't answer my question, Maddie." Paul's voice rises, making it a little clearer.

If Madison answers, I can't hear her. There's a brief pause, and then I hear Paul again. The sound cuts in and out, but I can make out some of what he's saying.

"That's not good enough. You know how I feel about women like her—" My whole body freezes. I wait with bated breath for Paul to finish what he's saying, but it never comes. I hear a few muffled sounds followed by static. He said, "women like her." Was he talking about me? I lean forward as though that might help make things clearer. I can still hear garbled bits of conversation, but nothing I can make out.

The static clears and I hear voices again. "I'm sorry. What do you want me to do? Please tell me," Madison pleads. My heart hurts at the pain I hear in her voice.

"You're not trying hard enough. I can hardly look at you right now."

Slimy pig. He's breaking her down. Whittling away at her confidence until there's nothing left. I wish she'd speak up for herself, but that's easy for me to say. Those bruises on her arm. The bruises on mine. They're just a prelude to what Paul is capable of.

"I know. I'm sorry." She sounds so defeated.

I hear the distinct *slap* of skin making contact with skin, followed by a stifled cry. I hear it twice more, and then the only sound is Madison's muffled sobs. I can't see it, but I've heard enough. It's what I expected, and I guess, on some level, it's what I was hoping for. No, that's not true. I wanted to be wrong about him, but I knew he'd only end up proving me right. I wouldn't wish this on anyone. Now that I know, I have to protect her. I have to do something.

I blink a few times and notice I'm on my feet. I don't even remember standing. The need to go to Madison is over-whelming.

"Baby, no. It's okay. Come here." Paul's voice is different. It's consoling and remorseful and meaningless, but I'm afraid Madison won't see it that way. "Don't cry, sweetheart. It'll be all right. We can fix it." I hear the sound of kissing. I can see what's happening without actually seeing it. He's turning it around on her, trying to force her to shoulder some of the blame. "You okay, baby?" More kissing. I feel bile begin to rise in my throat.

"Mm-hmm," Madison answers, and even though it upsets me, I understand it. She isn't absolving him. She's just surviving.

The kissing intensifies, and then the moaning begins. I can't listen to this. I tug the earbuds out of my ears and hurl them across the playground. They land on the merry-go-round with a *thunk!*

"Mom?"

Wyatt stands in front of me. I didn't hear him approach, thanks to the sound of Paul's diatribe broadcasting into my ears. I clutch my hand to my heart and suck in a breath. "Wyatt, you scared me!"

"I can see that." He shrugs. His forehead creases with concern and it surprises me. He's behaving like he cares, and I haven't felt that from him in a long time. "What are you doing here? Are you okay?"

I flop back down onto the swing and rest my hands on my knees. "I'm fine. I was just out for a walk and thought I saw the Thorn's dog run back here."

"Chester?" His voice is incredulous. "He barely walks, and I've never seen him run."

"Well, clearly I was wrong. It must've been a groundhog or something."

A shadow passes over his face. "What's really going on, Mom? It's late and you're out here alone." He pauses, deciding whether or not to continue, and then he adds, "I saw you throw your earbuds." He looks at me like he's the parent and I'm the kid he just caught in a lie.

I stand up so that we're eye to eye. "I already told you why I'm here, and as for my earbuds…I was listening to an audiobook and I didn't like the turn the story took, but since we're playing twenty questions, why don't you tell me why *you're* here? Is this your hang out? Do you come here with Gage to smoke and deface the equipment?" I regret the words as soon as they leave my mouth.

His posture deflates like a balloon leaking air. "Sure, Mom. Whatever you say." His voice is dejected and his shoulders sag. "You know what? Screw this. I don't even know why I tried." His expression hardens. By coming here, he opened a door to repair our relationship, but I just slammed it in his face.

"Wyatt…" But it's no use. He's already turned his back. The opportunity I've been waiting so long for is gone, and I was too wrapped up in my own thoughts to even notice it was there in the first place.

He shuffles back down the path. When he's almost out of sight, he calls back to me, "You should probably head home. Dad's starting to worry."

Chapter Ten

A BLESSING IN DISGUISE

THE FIRST RAYS OF MORNING SUN PEEK THROUGH THE SLITS IN THE blinds and rest on my face. I've been awake for hours, lying here replaying the events of last night over and over in my head. I let Wyatt down *again*. I jumped to conclusions, lumping him into a category based off of his clothing and attitude. Sure, he hasn't given me much to work with, but he's still my son. He deserves to have his mom in his corner.

I feel a deep ache in the pit of my stomach, and if I close my eyes, I can still see his face. His eyes swimming with disappointment. I've made it my mission to make Whispering Woods a safe place for my family to live, but my son doesn't even have that luxury in his own home.

Right now, I need to get my hands on that camera and once I know for sure what's going on between Paul and Madison, I can take care of that problem and then I'll be free to devote all of my energy into fixing my relationship with Wyatt. I'm not quite sure how to do that, but I'm very resourceful. I'm sure I'll figure it out.

I sit up, letting the covers fall off of me. Beside me, Frank quietly snores and rolls over onto his side. His sleep is peaceful. He has nothing to worry about. Sometimes, I envy the simplicity of his life. Everything has been laid out for him. He wakes up at the same time every weekday, goes to work at a job he does well with people he enjoys working with, eats three balanced home-cooked meals a day, relaxes in the living room, and then goes to bed. His sex life is fulfilling and never a guessing game. And on the weekends, he can sleep as late as he wants. Not a bad gig. I smile at his slumbering form. I wouldn't have it any other way.

My mother didn't speak often, but when she did, she'd toss out little anecdotes about life. One of the things she told me frequently was, "Keep your husband happy and everything else will fall into place." She didn't tell me that in passing. No, she drilled that into me from the moment I was old enough to understand what marriage was. I realize now that for her, keeping my father happy meant allowing his abuse and ridicule to continue without intervention.

Once, when I was maybe thirteen or fourteen, I asked her if the same rule would apply if I chose to marry a woman. She gasped and eyed me with suspicion. Then she waved her hand, dismissing me altogether. Still, the next time she uttered her famous advice, I noticed she altered her words. "A happy spouse is a happy life, remember that." My mother was ultraconservative, and I loved to challenge her ideals. Part of me did it because I enjoyed getting a rise out of her; it was nice to be noticed, even if it was in a negative light. But the other part of me, the stronger part, wanted her to see the world from a new angle. If you're stuck in the same place, you can't grow. I think about Wyatt and how he's always pushing me. It often feels cruel, but perhaps he's just trying to help me grow. Maybe there's more of me in him than I thought.

Saturday mornings are quiet in my house. Everyone sleeps in. Everyone but me, that is. I get to work whipping up pancake batter. It's the perfect weekend breakfast because I can make a stack and then my family can heat them up in the microwave when they're ready to eat. It frees me up to complete other household tasks. And today's is a big one.

Somehow, I need to retrieve the camera and microphone I hid in Madison and Paul's bedroom. I wish I could go now, but Paul is still home. I've looked out the window no less than eight times, and his truck is still parked in the same spot it was yesterday. Madison mentioned that he works for a roofing company, so I'm holding out hope that he'll have an install later today. It'll be hard enough coming up with a reason to be inside their house again. With Paul home, it'll be impossible.

IT'S STILL SPRING, but the weather in Pennsylvania is behaving more like July or August when the temperature has little to do with the time of day. It's hot at five in the morning, balmy at eight, sticky at noon, and disgusting in the evening. The humidity is so heavy, moisture builds up on your skin even when you're standing still. I rope my hands around my hair and hold it into a low ponytail, securing it with a hair tie. I've only been outside for a few minutes and already there's a sheen on the back of my neck.

I unlock the gate and step into my garden. I take in a breath. "Ahh…" This small patch of earth has healing qualities. I feed it, and it gives. New life from wasted life. It's the ultimate second chance.

The leaves on my spinach are vibrant and full. Perfect for harvesting. Speaking of perfect, I have an idea. I carefully pick the outside leaves of the spinach plants until I have a hearty bundle in my hands. I head back into the kitchen and find Gertie at the counter pouring maple syrup on a stack of pancakes.

She greets me with a bright smile. "Morning, Mom!"

"Good morning, my sweet girl. How'd you sleep?"

"Perfect. How about you?"

Barely. "Not too bad." I wash the spinach in the sink and leave it to dry on a paper towel. Smiling at Gertie, I pat her arm as I breeze out of the room. I stroll up to the bay window in the living room and peer out. Paul's truck is gone! It's now or never.

I walk back into the kitchen and pat the spinach dry, sliding it into a small round SnapLid container. "Gertie, I'm going to take this over to our new neighbor's. If I'm not back before your dad and Wyatt come down, please let them know I'll be back shortly."

She nods. "Okay, Mom."

Once I'm outside, I fight the urge to break into a sprint. My body practically vibrates with the need to get inside the Munch's house.

I only manage to knock twice before Madison answers the door. Her eyes widen. "Jeanette!" Her forehead creases, and she glances nervously at the empty driveway. "Did we have plans today?"

"Hi there, Madison," I say with a smile. "I was just dropping by to bring you some spinach. It's fresh from my garden. I just picked it this morning."

She eyes the container in my hands like a child tempted to take candy from a stranger. Her behavior would strike me as odd if I didn't already have an idea of the dynamics in her household. It's clear that Paul makes it his job to know everything that happens, and I'd guess he might notice a strange container of spinach in their fridge and start asking questions.

There's a war going on behind her eyes. She's trying to decide whether or not to take a small stand. Accepting a plastic bin of spinach from a neighbor shouldn't be a big deal, and yet, in her house, it is. She puts a tentative hand on the side of the bin and then pulls it away. "Umm, why don't we transfer it to the bin you already gave me."

"Aha, so you and Paul finished up the zucchini bread

already, huh?" I had almost forgotten about that. I was just trying to welcome her to the neighborhood, but now I hope it wasn't a problem for her.

A funny look flashes on her face, but she quickly replaces it with a smile. "We did." It's two simple words, but I can tell there's a whole lot more to the story than those two words can convey.

"Perfect." I tip my head toward her kitchen. "Shall we make the switch, then?"

She looks behind her and then again at the driveway before finally settling her eyes on mine. "Sure, come on in."

The last two times I was here, I didn't have a chance to really look around at any rooms besides her bathroom and bedroom. Now, as I follow her into her kitchen, I let my eyes wander. Madison's home is spotless and very sparse. We pass the living room and dining room. Both are nearly barren. The living room has a small white sofa that faces a large flat-screen TV mounted above a stone fireplace. There are two small light wood end tables on either side of the sofa and a matching coffee table. The room is fairly large and could easily accommodate a sectional and possibly a recliner. The dining room is even more underutilized. There's a tiny square walnut table with four chairs. It's pushed against the wall so that the fourth chair is completely inaccessible. It's not even positioned underneath the rustic chandelier. I know they just moved in, but the lack of furniture makes me feel very uneasy.

There are no knickknacks, paintings, throw blankets, or decorations of any kind. Nothing to make the space feel homey and lived in. It's as if Paul and Madison aren't even human. They're just pretending to be so that they can attempt to fit in as some sort of odd social experiment.

I clear my throat. "Are you and Paul almost finished unpacking?" I ask the question with a lilt of hope in my voice. Maybe there's another moving truck that has yet to arrive and it contains all of the items that would make this house a home.

"Just about." Madison's answer is like finding out your dog died on the same day you lost your job. I don't know how anyone could live this way.

I stare at her back as she floats into the kitchen. She's wearing a gray long-sleeved tunic and black leggings. Her feet are bare and her toenails are painted a dusty mauve. She strides with purpose toward a small cabinet next to her range. She kneels in front of it, and with the door open, I can see a metal organizer where all of her cookie sheets are arranged by size. She lifts the organizer out of the cabinet, and there in the very back is the SnapLid container I gave her the first time I stopped by. She holds it and looks up at me sheepishly. It isn't hard to connect the dots here. I'm guessing Paul never knew about the zucchini bread. She chews on her bottom lip, looking back down at the container with its patented leakproof lid. "You know, on second thought, maybe it would be better if I put the spinach in a plastic bag. It would take up less space in the fridge that way."

And Paul would be less likely to notice it, but I keep that thought to myself. She knows it, and so do I. "That works, too."

Madison nods and begins putting the contents of the cabinet back into place. The container is, once again, relegated to the back, obscured from view. I set the spinach on the island and lean over, offering her my hand to help her up. I can't resist the urge, even if it is completely unnecessary. She's young and agile, and here I am trying to assist her like she's my ninety-six-year-old grandma. But if it strikes Madison as odd, she doesn't say anything. She clasps her hand in mine, and I hold on to her upper arm to steady her. She flinches and sucks in a gasp, pulling her arm out of my grasp. She rubs at the spot I just held. I hadn't even applied any pressure, so her reaction surprises me. "I'm sorry. I didn't realize I was holding on to you so tightly."

She shakes her head. "You weren't. It's just…I…well, I took a little spill last night and banged my arm on the corner of my nightstand. I guess it's still a little tender."

And I'm sure the *spill* you took wasn't due to your own clumsiness. "That's too bad. Hopefully, it heals up quickly."

"Once it does, a new one will just take its place." I wonder if she realizes she said that out loud. She looks at me, and with a half shrug, she adds, "Paul's always reminding me what a klutz I am." Another one of his mind games.

"Here," I say, gesturing to the spinach. "Why don't you go ahead and rearrange things however you need to. I'm just going to quickly use your bathroom, if you don't mind."

"Of course. Go right ahead. Paul's at the hardware store so he shouldn't be back for another thirty minutes or so." As soon as the words leave her mouth, she cringes. "I just mean, um—"

"No need to explain. If Paul is anything like Frank, he needs to use the bathroom the second he comes home. I swear, that man would refuse a public restroom even in an emergency." I giggle, and she joins in. The panicked look in her eyes begins to dissipate.

"I'll be right back."

Madison smiles up at me. "Take your time."

I don't have that luxury. Experience has shown me that I can never be too careful. Paul isn't home right now, but that could change at any minute. I need to act swiftly to avoid another run in. As soon as I round the corner and am out of Madison's sight, I rush toward her bedroom.

The door is open today. Perfect. I breeze in and head right to the nightstand, sliding open the drawer and retrieving the pen/microphone. One down, one more to go.

I dash toward the dresser and palm the camera still suctioned under the counter. I drop it into my pocket and am about to leave the room when the window along the back wall catches my eye. It directly faces the playground. My mind drifts back to last night. I wonder how clear their view is. Curiosity gets the better of me, and I shuffle over to see for myself.

Holding back the sheer white curtain, I notice a clearing in the row of arborvitaes that line their backyard. Through that bare spot, I can see most of the slide and merry-go-round and part of the metal posts that make up the swing set. A large oak tree obscures the rest. I was completely shrouded in darkness last night, but I'm still relieved to see that there's no way they could've seen me from here.

"What are you doing in my bedroom?"

My body jolts at Paul's voice. I close my eyes for a moment and collect myself before turning around to face him.

His large frame fills the doorway, and his looming presence casts an ominous shadow on the white carpet. I'm like a mouse who couldn't resist the cheese and now I'm caught in the trap. My mind races with an excuse, but he doesn't give me a chance to speak. He strides across the room until he's standing directly in front of me. My eyes flit to the door, but he's blocking any chance of escape. Besides, depending on what I find on the camera in my pocket, I may eventually want to lure him to my house. I can't give his suspicions any more weight than they already have by dashing out of the room.

"I'm gonna ask you again in case you didn't hear me the first time. What are you doing in my bedroom?" His voice is a growl as he looms over me, spitting out the question.

I match his rigid gaze with one of my own, and when I speak, my voice never wavers. "I was on my way to the bathroom when I heard a loud thud coming from this room. It sounded like something hit your window, so I rushed in here and that's when I noticed the nest right there in your maple tree." I tap my finger on the glass, and his eyes follow. A nest of twigs and leaves rests on a high branch. Five tiny beaks stretch out in search of food that a busy mama bird keeps bringing to them. Right on cue, she soars through the air and hovers above them, dropping bugs into their hungry mouths.

I shift my eyes to Paul. He squints as he watches the nature scene outside his window. "I'm guessing what I heard was just a bird flying too close to your window," I say as I begin to slowly tiptoe backward toward the door.

He turns his head, regarding me with a look of disbelief. I expect him to challenge me, but he doesn't. There's some-thing else in his heady gaze. Something that stops me in my tracks. His eyes flick down to my feet and begin traveling slowly up the length of my body, finally settling on my face. His amber eyes turn molten as they assess me. It feels like a violation, though his hands never touch me. My traitorous body warms beneath his scrutiny. I'll admit, Paul isn't lacking in the looks department, but underneath that attractive facade lies a monster who preys on the weak.

I'm reminded of what I overheard him say last night. "You know how I feel about women like her." Is this what he meant by interesting? Is he attracted to me? Or to something about me? Maybe I can use that to my advantage. But for now, I need to remove myself from this situation. Fast.

I turn away from him and walk evenly out of the bedroom. The voice inside my head shouts at me to run, but I will my feet to move like a person who has nothing to hide. By the time I make it to the kitchen, Madison has finished packing up the spinach. She's wiping water droplets off of the counter when I waltz into the room. I arc my thumb behind me. "Paul's home."

Her hand stills and a look of dread flashes in her eyes. It only lasts a second, and then she resumes wiping the counter as though Paul finding me here wouldn't be the worst thing that could happen. "I didn't hear him come in." I wonder how he managed to sneak past her, but if her back was turned and she was making noise, then it would make sense that she didn't hear him.

I grit my teeth as I brace myself for what I'm about to say. "He caught me in your bedroom."

She lets the towel fall from her hands, and I watch it land at her feet. Her eyes snap to mine, and I see something unexpected in them—anger. "You said you had to use the bathroom. Why were you in our bedroom, Jeanette?" Her voice is even, but there's no missing the menacing tone. I'm surprised, but I'm also pleased. Despite living in these oppressive conditions, Madison hasn't completely lost her spirit. That may come in handy if Paul is a problem that has to be eliminated.

I cast my eyes to the ground, trying to appear apologetic. Madison trusts me, and if I'm going to be an ally for her, I need that to continue. "I heard something bang against the window in your bedroom and I ran in there on instinct. I saw a mama bird feeding her babies in the maple tree right outside. I must have heard her hit the glass when she flew to the nest. I got a little caught up watching the birds and that's when Paul found me."

She bites her lip as she considers my words. Her head lulls to the side, and a faraway look settles on her face. "I've watched her, too. Soaring back and forth for hours feeding mouths that never seem to be satisfied. How does she do it? Where does she find the strength to keep going?"

I get the feeling she's no longer talking about the birds.

I close the gap between us and bend down, picking up the towel she dropped. Handing it over to her, I catch her eyes with mine. "She does it because it's all she knows. Instinct is a powerful force."

"Well, isn't this cozy?" Paul's rough voice cuts through the air like a knife in softened butter. Our shoulders sag; the comfortable moment oozes out of the room and is replaced with a thick tension.

Everything about Madison changes. Her body curls into

itself like a snail seeking comfort in its shell. Where she was wistful, now she's alert. Where she was strong, now she's timid.

Paul glances at us as he strolls through the kitchen. Tugging open the refrigerator door, he plucks an IPA off of the shelf. He pulls his keys out of the front pocket of his jeans and pops the cap with a bottle opener that hangs from his key chain. Madison immediately moves as though she's on autopilot, scampering into the walk-in pantry and returning with a beer identical to the one Paul is holding. She opens the fridge and replaces the IPA with a new one, shuffling the bottles on the shelf so that the older ones are in front. He keeps an eye glued on her, and a glint of satisfaction passes over his features. He has her trained well. The camera inside my dress pocket feels like it has a pulse. I need to get out of here.

Paul leans against the counter, crossing his arms against his chest. When he tips the bottle into his mouth, the veins in his arm bulge. He's making a show of himself. Reminding us he's in charge. An immovable boulder in the road. A barbed wire fence keeping his prisoner trapped.

My hand rests on the pocket where I have the microphone and camera stashed away. "I think it's time for me to head home."

Chapter Eleven

THE LAST STRAW

MY HOUSE IS EERILY QUIET WHEN I RETURN FROM THE MUNCH'S. I've been gone a lot longer than I had planned, thanks to my run-in with Paul. I expected to find Frank and Wyatt eating pancakes in the kitchen, but judging by the sticky plates stacked in the sink, it looks like I missed them.

Frank left a note on the counter:

Accepted a last-minute invite to play a round at the club. Be home by 5.

A brand-new bottle of phenobarbital sits on top, acting as a paperweight. Frank always comes through for me. It's one of the many reasons I married him. He never lets me down. And his timing on this refill couldn't have been better. I'm pretty confident that after I watch the recording, I'm going to need it. I'll have to mix the crushed pills with a little water to make the medication injectable, but I can easily do that later.

His note is not at all surprising. If we had the space, Frank would have a golf course in our backyard. On weekends when the sun is shining and the temperature is bearable, he's always at the country club.

I amble down the hallway to check on the kids. Gertie's door is wide open, but she's not inside. That's not unusual for her. It's Saturday and she often spends a large portion of the day with her friends. I'm only surprised that she hasn't texted me. She usually keeps me in the loop when she has plans.

Wyatt's door is closed as usual, but it's not latched. A soft push on the knob is all it takes. He's not in his room, either, which is also not unusual. He's most likely playing video games at a friend's house. The difference is, I know and trust all of Gertie's friends, but Wyatt's are mostly a mystery. He hasn't texted me, either, but he never does, so it makes no sense for him to start now.

Actually, this couldn't be more perfect if I had planned it myself. An empty house means I can watch the video my hidden camera captured without any interruptions.

My laptop is on an antique desk in the corner of our bedroom. I carry it onto the bed with me, sliding back against my pillows. I crack open the computer and connect one end of the camera cord to the mini camera and the other to the port on my laptop. The photos app opens automatically, asking if I'd like to import the footage. It only takes a few minutes for the video to load, and once it does, I watch with rapt attention, barely pausing to take a breath.

Madison is the only one on camera at first. She's standing in front of her nightstand looking off in the direction I'm assuming Paul must be. Her arms are crossed loosely in front of her. Her lips move a few times and her head nods, and then Paul moves into the frame. His back is to the camera so I can't make out exactly what's happening, but there's quick movement and then Madison is on the floor. He scoops her up and pulls her to him so that she's flush against his chest. There's no audio, but I remember this well. It's where he starts comforting her after striking her. It was bad enough hearing this all play out last night, but seeing Madison on the ground incites a deep rage inside me.

I pause the video and stare at the image of my neighbor—my friend—cowering on the ground. I care about Madison more deeply than I realized. Watching this footage is all the proof I need to confirm my worst suspicions. I know what I have to do, but what about Madison? When I'm around the two of them, their behavior is hard to read. She seems afraid of him, but she also seems to respect him and she may even love him. She wouldn't be the first person to love someone who only causes pain. I made that same mistake a few times in my life. First with my parents and then with Derek. It happens whether you want it to or not. Would Madison be able to survive without Paul? Sure. But would she want to?

I saw a bit of fire in her when she realized I was in her bedroom. She still has some fight left in her. She may be hurting at first when she thinks Paul left her, but over time, when it's clear he isn't coming back, she'll be able to move on and she'll be all the better for it. And the best part is, she won't have to do it alone. I'll be there to help her. Paul supports them now, but Madison is definitely capable of supporting herself. I can talk to Frank and maybe he can get her a job working the cash register at the pharmacy. I smile. She'll be just fine.

There's also the issue of timing. It's only been a little over a month since I composted Henry. I wasn't planning on making this a monthly thing. I don't want to arouse suspicion, and two missing people in under forty-five days would definitely get some attention.

Henry just vanished, and I didn't worry about it. Maybe that was cocky of me, but luckily it all seems to have worked out. But I can't make that same mistake twice. No. I need to be more careful here. This is going to take some planning.

Paul will be the first person I take who leaves someone behind. Someone who will actually care that he's disappeared. Madison is the key here. I need to have her completely convinced that he isn't coming back and give her enough answers to fill in the blanks. Which brings me to his wandering eyes. Something tells me I'm not the first "other woman" to catch his attention. That thing he said to Madison last night about her knowing how he feels about women like *her*—well, I'm pretty sure *her* is *me*. And women, plural tells me there have been more before. I don't think it would be too far-fetched if Paul actually decided to leave her for one of these women. And it shouldn't be hard to convince her. I'll just need to gather some evidence, or rather create it, and everything else will fall into place.

So it's decided. Paul will be next.

I scrub the camera clean and do the same to my laptop, permanently deleting the video. It's for my eyes only.

My phone buzzes in my pocket with an incoming text.

Gertie: *Hi Mom, I'm with Becca. Sorry I forgot to leave a note! We're going shopping for new shoes. See you at dinner!*

That's my girl. Always the dependable one. I shoot off a quick response.

Me: *Have fun and don't spend too much money! *Wink emoji**

After we moved here, Gertie was able to realize her original babysitting dream. There were so many young children in the neighborhood, she's managed to sit for every family on our street at least once. It's become quite a prosperous business for her. She rarely ever spends any of the money she makes, preferring instead to save it for college. She's on track for a scholarship, but she told me she wants to be prepared to cover the cost of books and her dorm. She's so responsible. I just wish some of it would rub off on Wyatt.

He's only fifteen, but he's already managed to have and lose four jobs. He's proven to be incapable of scooping ice cream, bagging groceries, making photocopies, and slinging burgers. I'm not sure what else is left for a kid his age. It's not that he's physically unable to complete those tasks, it's more that he has no desire to please anyone. He has zero work ethic and very little respect for authority.

I give my head a shake. *Stay on task, Jeanette. You can't go down this road right now. Madison needs your help. Then you can deal with Wyatt.*

Now that the evidence has mounted against him and I have a plan in place, it's time to work out a method for luring Paul to my shed. The school year is over soon, which means the kids will be coming and going freely all day long. Not exactly a good environment for offing my neighbor and shoving his body into a steel compost bin in my shed. I'll need to move quickly before summer break. I wish I had more time, but I also can't stand the thought of Madison being stuck in that house with him any longer than necessary. Her physical and emotional wellbeing is at stake. There's no time for second-guessing here. I need to act fast.

———

MY SHED WAS BUILT three years ago and looks as perfect now as it did the day the walls went up. The roof has architectural shingles in the same shade of gray as our house. Not even as much as a drip of moisture has gotten inside. But Paul doesn't know that. Maybe there's a leak at the top where the pitch is highest. We had quite a storm the other night. Suppose I walked into my shed the next morning only to discover a large puddle of rainwater waiting for me on the floor. I couldn't have that. Not in the location where I store all of my inventory. It would definitely be a problem that I would need to address immediately.

I grin wickedly as I imagine Paul's burly frame filling the tiny space while I deftly maneuver around him to inject a lethal dose of phenobarbital.

He's significantly larger than Henry, so it's a good thing Frank refilled my prescription. I'm going to need all of it to ensure that Paul is thoroughly dead.

I've been keeping an eye on him, and he seems to leave for work every weekday around 7:30 a.m. I'll make sure I'm outside bright and early on Monday morning so I can catch him before he leaves. I'm so excited; I can hardly contain myself.

Chapter Twelve

SPEAK OF THE DEVIL

THUNK! THE SUNDAY NEWSPAPER HITS THE FRONT DOOR WITH such force, I can feel the vibration through the floor. I spotted the blue Volkswagen as soon as it turned the corner and started driving down our street, hurling rolled-up newspapers out of the windows, left and right. I tried to make it onto the porch in time before it reached our house. I have no idea who's behind the wheel, but whoever it is has a habit of carelessly tossing papers that wind up in flower beds, birdbaths, or even through windows.

When I crack open the door and lean out to grab the paper, I hear a familiar voice carrying through the air. It's faint at first, but grows louder and more hostile. It stops me in my tracks. Paul sounds upset. I can't quite make out his words, but it's the unmistakable tone in his voice that makes my blood run cold.

I peer around my porch just in time to see him stalk over to Madison. He wraps a large palm around the back of her neck and brings her face in close to his chest. It looks like he could be trying to hug her, but I can't be sure. She swipes at her eyes and he cups her chin, cradling her face. She pulls away, and he doesn't put up a fight. Her fingers probe the back of her neck, and he runs a hand down the front of his shirt, smoothing it out. He's shaking his head and he points a finger at her. She looks at the ground. "Goddamn it!" My eyes widen at his outburst. Madison jolts to attention, standing ramrod straight.

I wonder if anyone else is watching this. The whole neighborhood has a front-row seat since he's made his driveway the stage.

My eyes shift to Madison. If I squint, I can see her lips move, but the sound doesn't make it this far. She has enough sense to realize they probably have an audience.

Whatever it is she says, it seems to calm him slightly. His chest rises as he takes in a deep breath, raking his hands through his hair and pulling at the ends. When his fingers loosen, he turns his head and his eyes land on me.

Fear creeps up on me, but I swallow it down. I won't let him wield that kind of power over me. I try to make my legs move and take me back inside my house, but I'm frozen in place. Unable to look away. Curious how Paul will react when he realizes someone witnessed him in action. Witnessed, but didn't intervene. The thought settles over me like a fog. How many times has this happened to Madison? How many times has she waited for help and it never came?

Paul holds me hostage with his glowering eyes for a few brief seconds before turning away and hopping into his truck. He revs the engine, and the ladder in the bed of his truck rattles in response before he peels off, leaving a cloud of dust behind. It shields Madison from view. The black smoke covers her, making her invisible. The same way Paul's merciless treatment has done.

"Don't worry, Madison. Help is on the way," I mutter. I duck my head behind the wall of my porch and step inside my house. The door closes behind me with a soft click. I stand with my back against it for a moment and then I give my head a light shake and greet my family in the kitchen.

JUNE IS ONLY JUST GETTING STARTED, and we've already seen our fair share of storms with fierce winds and soaking rain. That, coupled with the heat and sun during the day, has left my garden looking a bit like a jungle.

I come out here every day, but I still have plenty of work to do. Weeds sprout overnight between the cobblestone walkway, and the stalks of my herbs begin to look leggy if I'm not on top of harvesting them.

I mill about on the path, plucking crabgrass out of the ground and depositing it into the bag on my arm. The dill catches my eye. I notice it's nearly begun to flower. It will taste best if I harvest it before the flowers mature, so I begin pinching off the leaves until a third of the plant remains. It will continue to grow this way. Herbs are the true gift that keeps on giving.

"Did you enjoy the show this morning?" A gruff voice startles me, and the dill I just picked floats to the ground. I snap up to standing and turn toward the sound. Paul stands just on the other side of the fence that surrounds the garden. His eyes are menacing as they bore into me.

I clear the cobwebs from my throat. He's trying to throw me off balance. I can't let him win. My voice lowers an octave and my eyes narrow at him. "You *were* performing for the whole neighborhood, you know. But to answer your question, no, there was nothing enjoyable about what I saw and heard." I deliver my response like a threat. He doesn't know I didn't hear most of what he was saying. He doesn't *need* to know. It only matters that he believes I did.

He lifts his hand and probes the metal wire that separates us with his finger. I can tell he's trying to remain calm, but judging by the way the muscles in his jaw tick like the second hand on a watch, he's fighting a losing battle. His gaze holds steady. His eyes are full of anger, but that's not all I see. The copper hues swirl with the same heat I saw yesterday in his bedroom. What is happening here? Does he have a thing for mouthy women? If that's the case, it's a bit contradictory when you consider Madison's meek personality, but maybe she didn't start out that way. Maybe she challenged him. Maybe she had a lot of fight in her. And maybe he pounded it out, beat it down to the ground until there was nothing left but a shell of who she once was. The same person she can be again once this tyrant is gone from her life. Which gives me an idea…

I tip my chin suggestively and watch as the cords of muscle in Paul's forearm dance beneath his skin. Neither one of us utters a word for a few minutes. Instead, we study each other like we're boxers in a ring just waiting for the bell to ding. His eyelids are at half-mast and he's practically salivating. It's disgusting, but also exactly what I was hoping for. "So, I hear you work on roofs?"

His chin lowers slightly. "You heard right." His voice is gravelly and a little strained. This is almost too easy.

"I seem to have sprung a little leak in my shed. Could I trouble you to take a quick look while you're here? That is, if you have the … *time*."

Paul swallows my suggestion whole. "I could do that. But you'll need to come out here and show me." His eyebrow lifts in a challenge. He thinks he's got me hooked on his line and he's about to reel me in. I almost feel sorry for him, but he's an abusive, manipulative waste, so no—I'm not sorry at all. In fact, I'm going to enjoy turning the tables on him.

"I'll be right out." I float toward the gate with a seductive sway in my hips. I don't have to turn around to know he's watching me. I can feel his eyes all over me, making my skin crawl. *You can do this, Jeanette. Just think about Madison.*

Once I'm outside the safety of my garden, it's like I've entered a lion's den. Paul pushes away from the fence and struts toward me. As he moves, his hips tip side to side and his arms hang away from his body, as though their size makes it impossible for them to lower. I notice a hint of a wing tattoo peeking out from under the sleeve of his shirt.

To anyone watching, the two of us couldn't look more mismatched. Him with his tight T-shirt stretched taut over his bulging biceps. And me with my navy and white polka-dotted apron dress, my slender arms pulled behind me with my hands clasped against my back. We're sizing each other up, trying to determine the best course of action. Confidence rolls off of him in waves. I'm no threat to him. He doesn't see me as a worthy opponent. But he's wrong to underestimate me. He looks more like a peacock preening its feathers than a lion poised to attack. I'm the only lion here.

"It's right this way." I wave my hand at the shed with obvious exaggeration. He knows where it is. He's blocking my way on purpose. The little twitch at the corner of his mouth confirms it.

He flares out his hands. "You lead and I'll follow." The sexual innuendo is dripping off of him. I feel nauseous.

When I reach the door to my shed, I turn and practically crash into him. He's standing impossibly close, making it so I have to tip my head in order to look him in the eye. This is what he does—his modus operandi. Dominate. Intimidate. Control. I want to laugh when I think about what's in store for him behind these walls. He'll never see it coming.

"You know, my husband could walk out any second." My voice is just above a whisper.

He grins. "He could…if he was home. But he's not, is he?" He looks at me pointedly. He already knows the answer. That's why he showed up here unannounced. He knew I'd be alone. Despite the heat, a shiver runs through my body.

I let out a defeated sigh. "No. He's not home."

"That's what I thought."

He steps closer, bringing his leg to rest between mine. *Dominate*.

"How about your kids? They around?"

I shake my head, afraid to speak. I don't want him to hear the waver in my voice. He's too close. His throat bobs with a slow swallow. *Intimidate*.

This situation feels like it's getting away from me. I need to put some distance between us. "So—" my voice cuts through the tension, alleviating some of the tightness in my chest—"if you want to walk around to the side, that should be a good vantage point for the leak. I'll go in here and see if I can tell where the water might be coming in."

He peers down at me, looking as though he might say something. His mouth opens slightly and then closes. He steps back and I feel his absence immediately. Not in the way he hopes I feel it—like I'm missing the touch of a lover. No, this feels like a boulder has been lifted off of me.

Once he's around the side of the shed, I key in my code and unlock the door. I don't have much time, so I zip across the floor and slide open the drawer of my work bench. I'm greeted by the syringe of phenobarbital that I stashed inside yesterday. I wrap my hands around it and then gasp as I feel a rough, calloused hand slide up the underside of my dress.

"Hey, now, think maybe I've found the leak." Bile rises in my throat and it takes everything in me to tamp it down.

I stand up and spin around so fast, his hand falls from my thigh. I take a few steps back until I feel the cold steel of my compost bin against my bare shoulders. Paul's massive body fills the tiny space, and my brain struggles to play catch up. I hadn't planned on doing this right now or even today. But I'm an opportunist, and when the perfect moment lays itself at my feet, I seize it. I flick my eyes above Paul's shoulder and notice the shed door still propped open. If Frank came home early from his golf game, he could walk right in. What would this look like to him? Would he see me as a victim or a willing participant? Either way, it wouldn't matter. My husband is half the size of the immense man hovering over me. It wouldn't be a fair fight.

Paul lays a palm flat on the steel bin behind me and lifts his other arm to do the same, attempting to cage me in. But I duck underneath it and skirt around him. Now I'm facing his back, staring at the carotid artery on the side of his neck. It jumps as blood pulses through it beneath his skin. He scoffs. "You gonna play hard to get now?"

Before I lose my nerve, I wrap an arm around his waist and press my body up against him. He groans, and my face screws up in disgust. My other hand, the one still gripping the vial, brushes leisurely up the center of his back. When I reach the back of his neck, I linger, running my finger along the collar of his shirt.

"You like a woman in control, don't you?"

He grunts.

"Bet it turns you on to think about all the ways you could teach me a lesson."

He widens his stance. It's working.

I step up on my tiptoes and lean to the right, bringing my lips closer to his ear and whispering, "Is that what you were doing with Madison this morning?" I hear his intake of air, and I tighten my grip on his waist. His shirt gathers in my fist. "Is it my turn now?"

His hand covers mine and his fingers knead the fleshy part between my index finger and thumb. He adds slight pressure, and I feel my knees buckle. What's happening?

He chokes on a laugh. "Someone's been holding on to a lot of tension. Looks like you could use a release." He presses harder and my vision blurs.

"What are you doing?" My voice barely sounds like mine and my speech is slow. I don't like where this is going. I try to pull my hand away, but he keeps it pinned beneath his. He's rubbing the same spot over and over.

"Reflexology." The word sounds foreign coming from him.

My mind may be fuzzy, but it's clear enough to know this is not something I would expect from Paul. "I thought you worked on roofs."

"I do. Someone I used to know taught me this. Relax." I hate that word. Whenever someone says it, my instant reaction is to do the opposite. But this time, my body betrays me by staying still.

I try to stay focused, but my brain feels cloudy. I think I had a plan, but now I can't remember what it was. I can still feel it, hovering nearby, just out of reach.

My free hand is resting up near the base of his neck. I wiggle my fingers, and something moves inside my palm. The syringe. My brain snaps back into action like a rubber band that's been stretched to the brink and then released. My eyes zero in on the needle hovering so close to Paul's skin. I just need to pull my hand back slightly and then I'll be able to inject him and end all of this.

There's no time for hesitation. I let the vial settle into my palm and curl my fingers around it. My hand quivers as I raise it above my intended mark. On a deep inhale, I lower the needle and—

"Mom?" Wyatt's voice blows inside the shed like a burst of cold air. The syringe tumbles out of my hand and lands with a *crack* on the hard cement floor. Paul's hand stills on mine. "Are you out here?" my son calls again. I know I need to answer him, but first, I need to find the needle. My eyes do a quick scan of the ground and I spot the white tip of the plunger lying in front of my shelves of SnapLid. It'll only take a simple flick of my foot to send it sliding underneath and out of sight. I'm not sure if Paul heard it fall, but I don't want him to hear the scrape of plastic against the cement when I kick it.

"Guess that's our cue. Looks like this little rendezvous has come to an end." My voice is barely a whisper.

I start backing away from him and inching toward the needle, but his body turns abruptly. He grabs my wrist and tugs me forward. I stumble over my feet and fall into his chest. He cups my chin with the same angst I saw in him this morning when he gripped Madison's neck. There's nothing romantic about his touch. It feels explosive. He lowers his face until it's inches from mine. "To be continued." His words are a warning. Little does he know, that's exactly what I'm counting on.

He releases me and brushes past, strolling out the door with purpose. "Your mom will be right out. I was just helping her work out a *problem*." Paul talking to my son does something to me. I feel my insides burn with fury. I almost ended that son of a b—. A few more seconds and he would've been eliminated. I can't believe Wyatt's timing. And why was he even looking for me? He barely speaks to me these days.

But what if Wyatt had come by a few minutes later and found Paul lying dead on the floor of my shed while I stripped him of his clothes? I close my eyes and suck in a quick breath. That would've been a disaster that I'm not sure I could've explained my way out of. It isn't fair to be angry with Wyatt. None of this is his fault. This is what I get for acting on impulse. I had a plan and I need to stick to it. I know better.

I drop my hands at my sides and trudge toward the door, giving the syringe a swift kick when I walk past. Wyatt stands statue still a few feet away from my shed. His face is twisted in confusion. He arcs his thumb behind him. "Who was that guy? And what the hell was he doing in there with you?"

I plaster on a fake smile and look past my son. Paul is nearly out of sight. I can just make out the back of his head as he drifts between the houses. He turns, and our eyes lock. Something unspoken passes between us. For him, a vow that we'll resume where he thinks we left off. For me, a promise that I'll finish what I started. I lift my hand in a casual wave, and Paul's eyebrow arches. I turn back to Wyatt. "He's a new neighbor who happens to fix leaky roofs. He's helping me in the shed. Sadly, we didn't get to finish taking care of the issue today, but not to worry. He'll be back."

Chapter Thirteen

GOING BACK TO THE DRAWING BOARD

MY GO-TO WORDS OF FRUSTRATION ARE USUALLY THINGS LIKE, "oh, sugar cookie" or "crap crackers," but given the situation, those are falling flat. There's only one word that would truly work here so I'm going to let myself say it, just this once. I give the kitchen a quick once-over, relieved that I'm still alone, and then I exhale low and slow, "Fuuuuuuuuck." My shoulders roll back, letting some of the tension fall. There, that's better.

I had him. That slimy dolt practically handed himself to me on a silver platter. If it weren't for his acupuncture-esque distraction tactic, I wouldn't have been momentarily stunned, losing sight of my goal. I underestimated him, but how in the world would I have known that he was familiar with reflexology. That's an odd piece of knowledge for anyone to know, but for Paul? It's baffling.

And then Wyatt showed up just as I was about to plunge in the needle, preventing me from saving Madison and the rest of the world from that disgusting brute. Wyatt. When I think about why he called for me in the first place, I want to scream. Not at him, but at myself. Despite the intrusion, I felt my hopes lift at the thought of Wyatt wanting to spend time with me. I should've known better than to expect anything more from him. I don't know why I keep setting myself up for disappointment where my son is concerned.

"What was it you needed, Wyatt?" I asked him after Paul had gone home.

He looked incredulous, like the answer should've been obvious. When I didn't react, he tapped his watch dramatically. "It's after five."

"You're looking for dinner." I sighed.

He nodded slowly. "I was surprised to come home and find you hadn't even started it. Are you feeling okay? Are we ordering pizza again?" On that last question, he cocked his head. It felt like his way of letting me know he's on to me. But he couldn't be. Could he?

I've always been careful when it comes to the contents of my shed. My family rarely comes in here because there really isn't a need. The last time any of them were inside for longer than five minutes was the day construction was completed. All four of us worked together to haul my boxes of SnapLid out of the basement. I had everyone stack the boxes in piles on the floor while I organized them on the shelves. My security measures have ensured that no one has been able to enter without me ever since. And given the recent activities, all it would take is one curious person to crank open the door of my compost bin before a body had finished curing. It's a risk I can't afford to take.

No, there's no way Wyatt knows about that. But the way he was looking at me with such suspicion in his eyes tells me he misread the situation between Paul and me. And that would make sense considering Paul misread it, too.

I shrug it off. I can't worry about that now. I have much bigger concerns at the moment. The first being how I'll be able to create another opportunity to be rid of Paul. This afternoon was perfect. It's going to be hard to replicate. Hard, but not impossible. After all, I've already laid the groundwork. I just need to get Paul back over here to "fix my leaky shed roof" at a time when there's no chance anyone will discover us.

"Hi, Mom," Gertie greets as she skips into the kitchen. She tugs open a cabinet and pulls out a glass, then dances over to the sink to fill it with water.

"Hi, sweetie. You're looking chipper this evening. Any reason in particular?"

Her cheeks flush as she takes a long sip of water. "I spent the day with Reed. I've spent quite a few with him, actually." She lowers her head, looking bashful.

"Is that so?" Her admission surprises me. She mentioned Reed, but that was over a month ago and she hasn't talked about him since. I assumed she'd tell me once she agreed to go out with him, and I guess I'm a little disappointed that she didn't, but I won't press the issue. I agreed to give her some freedom and I can't rescind it the first time I feel uncomfortable. "Judging by the shade of crimson on your face, I think it's pretty safe to say it's going well."

She nods. "Mm-hmm, he stopped home to check in with his dad, but I was wondering if you would mind if he joined us for dinner tonight. That is, if you've made enough?"

I cock my head and squint my eyes at her. She mirrors my expression. And then we both laugh. I always make too much food. It's a Singleton family joke that I could feed half the neighborhood and still have leftovers.

"Actually, I think that's a fine idea. I've been itching to meet this Reed ever since you first mentioned him to me. I hadn't realized you've been spending so much time with him," I chide, giving her a pointed look, "but that only makes me more anxious to get to know him."

She wears a goofy grin as she pulls her phone from the back pocket of her shorts. "I'll text him and let him know he's invited. Thanks, Mom."

She prances out of the room like a carriage horse. I shake my head, muttering to myself, "Ahh, to be young."

———

EVERY SQUARE INCH of the dinner table is practically covered in food. Two huge trays of baked ziti sit on matching hot plates in the center. A large bowl of salad greens is perched directly in front of Frank, and a slightly smaller bowl of homemade applesauce rests in front of me. A covered basket of garlic bread is the first to make the rounds. Frank takes a piece and hands it off to Wyatt, who stalls for what feels like forever. He's always loved my garlic bread, but he's very picky about what kind of piece he wants. Not too brown, but not too light. Just enough butter and heavy on the garlic. Once he's found the perfect piece, he leans across the table and sets the basket in front of Gertie. She huffs dramatically, but he just snickers. Younger brothers are so much fun sometimes.

She makes her selection quickly and passes the basket to Reed, who happens to be sitting next to me. He looks at her and then at me, clearly confused as to why I was skipped over.

I smile at him. "I'm told I make a mean garlic bread, but I'm not a fan of garlic so I never eat it."

"Huh." His eyebrows jut down slightly like he thinks my admission is odd. And then he turns his attention back to the bread in front of him. I watch him out of the corner of my eye. I have to say, when Gertie introduced us, his appearance took me by surprise. She hasn't brought many boys home, but the ones she has invited here have all had a similar look. They're clean cut with hair gelled in place and they usually wear clothing with an air of wealth, something that isn't odd around here considering Whispering Woods is a more affluent neighborhood.

Reed doesn't seem to fit that mold at all. He doesn't fit any mold, for that matter. He's not a slight boy. I was wrong to picture him that way, but Gertie mentioned he was shy, and for some reason I always equate timidness with physical size. I imagined him to be small in stature, possibly even shorter than she is. Not only is he *not* shorter, he towers over her—almost comically. He's broad chested with a muscular build, one that comes with effort. His hands are large and rough in a way that suggests he's used to hard labor. His midnight hair is loose and free, falling in front of his face. He runs his hands through it, absentmindedly pushing it out of his eyes. Eyes that are the color of a swimming pool in the sunlight. The first time they looked my way, I was struck by their effervescent quality and the hint of danger I saw lurking in their depths. I can't get a read on this kid, but something tells me there's even more to him than what I see before me. He hasn't been overly rude. Actually, by some standards, he hasn't been rude at all unless you count silence as rude, which I normally do. Although, in this case, I can chalk that up to what Gertie has told me. He's aloof and very intelligent. I'm sure it must be intimidating for him to be surrounded by curious eyes tracking him like a cheetah pacing in a zoo habitat.

"So, Reed," Frank pipes up. "Gertie tells us you're in her AP History class."

Reed bites at his lower lip while keeping his eyes locked on his plate. His head nods ever so slightly; it's almost undetectable, but it's enough for Frank.

"That final term paper Mr. McGrath assigned kept Gertie up late into the night for several days. Bet you're both happy that's behind you."

Gertie smiles wide at her dad. She can see that he's trying, and she appreciates the effort. Reed's gaze is still glued to his plate, but he nods again, and this time I notice a little more neck movement.

"Say, uh, what topic did you pick for your essay?" I've got

to hand it to Frank, despite Reed's reluctance to speak or even look at him, he doesn't give up easily. Watching him so in control is making me want to break the schedule for a Sunday night tryst.

Reed clears his throat, commanding our rapt attention. "The history of teenage childbearing as a social problem." I arc my brow and look over at Frank. His eyes are as wide as saucers. From his perch on the other side of the table, Wyatt snickers to himself.

"Go on, tell them what you learned through your research," Gertie coaxes.

I lean forward, resting my chin on my hand. "Yes, Reed, please tell us."

He lifts his head and his eyes land on me. Did I just see his lip quirk in a smug smile? I blink and his expression is stoic. Maybe I imagined it.

He shifts his gaze to Gertie, and when he speaks, I can almost see the tiny cartoon hearts pulsing from her eyes. "From what I was able to determine, teenage pregnancy was much more of a prevalent issue in the late 1950s and early sixties when it reached its peak. It was thought to be a much more serious problem in the mid-1990s, but as it turns out, that wasn't at all the case."

"Really," I muse. "And what exactly is the reason for that?"

He lifts his eyes to the ceiling and his lips twist in a wry grin. "Some of it can be attributed to a decrease in sexual activity, however, the vast majority is due to the multitude of birth control available." Who is this kid? I can tell by the dramatic flare of his tone of voice that he's trying to get a rise out of me. Great. Just what I need. Another teenage boy with an attitude. He may not be as direct as Wyatt with his jabs, but his intentions are the same. He wants to see me squirm.

He reaches for Gertie's hand and lifts it to his mouth, placing a kiss on her knuckles. It doesn't sit well with me, especially not after he openly discussed teen pregnancy and birth control. I'm not naïve. I know what a teenage libido is like. I had one, too, but this is my daughter and I don't know when they started dating, but it couldn't have been longer than a month ago. That's entirely too soon for him to be insinuating anything sexual. He tips his head until he's looking at me. His eyes sparkle with mischief. He's goading me, and it's working.

I keep my eyes trained on him while maintaining a neutral expression, giving nothing away. I'm not sure what he's up to, but I don't trust him. Gertie seems completely unaware of what he's doing. To her, he hangs the moon and the stars.

I hear a snicker on my right. Wyatt is trying and failing to mask his amusement with his hand rubbing at his eye. Of course, he'd fall for this behavior. It's exactly what I've come to expect from him.

I flick my eyes up to Frank and find him enjoying his dinner, looking totally unaffected. Whatever shock he felt upon first hearing Reed's paper topic has completely dissipated. As usual, I'm the odd one out. But I can't help the way I feel. When it comes to my family, I'm always on high alert and something about this boy doesn't sit well with me. I need to keep an eye on him. I may be wrong, but what if I'm not?

Quiet murmurs of conversation from the left side of me pull my attention back to Gertie and Reed. Their heads are bent toward each other and their whispers seem to carry plans and promises that I can't let happen. The smiles on their faces—hers innocent and sweet; his cunning and manipulative—tell me I'm going to have to act fast before this gets out of hand. I clear my throat, but it doesn't pop their bubble. It doesn't even leave a pin hole. Looks like I have my work cut out for me.

I open my mouth to say something, but Frank starts talking to Wyatt about major league baseball, and that piques Reed's interest. I can't even pretend to care about anything sports related, but at least it put some physical distance between the two lovebirds. They're no longer pressed together in an intimate, hushed conversation. Reed is discussing RBIs or ERAs or LOLs or some other shorthand baseball lingo that sounds like an entirely made up language to me. Gertie is helping herself to more salad, but keeps glancing up at Reed with stars in her eyes.

The rest of dinner was fairly uneventful with the natural evolution of baseball talk morphing into football. Even though I care even less about football than I do baseball, I didn't check out of the conversation completely. I sat back and assumed the role of quiet observer. The more I watched Reed talking animatedly about sports with Wyatt and Frank, the more ordinary and less threatening he seemed. That doesn't mean I've forgotten his grand dissertation, spewing facts about teen pregnancy being less of a problem because of condoms followed by his brazen act of affection with Gertie. He was clearly testing me, and I'm still trying to figure out why. Despite that, he no longer feels like a problem I need to focus on immediately. I'll keep my eye on him, but I can shift my attention back to the larger issue at hand. Paul.

"Well, I should get going. Thank you for dinner, Mr. and Mrs. Singleton." *Points for manners, Reed.* He turns to me. "Mrs. Singleton, the pasta was delicious."

"Thank you, Reed. I'm glad you could join us." I say the words with conviction. I'm still not sure how I feel about this boy, but I want him to feel comfortable in my home. After all, it's easier to keep tabs on someone when they're under your roof.

Reed walks over to Frank and shakes his hand. "Mr. Singleton, I'm sorry if I got carried away with the baseball discussion. It's just that my dad isn't much of a sports fan and it was nice to talk to someone who is, for a change."

Frank claps Reed on the back. "Anytime, son." The word sends ice water through my veins. I shoot a warning glare at my husband, but he doesn't see it. I'll have a talk with him later. I may be giving Reed some leeway, but it's a far cry from welcoming him into the family with open arms.

Gertie stands from the table, and her hands twist together nervously. Reed grabs her wrist and gives it a gentle tug. "Walk me out?" She giggles and runs a finger along her ear, pushing her hair back.

She looks up at me with wide eyes. "I'll be right back." Reed takes her hand in his, threading their fingers together, and they stroll out of the room.

The *clank* of a fork hitting a plate startles me. I turn toward the sound and head right into Wyatt's heated glare. "You're just gonna let her go with that guy? Alone?"

His question stuns me. "I thought you liked him?"

"Yeah, I thought he was funny when he said all that stuff about teenage sex," he scoffs. "But no, I don't like him and I don't think he's right for Gertie." In a low whisper, he adds, "I don't trust him."

I never would've pegged Wyatt as the protective brother. Probably because he's never assumed that role before. I'd be lying if I said my heart didn't swell at the thought of him looking out for his sister. They have the kind of sibling relationship that mostly consists of teasing. I've always hoped that if the moment presented itself, they would have each other's backs. I just always thought it would be Gertie sticking up for Wyatt and not the other way around.

I consider Wyatt's words. "I know. I had the same thought." I look to Frank for back up, but he's too busy laughing at something on his phone. It's funny to think of Wyatt as my only ally here, but maybe this will be good for us. I turn back to him. "I have an idea."

He cocks his head with interest.

"Why don't you keep a close eye on them? Him, in particular. I know he's in the grade above you, but he seemed to enjoy talking to you and Dad. I think you have an 'in' with him. And you're less threatening than an overbearing parent."

Wyatt puffs out his chest. "I can be threatening."

I chuckle and shake my head. "Yes, I *know* you can, but in this case, I think it's in your best interest to be less than. Don't you agree?"

He nods reluctantly.

I lean forward, catching his eyes with mine. "So, what do you say? Can I trust you to watch over your sister and keep her safe?"

He tips his head. "I'll do it."

Frank sets down his phone and barks out a laugh. "You two are ridiculous. That kid is great. There's nothing to worry about."

I roll my eyes at him. "I hope you're right, but I'd rather not take chances when it comes to *our* kids." All humor drains from his face. He looks like a wounded animal, and I feel bad for insinuating that he doesn't care. I know he does. Sometimes he just comes off as too flippant when it comes to our children. He's always trying to school me on giving them more freedom and not being so hard on them. And I've been listening. But sometimes I wonder if that that's why I have a son who can barely stand me and a daughter who brings home a boy with questionable morals.

Gertie floats into the room and starts collecting the dirty plates and silverware. "Thank you, sweetie." I stand up and take the bowls that she has stacked on top of the plates. "Here, let me help you."

When we're in the kitchen, we move as though we're two cogs spinning together, completely in sync. We stand at the sink and begin our nightly ritual of she-washes-and-I-dry. We've been doing this together for so long, it's like a perfectly timed ballet. Gertie hands me the first plate and I begin drying it. "So, Reed seems nice."

She sighs. "He is." Her words are like a song. She's already fallen hard.

"I didn't notice his car out front. Where did he park?"

Her face pinches with confusion. "Why would he drive when he lives so close?"

"Wait, he lives here in Whispering Woods?" I know everyone in this neighborhood. If he lives close enough to walk, wouldn't I have seen him before? Gertie said he was new here. I frown as I try to picture which house he could've moved into.

"Uh-huh, right over on the other side of Mr. Stuart."

The blood drains from my face. Somewhere off in the distance, I hear the *crash* of breaking glass as the plate shatters on the floor at my feet, followed by the panicked cries of Gertie as she rushes to clean up the mess.

Reed is Paul and Madison's son.

Shit.

Chapter Fourteen

TO MAKE MATTERS WORSE

My mind is a fury of questions. Why didn't Madison tell me she had a son? The Munches moved in a few weeks ago; why haven't I seen Reed at the house? I always know everything that happens in Whispering Woods. How could I have missed this?

"Mom? Are you okay?" Gertie's voice lifts me out of the torrent of thoughts swirling inside my head.

"What happened in here?" Frank booms from the doorway, bending over to catch his breath.

"Oh my! I guess I wasn't holding on to that plate as well as I thought. Here, let me go get the dustpan and broom." I start to walk toward the closet, but Gertie's gentle hand on my arm stops me.

"It's fine. I already took care of that." She waves the little blue pan and matching brush and looks at me sideways. "Maybe you should sit down."

That's the last thing I need to do, but I don't want to worry her or act out of character. I nod and plop down on the stool in front of the island.

Frank strides over to me, placing a hand on my shoulder. "You all right, dear?"

"Yes, yes, I'm fine. You can go ahead back to the living room and watch your show." I wink at him, and he smiles sheepishly. I watch his back as he lumbers out of the room, and then I turn to face my daughter.

"Sorry, sweetie, I guess I was just lost in thought." I want to steer the conversation back to Reed. I need to hear details, but I have to tread delicately. "When you told me Reed lived in the Munch's house, I was thrown a bit because I've spoken to his parents and they never mentioned him."

The side of Gertie's lip quirks as she sweeps away the broken glass. "That's probably because he doesn't actually *live* with them. Not full-time, anyway."

"Oh? And why is that?"

She stops sweeping and looks up. Her eyes dart around the room to confirm that we're alone, and then she leans in my direction and whispers, "Mrs. Munch isn't his mom. And apparently, his dad 'got around' when he was younger." She air quotes the words for emphasis.

Paul got around? Imagine that. "Hmm, so he lives with his mom, then?"

She shakes her head. "That's the thing. His mom was only sixteen when he was born. His dad was seventeen. Neither were in a position to raise a baby, so he lives with his grandma."

So his parents were teenagers when they had him, and now he's writing research papers about the rise and fall of teenage pregnancy. Interesting. "Does his grandma live in Whispering Woods?" My brain works in overtime trying to determine who she might be, but again, I would know because I know everyone here. Or at least, I thought I did.

"No, she lives over in Meadowbrook Estates."

My face scrunches. "But Meadowbrook is in Greenbriar County."

She nods. "Uh-huh."

"Reed goes to Vernon with you. Shouldn't he be at

Hillman instead?" As soon as I say it, everything clicks into place. "Oh, that's right, I remember now. You told me he transferred, but I thought you said he moved?"

"I thought he moved and I guess, in a way, he did. But that's not why he left Hillman. It turns out there was an issue so his grandma asked his dad if they could use his address, and that's why Reed is at Vernon."

"Issue? What sort of issue?"

She sighs in a way that tells me she's been dreading that question. Whatever led Reed to stop attending Hillman High School and transfer to Vernon is probably more than just a matter of "he wasn't challenged enough." She bites at her lip and doesn't meet my gaze when she answers. "It was kind of a bullying thing."

"Kind of a bullying thing?" There's an edge to my voice that I can't control. I had a bad feeling about that boy when I met him and finding out he's Paul's illegitimate son hasn't helped my opinion.

"Yeah, um, see, I know he warmed up to you guys tonight, but Reed is very shy. It's almost crippling at times. Most teachers are understanding and work with him, knowing he's never going to be a kid who willingly participates in class discussions. But at Hillman, he had this English teacher who didn't care about any of that. She demanded he speak up and started calling on him every single day. Then one day, he just snapped."

I keep my eyes on her while hers look everywhere but at my face. She's pausing here, and I could make it easier on her by offering up my quick understanding and expunging Reed from any guilt. After all, the teacher clearly had it out for him. But it's that word she used. *Snapped*. It stops me from absolving him before I hear the whole story.

On a long exhale, Gertie continues. "He stood up and swiped his desk clear. His notebook and pencil went flying across the room. He shoved his desk and it flipped over. He called the teacher a few names and I guess he scared her because she apparently moved away so fast, her back hit the chalkboard. Then he stormed out of the room and left the building."

"How do you know so much detail about this? Did Reed tell you?" I squint my eyes, scrutinizing her face for the truth.

She half shrugs. "Some of it. The rest I gathered courtesy of the Vernon rumor mill."

"Gertie," I chastise. "Haven't we talked about idle gossip? You know better than to believe what others tell you."

"You're right. I know that, which is why I went to Reed and told him what I heard. He didn't deny any of it."

So it *is* true. When provoked, Reed turns volatile and reactionary. Like father, like son. Gertie was right to be worried about me hearing this story. It makes him sound like a chip off the old block and certainly not the sort of boy I want my only daughter hanging around.

She's watching me. Her big round eyes are red rimmed with unshed tears. She already knows what I'm thinking, and I can tell by the quiver in her chin that she's bracing herself for what I'm about to say.

"Well, it sounds to me like Reed isn't who I thought he was."

Gertie's face falls. "Mom, please, if you would just give him a chance, you would see—"

I hold up my hand. "Let me finish, sweetie." I brush my fingers along the smooth waves of her hair. "What I mean is— he seemed very timid, and people like that are often easy to take advantage of. But Reed stood up for himself when no one else would. Sure, I don't condone his actions. It's important to respect authority, but on the flip side, it's important for him to feel safe and respected at school, and his teacher deprived him of that. To me, that says he's the type of boy who would stand up for you if you were threatened. How could I not admire that kind of strength?" My words shock us both, but I keep my expression soft.

The truth is, until the words left my mouth, I wasn't exactly sure what I was going to say. A few short hours ago, I nearly had Paul composting in my shed. Now I've learned not only that he has a son, but that son happens to be dating my daughter. Everything inside of me is screaming to put a stop to this. But then I remember that age-old saying about keeping your friends close and your enemies closer. Reed was unexpected, but that doesn't mean I can't use his connection to Paul to my advantage. Not to mention, Wyatt promised to keep a careful watch on his sister. This surprising turn of events may actually prove to be quite useful.

Gertie drops the dustpan and brush and launches herself at me, wrapping her arms around my waist. "Wow, Mom. I wasn't expecting that. I'm so glad you're giving Reed a chance. Thank you." She pulls back and looks deep into my eyes with adoration and affection. I feel a slight tinge of guilt for letting her think I'd even consider giving that boy a shot, but then I remind myself that everything I do is for the greater good of my family.

I wind my arms around my daughter and give her a squeeze. "There's one for the money."

She squeezes back. "Two for the show."

I feel confident that everything will work out exactly as it's meant to.

PAUL LEFT for work an hour ago. I stood and watched him from my window, toying with the idea of dashing out to greet him and make arrangements for him to come look at my roof. But then I remembered Reed. His existence complicates things.

Ty and Henry lived alone. It's a fact I used to think made

them more dangerous. With no one to watch over them, they were free to do whatever they pleased whenever they wanted.

Paul is different. He's married, a fact I knew from the start and in this case, it's the reason why he caught my eye in the first place. I pushed it aside, assuming I'd be doing Madison a favor. Paul as a husband garners no sympathy, but Paul as a father feels different.

Gertie mentioned Reed lives with his grandma. She never spoke of his biological mom. I have no idea if she's in the picture. It's possible she isn't. And if that's the case, can I really take this boy's only parent away from him?

I've never been a big proponent of "sons need their fathers and daughters need their mothers." I think it's more that kids need a grownup they can count on. One person can play the role of both. Maybe Madison isn't Reed's biological mother, but that doesn't mean she couldn't fill the role.

I need to do some more digging before I make a plan, which is why I've suddenly found myself strolling along the path leading up to the Munch's front door. It's odd that Madison never mentioned Reed. I think it's time I got her side of things.

My knock is more forceful than I intended—I put all of my questions, frustrations, and intentions into my clenched fist and slam it against the worn front door. A few seconds pass, and it's in those that I gather all of my negative energy and push it down deep into my gut. I need to maintain controlled behavior. If Madison opens the door and I unleash all of my pent-up hostility onto her, she's going to feel backed into a corner, more so than she already does.

I close my eyes, inhaling through my nose and exhaling out of my mouth. I count each breath and on three, the door creaks open. Madison's smile is warm and inviting. The shift in her demeanor is subtle, but noticeable. She doesn't look at the driveway; rather, her eyes stay locked on mine. There's no mistaking what I see before me—confidence. The first few times I visited her, I frightened her. She's slowly warmed up to me, but even still, her behavior now is surprising.

"Hi-ya, Jeanette." A tiny hint of crow's feet stamps the corners of Madison's eyes. I don't think I've ever seen her smile this wide, except maybe when she was wandering through my garden.

"Hi, Madison." My greeting sounds warm, even though I feel far from it. I can't shake the peculiar feeling that there's more going on inside this house than I realized.

"What brings you here?" Her eyes flick down to my hands, but they're empty. She's used to me bringing gifts, but this isn't a social visit.

"Can we talk for a few minutes?"

The broad smile melts off of her face, and a fractured one settles in its place. Her eyes dart to the driveway, only this time I wonder if she's hoping to find Paul's truck there. "Sure." She nods somberly. "Come on in."

The last time I was inside this house, I was struck by how barren it was. I was so distracted by what I *didn't* see; it kept me from noticing the small details. That was before I knew Reed was living here. Even if it is only part time, it's hard to mask the presence of a teenage boy. And now that my eyes are open, I see evidence of him everywhere.

A pair of worn Nike cross trainers rests against the beige rug next to the door. They're laying in a way that suggests they were removed quickly and haphazardly tossed aside. On one of the end tables sits an open can of Crush orange soda. There's no coaster underneath and something tells me if I lifted it, I'd find a sticky ring in its place. The dining room chairs are all pushed in, but on the cushion of one I see a rolled up faded black T-shirt similar to the one Reed wore to dinner at our house.

Madison leads me to the kitchen and waves a hand at the

breakfast nook in the corner. "Have a seat. I'll get us some iced tea."

I want to tell her not to bother, but it wouldn't make a difference. I can tell she's nervous to hear what I came to say. Keeping busy helps her relax.

A few minutes later she places a tall glass of iced tea in front of me and takes the seat opposite me. The glass has already begun to sweat from the cold liquid and ice. Tiny droplets of condensation form and I watch as one starts to make the journey down the glass toward the table. It collects other drops along the way and by the time it reaches the bottom, it's grown much larger. We don't speak for a minute, and I keep my eyes on the glass, following more drops as they slide down. I tap at a few and they immediately join together. It's momentum in its purest form. Something starts out tiny, even microscopic, but slowly as it moves, it starts picking up speed. It gets passed around and adopted by others until it's ten times larger and more powerful than it was when it started. It's the very core of humanity. Alone we are small, ineffective, but whenever we connect with another person, we grow. We thrive.

Madison clears her throat, shaking me out of my deep concentration. "You said you wanted to talk?" she asks with a tentative voice.

I smile at her and notice the subtle relaxing of her shoulders. "The last time I was here, things were a little strained—"

"Strained?" The skin of her forehead folds like an accordion.

I scratch at an imaginary itch on my chin. "Maybe strained isn't the right word. But after I told you I had wandered into your room and Paul discovered me, it felt like something shifted between us." Her head bobs in rapid, jerky movements as though it might have the power to fast forward this conversation.

She tries to dismiss my concern with a flap of her hand.

"Oh, that was nothing. Just a little misunderstanding, but it's all water under the bridge now."

I let out a relieved sigh. "Well, I'm certainly glad to hear that. I feel like you and I were becoming friends and I would hate to have done anything to jeopardize that."

She shakes her head. "Not at all, Jeanette. You've been so kind and welcoming. I couldn't ask for a better neighbor."

Thanks for the perfect segue, Madison. "I feel the same way. It's a good thing, too, since our kiddos are spending so much time together lately." I keep my tone light and laugh softly.

Madison laughs, too, but hers is heavy, weighed down by guilt. She shifts uncomfortably in her seat, changing positions every few seconds. If she has anything to add, she keeps it to herself. I can't say I'm not disappointed. I thought she might come clean right away.

"Did you tell me that Paul had a son? I was surprised when Gertie mentioned it, but then I wondered if maybe I knew and just forgot." We both know she never told me. I'm giving her a lifeline. Now to see if she takes it.

She bites at her lip and lowers her eyes to the table. "Sorry, I guess I never mentioned Reed." She rubs her fingernail back and forth, scraping at a mark on the wood. "He wasn't around much at our last place, and honestly, I didn't think he'd be around much here, either."

"What changed?" I hate how my question sounds, like I'm desperately seeking information. But the truth is, I am. I need more answers. About Paul, but also Reed. He's dating my daughter, and Madison's withdrawn behavior isn't doing much to alleviate my concerns.

"So much has changed. He's been living with Paul's mom, Amelia, since he was born."

"Why didn't Reed live with Paul or with his mom? Does he have any contact with her or his other grandparents?"

She cradles her neck in both hands and massages the base of her skull. This is clearly not a topic she enjoys, but I can't let her off the hook. She lets out a long exhale. "Stacy and Paul weren't really ever together aside from that one night, but everything changed when she found out she was pregnant with Reed. Her parents are wealthy and very fixated on social status. An unwed pregnant teenage daughter was not acceptable. They wanted her to terminate the pregnancy, but she wouldn't hear of it. So they disowned her."

I gasp. "That's awful!" I think about my own daughter. Suppose she found herself in this same situation. How would I react? I guess I can't say for certain, but I'd like to think I'd support her no matter what she decided. I can't imagine abandoning her during such a tumultuous time in her life.

Madison tips her chin solemnly. "I know. It's so cruel. And I sympathized with Stacy, I did, but there's more to this story. Paul promised her that he would be there for her and the baby and help them in any way he could. But Stacy had other ideas. She became obsessed with Paul and tried to use the pregnancy to trap him. You can't believe the lengths she went to." Madison rolls her eyes. "She had some crazy notion that Paul would be more attracted to her if she was more independent. She got a job doing some kind of weird pressure point therapy and when that didn't seem to get the attention she wanted, she stooped even lower. Even going so far as to move in with his own mother just to be close to him. Amelia wasn't much better. She believed Paul should marry the mother of his child. And she kept on believing that, even after he and I met."

I grit my teeth. So that's where Paul learned that weird trick he did with my hand. But if he and Stacy weren't close, how would she have taught him? Something doesn't add up, but this all happened before Madison came into the picture. Maybe she doesn't know the whole story. Paul probably only gave her the highlights he thought she needed to know. I scrunch up my nose. "That sounds like a tough situation for you."

"You don't know the half of it. I won't lie. Paul was a terrible father to Reed. He was never interested in being a dad. It was like trying to force a round peg in a square hole. He'd provide for his child, but that was as far as his parental instincts went. Paul's own father deserted him and his mom when he was only six years old, and he used that as an excuse for his behavior. Most people would try to learn from the mistakes of their parents, but Paul emulated them." She shakes her head. Paul isn't winning any points with me. I had awful parents, too, but the way I see it, you have two choices. You can learn from their mistakes or you can use them as an excuse. I may take lives from time to time, but only to protect those I love. That's the difference between my parents and me. I *can* and *do* know how to love; they never learned how.

I notice a change in Madison as she tells this story. She's reciting it like she's exorcising a demon. Her eyes are manic, darting all around the room. Her tone is nearly menacing. If I could see inside her head right now, I'm certain I'd find confirmation of her true, unabashed hatred for Stacy.

"I hope Stacy isn't still causing problems for you."

"Not anymore. She's not causing problems for anyone, actually. Stacy's dead."

I'm getting whiplash from all the twists and turns in this story. "Dead? How?"

"Car accident." Madison responds like I asked her, "what is two plus two?" She sounds bored and completely unaffected. I understand what she's feeling. It's hard to have sympathy for someone who's done nothing to deserve it.

"When did that happen?"

She takes a long sip of iced tea. "Two years ago. She drove straight through a solid red light, slamming into the back end of a tractor trailer." I suck in a breath. Such a violent end for Stacy, but considering all that Madison told me, maybe the ends justify the means.

"That's when everything really changed with Reed,"

Madison continues. "Before then, Paul was more of an uncle to him than a father." Her words are like salve on a wound. If Paul isn't a father figure, maybe he hasn't had a chance to corrupt Reed. But then my mind replays what she said and catches on a word, *was*. "These last two years, Paul decided Reed needed a man in his life and he started spending a lot more time with him. Paul isn't one to watch sports, but he found other ways to bond with his son. He took him fishing and to the shooting range, just trying to connect with him on some level."

I'm reminded of the night Reed ate dinner with us and fell so easily into conversation with Wyatt and Frank. They jumped from baseball to football with no hesitation, and Reed's face lit up with an almost child-like joy. He mentioned his dad wasn't a fan of sports. I didn't pay much attention to that since I didn't realize who his father was, but now when I think back on it, it was clear that Reed was looking for more.

"I'm sure it can't be easy trying to bond with a teenage son who you aren't very close to."

"No, it hasn't been easy at all. Paul's had a pretty rough go of it and he knows he deserves it. But he keeps trying. He even got him a job at the roofing company and bought him a used truck. It's just…Reed's different. He's prickly."

"Prickly? Well, I guess that's understandable given what happened to his mom and his lack of a relationship with his father. I was only with him for dinner the other night, but once he warmed up to us, he seemed pretty easygoing." I don't mention the part about him diving into a dissertation on teenage pregnancy. Given all that Madison has just told me, I'd say he's a kid who's been tossed around and he was just testing the waters. I'm still a little leery of him, but my heart has definitely softened.

She coughs on a laugh. "I'll say this, I would never describe Reed as 'easygoing.'" She pauses, seeming to get her thoughts together. "Listen, Jeanette, he's my stepson and I'm supposed to care about him." She shakes her head. "I mean, I *do* care about him, but if I'm honest, I don't like him very much. He has a temper. I've only seen it briefly, but it was enough for me."

"Hmm, I'm glad you brought that up. I heard a story about how he came to be a student at Vernon. Something about an incident with a teacher at Hillman High? It sounded pretty intense."

She's quiet for a beat and then she waves her hand, dismissively. "Oh, that was nothing. Just a big misunderstanding, really."

"He changed schools midyear. That must've been *some* misunderstanding."

She shrugs. "A teacher had it out for him and Reed overreacted and then the school *really* overreacted."

I bite my lip, unsure of her version of the story, but she just admitted she didn't like Reed very much. Why would she lie about this? She leans across the table and takes my hand in hers. "Listen, Jeanette, I shouldn't have said anything. I know he's dating Gertie, but you have nothing to worry about. Reed is a typical angst-ridden teenage boy most of the time. He's just always had a little extra baggage, and after what happened, it's gotten a little worse. He's under a lot of stress, but that's all it is."

It sounds like she's trying to smooth over the jagged edges of her candid confession. I want to believe her and I think I do, but I can't shake the feeling that there's more to this story.

Chapter Fifteen

A CHIP OFF THE OLD BLOCK

I'M TRAPPED IN MY OWN HEAD AS A BARRAGE OF THOUGHTS assault me from every direction. When I left Madison's house, I had no clear picture of what to do next, which is highly unusual for me. I pride myself in always having a plan. I don't like curveballs, but I've never encountered one I couldn't handle. Until now.

I've been sitting on the bench swing outside of my shed for the past few hours. Unable to move. Just a couple of days ago, I had Paul right where I wanted him. Well, almost. He was inches away from becoming compost. Everything was much simpler then. More direct. Paul was an abusive husband. Madison was living in danger. I had the perfect solution. But now everything has changed. It's become more complicated. Paul is a father to a boy who lost his mother. A boy who has been dealt a cruel hand in life and who has been acting out as a result. Also, a boy my daughter is enamored with.

And then there's Madison. After she told me all about Reed and Stacy, I asked her how she came to meet Paul. She looked at me with humor sparkling in her eyes. "It's a romantic story, but it won't sound that way."

I cocked my head. "Now I'm intrigued."

She laughed. "We met at a gas station. We were filling our tanks across from each other."

"You're right. That doesn't sound very romantic."

She holds up her hand. "That's because you don't know the backstory. See, I had never pumped my own gas before that day. My dad had always done it for me." Her eyes were downcast and sullen. "Pneumonia took him from us so fast. It's been four years and I still can't quite wrap my head around it. My mom died three months later. Her heart was too broken to keep beating." She shivered and wrapped her arms around herself. "Anyway, I put off filling up my tank for as long as I could. It sounds crazy to say it out loud, but my dad had been the last one to put gas in my car and when the empty light came on, it felt a bit like losing him all over again." I leaned in and placed a comforting hand on her forearm.

"I'm so sorry. My parents are both gone, too. It's a wound that never fully heals." Only my wounds were caused by my parents when they were alive. I don't have the luxury of happy memories like Madison does.

She nodded. "So if you can picture it, there I was, standing in front of a gas pump, completely clueless and sobbing like a fool. I heard someone clear their throat. I looked up and there was Paul. I can't describe it, even now, but there was just something in his eyes. It was like he knew my whole story before I uttered a word. He walked around the pump and stood right next to me. But instead of taking over, he put his hand over mine and led me through the process. His voice was so calming. It was like being wrapped in a blanket. At the time, I was so cold, all I craved was that warmth. And now here we are."

Hearing her tell that story did something to me. It made me sympathetic toward Paul. It gave his humanity a pulse. Up to that point, I had only viewed him as a problem that needed to be solved. Goodness didn't exist in him. Or so I thought. But Madison had just proved otherwise. It doesn't erase what I've heard. What I know. What I saw. But it blurs the edges a bit. Making them fuzzy and unclear.

No matter what I do, there will be a direct outcome and I need to determine if it's one I can live with. *Every action has a consequence.* My dad's words still ring true, now more than ever. He drilled them into my head over and over.

I glance down at my left hand, flexing my fingers one by one. They've been healed for years with nothing but a tiny white scar across the knuckle of my middle finger. That's not to say my father's punishment didn't leave a mark. It's just on the inside where no one else can see.

"Mom," Wyatt whispers with a hand on my shoulder, gently shaking me.

I blink open my eyes and find him crouched down at my feet, peering into my face with concern. "Hi, kiddo." I smile at him.

The corner of his lip quirks slightly, but the worry doesn't leave his eyes. "Were you sleeping?"

I shake my head. "No, I was just dreaming awake."

"Huh?"

I chuckle. "I was remembering a time when I was little, and I guess I just got lost in the memory." I look around and notice the backyard is mostly shaded. "What time is it?"

"It's a little after four." His brow furrows. "How long have you been sitting here?"

I shrug. "A while. It's hot, but there's a nice breeze in the shade. It felt good just to let myself be for a change."

He nods like he understands. And maybe he does. I always think of Gertie as the one who's always trying to top herself, never stopping to smell the roses along the way. But Wyatt isn't quick to cut himself some slack, either. He's too focused on reinventing himself, either to shock me or to keep life interesting, or both. He never settles. I've never pegged

Wyatt as being driven, but maybe, in his own way, he is. He and Gertie just wear it differently.

"Okay, so listen, I did what you said. I've been keeping an eye on Reed."

I sit up and place a hand on his shoulder. He glances at it for a second before looking back at me. It makes me realize I don't touch him very often. I can't even remember the last time we hugged. I keep my hand where it is because I'm his mother and affection from me should not be shocking.

"We have lunch during the same period," he continues. "But today, he never showed. He wasn't at his usual table, and when I looked around the cafeteria, I couldn't find him."

I shrug. "Maybe he stayed after class for some reason or had a doctor appointment."

"Well, yeah, you might think that and I probably would've, too, but this is too much of a coincidence."

I lean forward, letting my hand fall from Wyatt's shoulder. "Coincidence? How?"

"Today someone took Mr. McGrath's car keys and cell phone and put them up on the roof of the school."

"You're kidding! Who would do that?"

Wyatt smirks. "Someone who wanted to send a giant 'fuck you' to a teacher who screwed them over."

I squint at my son, who seems to be leaving a trail of breadcrumbs for me. "My interest is piqued. Go on."

"Wait, are you not going to say anything about my *crass* language?"

I shake my head. "I'm learning to relax, Wyatt. Try to keep up." I grin.

His eyes tick-tock between mine. "Are you sure you're feeling okay?"

I wave away his concern. "I'm fine. More than fine. I promise." It's not a lie. I'm having a real conversation with Wyatt. No one is yelling. No eyes are rolling. No one's defenses are up.

"Well, okay then. Where was I?"

"You were about to tell me why you think Reed put Mr. McGrath's things on the roof."

He cocks his head. "Ah ha, so you *are* paying attention!"

I laugh. "Just trying to keep you on your toes. Please, continue."

He makes a grand show of clearing his throat. He's enjoying this way too much. This son of mine is pretty funny. How have I never noticed that before? "So, as it turns out, McGrath gave Reed's teen preggo paper a B minus, which, according to Gertie, was not acceptable."

"Gertie told you about this?"

"Uh-huh. I saw her before third period. She was leaving AP History and looked really upset. I asked if she was okay and she told me about Reed's paper. She said, and I quote, 'He was angry in a way I haven't seen before.'"

A shiver rolls down my spine. Wyatt clocks it and gives me a grim nod. "I know, that was my reaction, too."

"Did she say anything else?"

"She said when the bell rang, Reed told her he'd catch up with her later and he rushed out of the room, but not before he went up to McGrath. Gertie couldn't hear what he said, but she could tell he was pissed."

"Wow. Still, how do you know he was the one to put the keys and phone on the roof?"

Wyatt taps at his temple. "Elementary, my dear mother."

"Oh jeez," I huff. "Get to the point, my dear son."

"It's simple, really. McGrath had his phone during fifth period. I know this because he used it in every class today. He made them all listen to Billy Joel's 'We Didn't Start the Fire.' Apparently, he believes that everything we need to know about history is in that song." He pauses, pushing his lips together and shaking his head. "Those poor kids," he mutters. "Anyway, back to the phone. McGrath also has sixth period. From what I've heard, he always leaves his suit jacket on the back of his chair with his phone and keys in the pocket. When seventh period rolled around, he reached for his phone to play that damn song again and *dun dun dun*, it was missing. Then, Ms. Warner started squawking over the loudspeaker asking if any of us had seen the phone. McGrath was using Mrs. Anders' phone to continuously call his, hoping he'd hear the ringing from wherever it was stashed. A few kids in study hall volunteered to go outside to search, and that's how they discovered where it was. And get this, his ring tone? It's the theme song to *Days of Our Lives*." He snickers.

"Well, this certainly sounds like a banner day for poor Mr. McGrath, but really, Wyatt, that still doesn't prove it was Reed." I pause to consider the logistics of such an elaborate prank. "How do you even access the roof? There must be a door or something."

"There is, but this is where it gets interesting. See, last week, someone graffitied the walls of the stairwell that leads to the roof—"

"Someone like Gage McNamera?" I narrow my eyes and Wyatt rolls his.

"That's not important. Anyway, the walls were being painted today so that part of the stairwell was blocked off." He pauses for dramatic effect.

"And? What aren't you saying?"

"Come on, Mom. You're smarter than that. Think about it for a minute. If the door to the roof wasn't accessible, how else could you get up there?"

I drum my fingers on my chin. "A suppose a ladder would be an option…" Madison told me that Reed had started working with Paul and recently got a used truck. I haven't seen it parked in their driveway, but chances are, he has a ladder just like Paul's.

Wyatt sees the moment it all comes together and nods triumphantly. "See? I knew you'd figure it out."

I shake my head. "Wyatt, listen, I'm not one to approve of

petty pranks, but that's all this was. It sounds to me like Reed overreacted, but at the end of the day, no one was hurt and it was just a harmless joke."

"Harmless, huh?" Wyatt hums. "I guess I forgot to mention the punchline. Not only did he stash McGrath's phone and keys on the roof, he also decorated his Subaru."

My brows pinch severely. "What do you mean?"

"Oh, nothing really. Just etched 'Mr. McPrick' right on the hood of the car."

"You're serious?"

"As a heart attack," he affirms.

"All of this over a B minus on a paper?"

"Seems a little strong of a reaction, don't you think?"

What it seems is that Reed is a lot more like his dad than I realized. Madison said he had a temper and she's clearly uncomfortable around him. But this is extreme. "I know all signs point to Reed, but are you really positive it was him?"

An impish grin curls on his face. "I am. But don't take my word for it. Ask him yourself. He's right inside."

Chapter Sixteen

EVERY CLOUD HAS A SILVER LINING

Dinner is a disproportionate medley of throats clearing, silverware scraping, cups clanking, and the occasional quip about the latest news headlines. Those come courtesy of Frank, who's totally oblivious to the tightness in the room. Whenever he offers a morsel of conversation, Gertie jumps on it. She feels the tension, but she's quick to mask it. Wrapping it up in bandages in a fruitless attempt to conceal the obvious.

Wyatt was right about Reed. When we walked back into the house after our discussion, Gertie and Reed were in the kitchen. Her shifty eyes danced everywhere but on mine, and he looked smug, leaning against the counter with a can of Coke in his hand like he lived here. My son took a paternal stance with his hand resting on his hip. "So, how was everyone's day at school?" His accusatory tone rippled through the room. Gertie's eyes snapped to Wyatt's, and her jaw clenched. They've always been able to communicate with just a look. And hers said everything.

But the final nail in Reed's coffin came from Reed himself. He laughed at the question, and the throaty sound bounced off the walls as he crossed the room to stand directly in front of Wyatt. Reaching into the pocket of his jeans, he pulled out

Wyatt's key chain and dangled it in front of him by the lone front door key. "You left this on the table by the door." He moved to hand it over, but as Wyatt went to grab it, Reed snatched it back. "Probably not a good idea to leave keys unattended. They could wind up in the wrong hands." Wyatt's eyes narrowed into slits as he swiped the keys. Reed snickered and palmed Wyatt's cheek, giving it a patronizing pat before turning and strolling out of the room. Gertie followed closely behind, disappointing me more with each step.

Now we're all sitting around a table looking like one big happy family, and it's all a lie. I can pretend better than most people. But I've never had to pretend in here. Not in my dining room.

I glare at Reed as he nimbly eats the dinner I prepared. The only thing that isn't tough in this room is the medium rare steak he's chewing. He brought this discord into my home. He *and* his wayward father. It always comes back to Paul.

"So, tell me something, Reed." My voice cuts through the silence. All eyes are on me. "How do you like living in Whispering Woods?"

"I like it more now that I've met Gert." He nudges Gertie with his elbow, and she lights up.

Gert, huh? I suppress the urge to roll my eyes. "I understand you've been splitting your time between two homes. That must be a little rough."

He looks at me like he's trying to see through mud. He has no idea where I'm going with all of this, and truth be told, neither do I. But I'm sure I'll figure it out along the way. "It's not too bad. I keep duplicates of the important things at each house and that makes it easier."

I nod. "It must be a little strange living with your dad after all of this time."

His expressions twists with confusion, causing the skin

between his eyes to wrinkle as he stares intently at me. "It's an adjustment."

An adjustment I'm afraid he's thriving in. "I was so sorry to hear about your mother."

The muscles in his jaw tic, and his eyes drop to his plate. He remains quiet, clearly hoping this line of conversation changes. Unfortunately for him, I'm just getting started.

"At least you have Madison. I'm sure her presence has been a comfort—"

"That woman is NOT my mother." A barely controlled fury boils behind Reed's eyes that are now locked on mine. I poked the bear and got the reaction I was looking for. He has a hair trigger, and if I were to push just a little harder, I think we'd meet the kid who was capable of carving up his teacher's car. I don't need to do that, though. I've seen enough.

Before I heard the story from Wyatt, I was toying with the idea of dropping my plot against Paul Munch. Reed lost his mother. Should he lose his father, too? Is it fair of me to sentence him to a life without his parents?

But then I think about my own father and the paternal guidance he gave me. And look how I turned out? Sure, I may do things that an ordinary person wouldn't, but only when it fits my code. I have a husband that I love and two children I adore. I've made a life for myself, not because of my father's influence. In spite of it. I know Paul has only recently entered the picture with Reed. I don't think he's been around long enough to have done any lasting damage, but it's better for Reed if he never has the chance. It may be too late for Paul, but there's still hope for his son. And I think the fury behind Reed's poor choices stems more from feeling discarded rather than how he was raised. He and Madison are clearly not close, but maybe they could be. Maybe in their shared grief over Paul's absence, they could connect in a way that helps them both thrive.

I give him a sympathetic look. "Of course. I didn't mean to imply anything." I still don't trust Reed with Gertie, but I can relate to him. It's an odd feeling. To be cautious around someone that you also feel protective of.

He nods curtly, and then we're back to where we started. Eating dinner in silence.

―――――

AFTER DINNER, Frank takes Reed into the den to show him a video of "the greatest triple play in baseball history." Frank didn't seem to notice the tension during dinner, but why would he? He has no idea what transpired at school, and I feel a little guilty keeping it from him. If he knew what Reed did, I'm sure he wouldn't want Gertie anywhere near him. I don't really want him near her, either. But I also understand more about Reed's upbringing than anyone else at that table, and I think having someone like Frank to talk sports with may be exactly what he needs right now. Wyatt has never been a true fan. He's always humored Frank by watching games with him and listening to all of his theories, but he doesn't share the same devotion. Still, Wyatt catches my eye when Reed leaves the room with Frank. He gives me a tiny nod and follows them into the den.

It dawns on me that only a few days ago, I viewed Wyatt as a roadblock in this house. Something to move around and avoid for fear of the repercussions that might come from running into it. But now, he's more of a partner. We're sharing secret looks and communicating without words. We're a team. Sure, it's all because we're conspiring and keeping secrets, but in the name of repaired relationships, I'm calling it a win.

Gertie and I clean the table, collecting silverware and stacking dishes in a synchronized dance. We don't speak. The tension from earlier during dinner has dissipated a little, but hints of it are still there. I catch her giving me a few sideways glances, testing the water. I could make it easier on her and normally I would, but she let me down. I don't know what she sees in Reed, but to stick by him so intently after the behavior he's exhibited makes no sense to me. I may understand his actions, but I definitely can't excuse them and neither should she. It's completely out of character for her. It's almost as if she and Wyatt have switched roles. I used to be able to predict her every move, but right now I can't even pretend to know what she's thinking. As her mother, I could forbid her from seeing him, but we've all read that story or seen that movie. We know how it ends. As soon as a parent labels something "off-limits," it becomes much more enticing.

Which is why my plan feels even more dire now. Removing Paul is what's best for Madison *and* Reed. I hope they'll lean on each other, but even if they don't, they're much better off without his dark presence looming over them. Maybe Reed won't stick around after Paul's gone. That wouldn't be the worst outcome, either. No matter what way I look at it, it's two birds, one stone.

Gertie's scrubbing a plate under running water, working the rough side of the sponge against the soiled china. Without warning, she plunks the dish into the sink of soapy water and shuts off the faucet. Leaning against the counter, she angles toward me. "Even though I know I won't like what you have to say, I still wish you'd say it. Just to get it out in the open. Because this"—she moves her hand back and forth between us—"is making me crazy. It's not us."

She's right. We've always been open and honest with each other. And up to this point, I never would've held back with her. But I also never had a reason to. She's played her role dutifully, and I'm beginning to think I've been putting an unfair amount of pressure on her to continue behaving in the manner in which I expect. She's human and we're all flawed, no matter how hard we try not to be. I think Reed is a mistake, and based on what she's just said to me, she already knows that.

I set the fork I'm drying into the rack and let my eyes drift over my daughter. I see her. *Really* see her. She's always so put together. From her carefully styled hair to her expertly applied makeup to her perfectly manicured nails. When I look at her now, I see the spot on her chin where her foundation has rubbed away from the constant worrying of her hand. Most of her hair is still secured in a French braid, but pieces have fallen out of the plait and a few land in front of her eyes where she furiously swipes at them. The polish on her nails has been picked clean and some of her cuticles look raw. Her misery has become a second skin. So I ask the only question I can. "Why him, Gertie?"

She lets out a long sigh. "I could explain, but I don't think you'd understand."

I take her hands in mine. "Well, then, make me understand. Because from where I'm standing, all I can see when I look at you is despair."

She bites her lower lip and nods sadly. "I do feel that way, but it's not for the reason you think it is. I know Reed doesn't seem like the ideal boyfriend, but listen, Mom, you don't see him the way I see him. He's been hurt, badly. He's been dealt one awful hand after another. Deep down, he feels unwanted. Can you imagine what that must be like to live with the constant feeling of abandonment?"

Actually, I can. It's crippling. "I know his life hasn't been easy, and I can give him a pass on being less than pleasant, but honey, he vandalized private property. I can't make excuses for that, and you shouldn't either." I level her with a pointed look.

She responds with a shake of her head. "I can't abandon him right now. I won't." She turns back to the sink and resumes washing the dishes. She's made her decision and she's closing the door on any discussion of the contrary.

A part of me respects her tenacity. She believes in Reed, and she's bound and determined to stand with him when the rest of the world seems to have turned its back. It's honorable, but it's also a problem. If she becomes the *only* person he can trust, I fear that puts her in a very dangerous position. I know I won't be able to get through to her, not when she's convinced herself that she's all Reed has. Which brings me back to square one. Paul. If I get rid of him, then the problem is gone. Maybe Reed will stay; maybe he won't. Either way, it'll be better for him. And for us, too.

Gertie hands me a plate. It's dripping wet, and I watch the water droplets move around. Just like the glass, they glide and connect, spreading as they move. Paul's evil is just like that first drop of water. It slithers around until it finds another lonely drop and then it attacks, first connecting and then overpowering. I think about everyone that's been affected by Paul. Madison was vulnerable at that gas station. She never saw any of this coming. And Reed didn't have a choice. You can't pick your family. And now it's here in my house infecting all of us. It's like a virus. It needs to be snuffed out. I swipe at the drops with my towel and they smear along the china, coating the surface. I stopped the movement, but I didn't stop the spread. I've only managed to mix everything together. One more furious wipe of the towel rids it of all moisture. The threat is gone. The surface is clean.

Chapter Seventeen

THE DEVIL IS IN THE DETAILS

I'M NOT SURPRISED THAT REED ISN'T A FAN OF HIS STEPMOM. Even knowing how sweet Madison is, it's often rare for kids to readily accept a stepparent, especially one they feel is a replacement for someone they've lost. Stacy died, leaving Reed without a mother. It's unclear how close he was to her, but I can only imagine how difficult that must've been for him. It's one thing to have no relationship with a parent; it's another to know they're gone for good. When that happens, any dreams of a magical reconciliation die along with them.

Despite his feelings being logical, I still need to investigate them. If I hope to have them bond once Paul is gone, I need to understand how deep their bad blood runs. Maybe there's still hope for them. Which is why I find myself outside the Munch's house bright and early the next morning.

Madison answers the door before I even have a chance to knock. "Hi, Jeanette! I was just standing by the window finishing up my coffee"—she lifts the mug in her hand—"and I saw you coming up the walkway."

Her sunny disposition throws me off a bit, but I recover quickly and find my smile. "Actually, I was just popping in to check up on you."

She tilts her head. "Check up on me? Why?"

"Oh, it's nothing really." I flap my hand. "It's just when I was here yesterday, we got into some emotional territory, and I wanted to make sure you were doing okay—that *we* were okay."

She buzzes her lips. "Of course! You and I are friends and in a true friendship, there's always heavy lifting involved. We're totally fine. As a matter of fact, I was just about to refill my cup. Come on in and join me?"

She's awfully chipper today, almost uncharacteristically so. But that could work in my favor. She may be more willing to divulge information if she's feeling relaxed. "Sure, I'd love some."

Madison pours our coffee while I retrieve the half-and-half from her fridge. It strikes me then. I've been in her home a few times, but she has yet to be inside mine. I wouldn't say I'm comfortable here—far from it, but there's a familiarity that comes from having already been somewhere. Once Paul is gone, Madison will need a comfort like that. "I have to say, I feel a little guilty here, Madison."

She scrunches her face. "How so?"

"It's just, I've been in your home a few times now and you're always so hospitable. I need to return the favor. You should come over some time for a girls' night on the patio. We could have wine. It would be fun! What do you say?"

Her expression turns timid. "Well, um, sure, maybe we could do that."

She's saying no without ever uttering the word, and I know why. I smile at her because I have a secret. Soon she'll be able to say yes without hesitation. "Where, again, do you keep your sugar? I can't remember."

She grins. I didn't press the issue, and her relief is palpable. She points to a small cabinet above the microwave. "It's right in there."

We take our coffee out to the deck and sit in amicable

silence for a beat. The view from here is remarkable. The backyard is sloped, making the first floor seem like the second from out here. The deck sits at least twelve feet off the ground. It's an excellent vantage point for watching the deer that often wander over from the forest nearby. Forty years ago, when this land was sold, Whispering Woods was built among the trees. It was a revolutionary idea at the time because it was more fashionable to clear the land entirely, build new homes, and then plant new trees. But not here. Here we have trees like the maple behind the Munch's house that are over fifty years old. A fawn and her doe push through the overgrowth that separates the yard from the playground and sidle up to the base of the tree to snack on grass.

Madison lets out a delighted gasp. "This is my favorite part about living here," she whispers.

"You have the perfect view, that's for sure."

We watch the deer as they meander around the yard, stopping to munch along the way. "It's adorable the way the baby follows its mother, isn't it?"

She nods. "Mm-hmm."

"It reminds me of when my two were tiny. They were my little shadows. Gertie always followed everything I did, right down to the way I brushed my hair every night before bed." I run a hand through my hair, recalling the way my daughter would sit beside me and we'd brush our long locks with even strokes. I steal a glance at Madison and find her leaning forward, her elbows on her knees and head resting on her hands. She looks almost childlike as she marvels at the deer. I turn my head back to the yard and watch as the little doe dutifully follows its mama. I think about Reed and his mom. She's gone now, but was there ever a time when he looked at her with as much awe as this baby looks at her mother? "Poor Reed. I know what it's like to lose a mother at such a young age. I'm sure it's been really difficult for him. He must miss her terribly."

I watch Madison for a response, and it comes in the form of a slow swallow. She keeps her eyes fixed on the deer and never utters a word. Reed said she was no mother to him, and her lack of sympathy isn't shining the best light on her. We stew in the uncomfortable quiet for a few more minutes when she finally turns to me. "Well, I guess I better get started on the laundry. It won't wash itself, unfortunately." She chuckles at her attempt at humor, and out of pity, I join her.

We stand and take our cups back into the kitchen. She heads toward the sink and motions for me to follow. She sets her mug on the counter and runs a finger along her ear, pushing her hair back. It's then that I see it. A round bruise, about the size of a half dollar, on her neck, just below her earlobe. It's purple and angry and looks slightly raised. "Oh, Madison! What happened?"

"Huh?" She looks at me, and for a brief moment seems completely perplexed. My eyes stay glued to the bruise and when she catches my line of sight, her hand moves instinctively, tugging her hair back over her ear. But it's too late, and she knows it. I can almost see the excuses flip through her brain like a card catalog. Just as she seems to have settled on one, a deep voice bellows from the doorway, startling us both.

"Maddie tripped last night and hit her head on the corner of the dresser." How a man the size of Paul manages to tiptoe around, I'll never understand. He's not there, and then he is. And here he is again, offering up an excuse for Maddie. And she clings to it—only her voice is less assured, more shaky.

"Y-Yeah, I, um, somehow always manage to trip over my own two feet." She stares at Paul as she speaks, like she's passing the words through him for approval. He nods, and then his eyes are on me. They widen slightly, and I don't miss the subtle sweep as he takes me in. What a brazen son of a—. He's checking me out right in front of his wife.

My fingers curl around my hip as I match his defiant stance. "So, what brings you home, Paul? You must have a very understanding boss, seeing as how you seem to be able to pop home anytime you want." It's a bold statement, but I do my best to mask the accusation in my voice. Madison doesn't seem to notice, but the lift of Paul's eyebrows tells me he picks up on it.

He clears his throat in an obvious attempt to tamp down his irritation. "I could ask you the same."

"Really? How so?"

"Well, this is my home, but lately it seems like you're always in it." His gaze slides to Madison, and she visibly squirms. Bastard.

He stalks toward the fridge and yanks it open, plucking a wrapped sandwich from the shelf. He holds it up, turning his hand around to show it from all angles. He glares at me, daring me to challenge him. I shake my head and lift my eyes to the ceiling.

He sets the sandwich on the island and leaves the room, calling over his shoulder, "Now I'm going to use *my* bathroom before I leave *my* house."

When he disappears around the corner, I turn my attention back to Madison. She was in such a happy mood when I first got here, but all traces of it are gone now. She's back to looking sullen and withdrawn. "I-I'm so sorry about that. He's just been working so much lately and—"

"You don't have to explain anything. He *is* right, after all. This is his house. And I think I should probably go home."

She looks so defeated, but she doesn't bother arguing with me. We both know it will be worse for her in the long run if I stay.

I take hold of her hand and squeeze. "Listen, think about my offer, okay? I'd love to have you over for a glass of wine later this week."

She nods and a small smile plays on her lips, but it doesn't reach her eyes. I'm going to fix that.

———

THE HUMIDITY HAS BEGUN to settle in for the day. A curtain of sweat immediately begins to form on my forehead as I stand on the sidewalk in front of the Munch's house. I'm waiting for Paul, using his truck to obscure me from view should he or Madison look outside. I take notice of his personalized license plate emblazoned with the letters *GTYIUP*. That sounds about right.

I pretend to be sending out a text in case there are any curious eyes on me. Sometimes it feels like I'm the only one who pays attention in this neighborhood, but maybe I'm just the only one who takes any action.

Paul is like a dark cloud forever looming in the sky. Worse, actually. His thunder is more menacing and his lightning always strikes. Tonight, it's his turn to get caught in the storm.

The front door closes with a *BANG!* This man is infuriating. He's either loud and impossible to ignore, or he's sly and lurking in doorways. There is no in between.

He struts across the driveway and right up to me as though he's known I've been here all along. He crosses his thick arms, machismo radiating off of him. "You like that performance in there?" He juts his chin in the direction of his house.

"Performance, huh? Is that what you're calling it? Because I've gotta tell you, nothing about it felt rehearsed."

"I didn't need to rehearse. I know my wife. I threw all of that '*my* house' shit in there to keep her off the scent." He chuffs, looking proud of himself.

I shake my head. "Well, then, I suppose I should say, 'Bravo.' Because I'm fairly certain the only thing she picked up from you is fear. It seems you've done a good job of planting that seed. What is it that she sees in you, anyway?"

He narrows his eyes. "You should talk. You're the one out here waiting for me. It's clear you're ready to buy anything I'm selling."

He's so cocky. It's repulsive, but it's also quite useful in this situation. "Speaking of being ready…" I let my words dangle and watch them wrap around him, pulling him right into my web. "How about we *connect* later tonight to fix that leak."

He strokes his chin in contemplation, but the flames in his eyes tell me there's nothing for him to think about. The decision is already made. "What time?" His voice is low and gravelly. This conversation is foreplay for him.

Frank has golf and beer plans tonight, and I'm sure Gertie will be off somewhere with Reed. Which leaves me with Wyatt, but I'll think of some way to distract him. "Seven thirty. My backyard. Bring your *tools*."

"Count on it." His eyes dip down and slowly travel back up my body. When he meets my waiting gaze, I make sure he can see desire staring back at him. I have to dig deep to find it when all I really feel is nausea. But in the name of offing this creep, I'll pretend he has the effect on me that he thinks he does.

I turn on my heel and strut down the sidewalk. I know his eyes are on me, but I never turn around to check. Even though I've laid the groundwork for what he can expect tonight, I still want him to think he has to work for it. Paul likes a challenge. That's my insurance policy.

Chapter Eighteen

NEVER JUDGE A BOOK BY ITS COVER

"Wow, hun, you've really outdone yourself tonight," Frank pipes up from his seat at the table, contentedly patting his full stomach. He's right. I prepared a feast for dinner. A small smattering of white and dark turkey meat and a spoonful of stuffing are all that remain from our Thanksgiving in June.

My reason for the elaborate dinner is two-fold. First, I enjoy feeding my family and sitting around our table talking about our day. It's one of life's highlights. But second, I wanted to appeal to everyone's good graces. If they're wowed by the food I made, it's my hope that they'll be much more susceptible to playing into my hands. I need to make sure I'm alone here for at least a few hours tonight in order to carry out my plan. It's like that old saying goes, a way to a man's heart is through his stomach. I've found that's true for anyone. Fill their bellies and they're putty in your hands, which, in this case, equates to making sure the coast is clear for my backyard compost party later.

"I'm happy you all enjoyed it," I say with a proud smile. "So, tell me, what's everyone's plans for tonight?"

"Let's see. On this fine *Tuesday* night," Frank says with a cheeky grin, "I'm meeting the guys for a round of sunset golf." He peers down at his watch. "Actually, I ought to get a move on if I want to make it in time." He rises from the table and strides over to me, bending down to place a kiss on my temple. He lingers for a moment, whispering, "I'll try to be home by eleven. Be ready for me." I give him a smile, and he saunters out of the room. A few seconds later, I hear the sound of his car starting up in the garage.

I turn my attention to my kids. Wyatt is working his thumbs over his phone screen, furiously texting. Gertie is pushing around the last few kernels of corn on her plate, wearing a contemplative expression. "How about you, Gertie? What are you up to this evening?"

She lifts her eyes to mine, and the right side of her lip quirks. "I was actually thinking about going golfing, as well."

"Really?" My brow creases.

"The miniature variety, I mean," she says, laughing.

"Ahh, that makes more sense. Are you meeting friends?"

"Just Reed." She casts her gaze back to her plate, and I steal a glance at Wyatt. His eyes are wide and on his sister. I catch his attention and silently reassure him with a subtle nod..

"Wyatt, why don't you join your sister?"

"Huh?" they both respond in unison.

"The two of you rarely spend any time together, and Gertie, you'll be a senior next year and before you know it, you'll be off to college." I give her my best don't-argue-with-your-mother look. "I think it would be good for both of you. You could go play mini golf and then catch a movie at the Promenade. I think I saw *Back to the Future 1* and *2* were playing in a double-feature this week." I slide my eyes back and forth between the two of them. Gertie looks horrified by my suggestion, but Wyatt is on to me. He knows what I'm really asking here, but he still has a part to play. He schools his features, wearing a look of disgust. "Oh, come on!" I add. "It's my treat!"

Wyatt shrugs. "Why not. Whatdya say, Gert?" I don't miss his use of Reed's nickname. This kid.

She nods. "Okay. Let's give it a try, but I'm warning you. If you so much as make one snide remark about anything, I'm dropping you back home."

I can't have that. "He'll be on his best behavior. Won't you, Wyatt?" I glare at him.

"Yeah, yeah." He rolls his eyes.

"You know…you could bring a date." I can't help myself.

Now it's his turn to glare. "Don't push it."

ONE HOUR LATER, the house is blissfully quiet. I glance at the wall clock in the living room for the hundredth time, only to confirm that it's exactly thirty seconds later than the last time I checked. Paul isn't due for another fifteen minutes. I can't just stand here waiting around. I need to keep myself busy and avoid getting lost in my head. I plunge my hand into the pocket of my dusty pink A-line dress. My fingers make contact with the syringe. It's filled to capacity with phenobarbital, but Paul is a large guy. I can only hope it'll be enough.

I stroll through the house and out into the backyard. A quiet walk through my garden is just what I need. A slight bit of movement in my herb planter catches my eye. I squat down and watch with wonder as a plump striped caterpillar lazily munches away on the fronds of my Italian flat leaf parsley. He's already remarkable with black and lime-green stripes dotted with yellow, but one day soon he'll form a chrysalis and transform into a beautiful black swallowtail butterfly. This small creature is the very essence of my garden. In here, the ordinary transforms into something astounding. Old begets new. Evil becomes good.

"I'm beginning to think you live in here." Paul's gruff voice breaks through the stillness, invading the peaceful moment. The caterpillar curls into itself as if sensing the nearby threat.

I blink three times, willing myself to remain stoic. I have a job to do. The last time he was here, he managed to gain the upper hand. I can't let that happen again.

"You're right on time." I stand and regard the man who always seems to materialize out of thin air. "I didn't hear you open the gate."

"That's because I didn't."

I narrow my eyes at him, and he answers with a snicker. "What, you think it's a good idea for me to just waltz right in here?" He does have a point. The curtains in this neighborhood are always open. And curious neighbors have a tendency to talk.

"True. But if you didn't come through the side entrance, how'd you get in here?"

His lips turn up into a sly smirk. "I have my ways."

I roll my eyes. "So it's like that, huh?"

He nods. "It's like that." His voice is gravelly and filled with yearning.

We stare at each other for a few long seconds. His nostrils flare and his eyes widen. His intentions have been obvious for a while, but right now, they've never been more clear. I can feel the desire rolling off of him. Time to get this over with. I lift my chin. "So, the leak."

"Yep. The *leak*." He grips the wired fence with both hands. Hands that are not carrying any tools because there's no leak and we both know it.

I huff out a shaky breath and pray he didn't pick up on it. The first rule in tracking an animal is to never let them know you're afraid. Once they sense your fear, you're as good as dead. In a few moments, I find myself on the other side of the fence, completely unaware of how I got here. I'm standing a few feet away from Paul, but I may as well be pressed right up against him. His needy eyes assess my body, lingering on every curve.

He splays out his hand toward my shed. "After you." His voice has a bite.

I saunter past him and never look back as I key in my code and unlock the door. Once inside, I feel as if I'm floating, drifting across the small space until I'm facing my bin. I rest my palms on the cold steel, allowing it to rouse me from this spell. Paul clears his throat, and I spare a small glance over my shoulder. He fills the doorway where he leers menacingly at me. To him, I'm nothing but a snack that he's poised to devour. I close my eyes and try to picture Madison on the receiving end of this intensity. I come up empty-handed, and maybe that's why he's here. He has unfulfilled desires, and in me he sees a vessel he can pour them into. Little does he know, I have desires too, but they all end with him inside the bin I have my hands pressed against. My lip quirks and he clocks it, mistaking it for shared desire. He ducks his head and steps inside the shed, slamming the door behind him. My fingers twitch with the memory, but that was my father's rule. Not mine. My rules are far less trivial, and the punishment is much more severe.

All the air seems to leave the room as Paul crosses the space in two strides. I lower my head until I feel it make contact with the metal. Rolling my forehead back and forth along the bin, I feel his hard body press against me, the root of his hunger probing the small of my back. I swallow and think of my husband. I don't want anything to do with the man standing behind me. It's a means to an end. It's the only reason I'm here. I had to lure Paul with lies. He would never have come if I told him my true intentions. But being here like this still feels like I'm hurting Frank.

But then I think of Madison. She's locked in a cage and

Paul holds the key. He's not just the root of the problem. He *is* the problem.

His hands grip my waist and I spin around to face him. Black soulless eyes hide behind thick lashes. A low rumble sounds in his chest as he pulls me close. I wrap one arm around his neck and the other rests against his hip. His eyes dip low, tracking my body from the ground up. "I gotta say, this whole Donna Reed thing you've got going on is really working for me."

I'm reminded of the time I first met him. "That day when I walked into you after leaving your bathroom, you called me interesting. Why?"

He leans in, and the smell of peppermint wafts from his mouth. It's surprising. I expected tobacco mixed with cheap beer, but the minty aroma fills my nose and throws me slightly off balance. He presses his lips against my ear and whispers, "Let's just say I have a type. And you're it."

The expression on my face twists, "What does that mean, exactly?"

"Not important. No more talking." And then his lips press against mine and his tongue probes the seam, coaxing my mouth open. Kissing Paul was not on my agenda, and I hate it with every fiber of my being. His hands fist my hair and he lifts my legs, encouraging them to wrap around his waist. I oblige, but only because I plan to use all of this to catch him off guard. He's so intent on what he's doing, he isn't paying attention to anything else.

He walks us back until I'm pressed flush against the compost bin. My eyes spring open. Paul's are clenched tight. His bushy brow is drawn and his forehead creases with sever- ity. He looks every bit the villain that he is. But I won't let him win. I haven't lost sight of my purpose, and it isn't to satisfy his lustful needs. I rake my fingernails against his scalp and grab a fistful of his hair, continuing the charade. He groans and presses his pelvis against me. I let my other hand fall from his waist and dangle at my side, slowly creeping it toward my pocket. Paul cups my bottom and shifts me closer. I take advantage of the movement and thrust my hand into my pocket. As soon as my fingers make contact with the needle, I sigh in relief, which Paul mistakes for enthusiasm. He pulls back, eyeing me with a pointed look. "Hot damn, woman." His words are meant to be my undoing. Instead, they're like gasoline on a raging inferno. I crane my neck and fuse my lips to his, distracting him from what's about to happen.

My hand curls around the syringe as I lift it from its hiding place. Raising my hand to his neck, I'm hit with a sudden surge of déjà vu. Last time was unplanned, and we were interrupted. This time, I thought ahead and made certain there would be nothing standing in my way. With a lift of my hand, I bring it down hard, plunging the needle deep into the artery in Paul's neck. Depressing the syringe, I push the phenobarbital, a dose four times the prescribed amount, deep into his bloodstream.

He pulls back, and the expression on his face surprises me. He looks even more aroused. "I didn't take you for the kinky type." But as the last few words leave his mouth, there's a slowness that takes over. "Whaaaa happen..." he slurs. His hands release me, and he tries to hold them up in front of himself, but they have a mind of their own. He looks as though he's moving through water. His arm lifts and his fingers probe the needle still jutting from his neck. His eyes widen in shock.

"There it is. You know, I was beginning to wonder if this would even take on a man of your size." I smirk.

His face fills with anger, but there's no action behind it. The drug is fast acting and already making its way through his system. He drops to his knees. "You f-f-f-u-c-k-i-i-n-g bit—"

"Now, now," I tsk. "There's no need for name calling.

After all, this isn't my fault. You earned this fate fair and square."

His palms drop to the floor and he slowly splays out in front of me. His fingers twitch and his eyes become glassy. A loan tear seeps out the corner of his left eye, and he has no choice but to stare straight ahead. As luck would have it, he's facing my enormous compost bin. I tap my hand against it, and the *tin, tin* of the metal answers. "Don't worry, dear Paul. It's nice and cozy inside here. It's like your own personal cocoon, and in thirty days, you'll be a perfect butterfly."

"W-h-y," he whispers, almost inaudibly.

I lower myself until I'm lying on the hard concrete beside him. Our eyes lock as his blinking slows to a stop. "You've been hurting her and with your absence and then your sudden presence, you've been hurting your son, too. And now, thanks to this"—I yank the needle from his neck, but he barely registers the movement—"your reign of terror is over." I grin and lift up to my knees. "Now, let's get you ready for your metamorphosis." I roll him over and untie his boots, sliding them off along with his shoes. Next, I undo the buckle and snap on his jeans. Lowering them to his ankles, I notice his arousal is still intact. "You won't be needing that anymore. How many times did you use it to intimidate Madison? And how many others were there before me?" I look up at his face, but if there's any awareness left, it's impossible to see.

"Let's see. Where's your phone, hmm?" I plunge my hand into the back pocket of his jeans and find his cell phone, powering it down immediately. I'll wipe it clean and hold on to it until I can plant it back inside his house. I check his other pockets and the only thing I find is a crumbled piece of paper. It looks like a supply list for work. There are various measurements and colors written out along with a few types of shingles. It gives me an idea. I shove it into my pocket for safekeeping.

I make quick work of the rest of his clothes, depositing

everything inside an unmarked tote bag, except for his under-shirt. I'll need that later. I'll keep the bag locked in here for a few days and then I'll begin burning each item, one piece a day in my chiminea.

With Paul naked and lying prone on the floor, I openly gape at him. In this vulnerable state, he no longer looks like a monster. "An evil soul producing holy witness is like a villain with a smiling cheek, a goodly apple rotten at the heart." I cackle as the words leave my lips. "Maybe that's a better Shakespeare quote for Gertie. It's a good reminder that evil lurks everywhere, and when it appears it's all been snuffed out, that's when we need to arm ourselves. Because when it comes to true wickedness, it's often where you least expect it." I spin until I'm face-to-face with my compost bin. As I crank open the door, I have a thought. "Maybe evil does have an expiration date. In here, it turns to dust. In here, it decomposes."

Chapter Nineteen

YOU CAN'T HAVE YOUR CAKE AND EAT IT TOO

THE WATER FALLS ON ME LIKE A BAPTISM. IT WASHES AWAY MY sins of the evening. And let me be clear, composting Paul was not a sin. No, that was a necessity. I'm referring to the means I used to get him there. I close my eyes and lean my head against the cool tile in the shower, but all I see is his mouth on mine and his hands all over me. I know I didn't have a choice, but it still doesn't feel any less vile.

I squeeze some floral-scented body wash onto my sponge and run it under the cascading water. The rich lather builds as I furiously swipe at my arms and legs, trying to scrub away the filth. But no matter how hard I try, I still feel dirty. It's impossible to wash away the grime when it lives deep underneath your skin.

Frank juts his head into the shower and squints at me through the steam. "Is there room in there for one more?" The lust in his voice is like a living, breathing entity. I swear I could reach out and touch it.

At the moment I feel like I'm drenched in shame, but if I let him join me, maybe he can help me rewrite the narrative I've been berating myself with. His touch is welcome. His touch will erase all others.

Without any more forethought, I reach out and wrap my fingers around his neck, tugging him inside. I pull him toward me until we're staring directly into each other's eyes. A thin stream of water is the only thing separating us. Our chests heave with unspoken hunger as we continue gazing at each other. Both of us silently daring the other to make a move. Frank lifts his hands to cradle my face, and the act is so pure and so sweet, it almost brings me to tears. Despite standing in the shower, I'm unclean, unworthy. I need my husband to fix me and make me whole again. So I do the only thing I can. I grab Frank's forearms while he still holds my face and I tug hard. His lips crash against mine and I assault them. Everything I've felt. The disgust. The anguish. The ruin. I force it onto my husband. And he isn't ready. He's not prepared for all that I unleash upon him, but he holds his own, matching my licks and mirroring my moans. I launch myself at him, wrapping my legs around his waist. We grind our bodies together like a song. His a sweet melody of love and devotion, mine a ballad of heartbreak and apology.

Frank pulls back for a moment and gazes at me through jet black lashes dusted with water droplets. His mouth parts and a groan escapes. "My God, you are remarkable." His whispered devotion breaks me. I come apart in his arms, kissing him wildly, sucking his lower lip into my mouth and biting until I taste blood. My aggression does little to quell his desire, in fact, it spurs him on. His hands grip my curves and he raises me slightly, only to bring me down hard against him, filling me to the brim. He walks us back until I'm pressed up against the smooth tile. It's slick with water and I glide easily as he lifts and lowers me with measured precision. We match each other's thrusts, pushing our wants and needs inside the other like we're burying a secret. His is laid bare for me, but mine is something he can never know.

On a final shared moan, we come undone together, our bodies quaking and our mouths still fused. When we finally break away, our foreheads kiss and we stare deeply into each other's eyes. My husband's love is aglow in the crystalline blue of his irises. I still feel like a sinner, even though he holds me like a saint. I blink slowly and allow myself to feel every moment from this night all at once, and then I close my eyes one final time and will it all away. Paul is dead, and I did what I had to do to make that happen. I make myself repeat the words inside my head until I believe them.

MY SLEEP IS FAR from restful. All of my dreams turned to nightmares and my nightmares turned to dreams. The morning light kisses my bare arm as I lie in bed, turning the next part of my plan over and over in my mind. I list it off like a grocery store list.

1. Compost Paul…CHECK
2. Recover his phone and turn it off…CHECK
3. Plant his phone back in his house…TO DO
4. Prepare other evidence and hide it for Madison to find…TO DO

I'm not worried about his phone. I can easily stash that back in his house and I'll power it on before I hide it so that location services will place it in the home. I need to do it today. I can't take the risk of letting more time pass. He's been gone all night; chances are, Madison is going to try to find him soon. She may have even started looking already.

I considered getting rid of his truck, too, but it feels too risky. I'm not sure how I would go about driving away in it without being noticed and where would I dispose of it? If he leaves it behind, it may seem suspicious, but that's where my "other evidence" comes in. I have some items to stash in their home—a manufactured motel receipt, a lipstick stain on the undershirt I saved from him last night, a few travel brochures with some destinations circled. But I've been thinking of ways to solidify the idea that Paul left Madison for another woman. I don't think it'll be far-fetched. After all, the last time I was with both of them, he blatantly checked me out in front of her. She didn't acknowledge it, but there was no way she missed it. He told me last night that I was his type. Madison and I are nothing alike; both in looks and personality, which leads me to believe there must've been others before me.

I've decided to write a letter from Paul to Madison. That's where the supply list I found in his pocket comes in. It isn't much to go on, but I think it'll be enough for me to emulate his handwriting so that it's believable. In person, Paul was a man of few words. I'm pretty sure he'd be the same way in a letter, too. All I need to communicate to Madison is that he's met someone and he left with her. He's starting over and leaving everything else behind. She'll be devastated at first, but she'll survive. And if the police get involved, I'm not worried. Spouses are always considered suspects, but Madison will pass with flying colors because she's truly inno-cent. She has nothing to hide and she'll be visibly grieving, which will only help her more.

Which brings me to Reed. I could write him a letter, too, but I think a clean break is what he needs. It may seem harsh for Paul to not even say goodbye, but he's barely been around until recently. It will only drive home the point that he's been a terrible father. Reed will be better off without him.

Time to get up and finish my plan. Frank is already out of bed. He's probably in the den watching the news. I practically sprint across the room and peel back the curtains. From here I have a pretty clear vantage point of the Munch's driveway. Right now, the only car I see is Madison's tiny hatchback. Huh. That's interesting.

I think back to last night and recall Paul telling me he didn't use the side gate. He was playing coy and wouldn't say how he got into the yard, but it must've been through the tree line at the back of our property. He probably parked his truck somewhere less conspicuous and then snuck in through the trees, completely unnoticed. It feels like more proof that this wasn't his first rodeo. He's obviously a seasoned veteran when it comes to sneaking around on his wife. The bastard.

But what now? If his truck isn't in the driveway, where is it? And wherever it is, I hope it doesn't give away any unwanted clues. The last thing I need is for any of this to lead back to me.

I hustle into the bathroom to grab a quick shower. I'll send my family off with a filling breakfast and then I'll go for a little walk. Maybe I can locate Paul's truck. I don't know what I'll do if I find it parked in the *wrong* place, but I'm resourceful. I'll figure it out.

FROM THE TOP of the stairwell, I hear the distant murmur of voices in the kitchen. I glance at my watch. It's still only a few minutes after seven. I'll admit, I'm a bit off my game this morning, but it's still early. I can't imagine the rest of my family is awake before me.

The voices become clearer as my foot hits the final step. "Do you have any idea where he might've gone?" Frank's voice is laced with worry, and my ears perk up.

I rush into the kitchen and find Madison slumped over on one of the stools. There's an untouched cup of coffee in front of her. Her elbows sag on the counter while her hands worry through her hair. She hasn't noticed me. Frank is standing beside her, a comforting hand resting on her shoulder.

He looks up as I enter the room, a pained expression on his face. Madison speaks through sniffs, her voice muffled by her hands. "He said he was leaving and that I shouldn't try to find him."

I don't understand. Why would Paul tell Madison he was leaving? Or is she talking about Reed?

I look at Frank, unable to mask the panic in my eyes. He furrows his brow and opens his mouth to speak just as Madison lifts her head. When she sees me, her whole body sighs with relief. And then she's up on her feet, racing across the room to me. She launches herself, clinging to me like a lifeline.

"Oh, Jeanette! Paul is gone!"

I grip her shoulders and push her at arm's length. I'm probably being too rough, but I can't think about that now. "What do you mean he's gone?"

Tears pool in her eyes and cascade down her face. "He, he," she stammers. "Oh, God, he left me!"

"Madison." My voice is even and almost stern. "How do you know he left you?"

She sucks in a shaky breath. "He wrote me a letter."

Chapter Twenty

THE BEST OF BOTH WORLDS

WHAT FLIPPING LETTER? WHO AM I KIDDING? WHAT FUCKING letter is she talking about? I know I didn't write it. I planned to, but that's as far as I got.

I feel a bit like I'm on the outside looking in through foggy glass. Nothing is clear. "A letter?"

"Uh-huh." She nods, sniffing a few more times before Frank hands her a tissue. She peers up at him with kind eyes. "Thank you."

"Sure thing." He smiles warmly. When his eyes meet mine, I see an apology swimming in them. "Honey, can I talk to you for a minute?"

My husband has no idea the war I'm waging inside my head right now. Madison's news is like a hurricane when I was preparing for a rain shower. How am I supposed to walk away from her right now?

As if sensing my reluctance, he places a hand on my forearm, leading me away from the emotional wreckage in my kitchen. "I just wanted to go over a few quick things before I leave for work. It'll only take a second. Walk with me?"

On a sigh, I turn to Madison, but she's back on the stool, gulping down coffee like it's manna from heaven. I trudge along beside my husband while he prattles on about a new medication that's being used to treat fibromyalgia. Once we're inside the garage, he pushes the door shut and leans in. "Listen, honey, I'm sorry about that." He just his chin toward the door. "She just showed up, and when I saw the condition she was in, I had no choice but to invite her in."

"It's fine. I can deal with it." The words practically launch out of my mouth. I'm desperate to get back inside to Madison.

"I'm sure you can. I'm just sorry I won't be here to help. We have a shipment coming in this morning and I need to be there to accept it."

My brow furrows. "But you didn't eat breakfast?"

He smiles with kind eyes. "I had cereal. Honey, it's not your job to make a full breakfast every morning. A bowl of Rice Chex every once in a while won't kill me."

I nod. Normally, I'd argue with him. It *is* my job to take care of my family, but right now, I have a hysterical neighbor to contend with and more importantly, a mysterious note to decipher. I give Frank a hug goodbye and then I hurry back inside.

Madison's still perched on my kitchen stool, right where I left her. Her hands are wrapped around her mug as though she can't bear to let it go. Her body shivers from shock, but her arms are still thanks to the warmth of the coffee cup. I clear my throat and her head snaps up. She glances around the room as if seeing it for the first time, and then she's on her feet. "Jeanette, I-I'm sorry. I've taken up enough of your time. I should go."

"No!" I don't mean to shout, but that's exactly what I do and it startles us both. I chuckle and smile at her, but she eyes me warily. "What I mean is, you shouldn't be alone right now. I was just about to go for a walk through my garden. Why don't you join me?"

I can see the hesitation in her eyes as she looks to me and

then at the hallway leading to the door. I can't let her leave, yet. Not until I hear more about the letter. So, I give her another nudge. "You know, strolling along the path among the herbs and vegetables is such a uniquely peaceful experience. It's the only place where I ever feel truly at ease. If I believed in such a thing, I might be inclined to think it holds magical powers. Do me a favor and humor me, please?"

She nods reluctantly, following me to the back door.

As Madison and I stand among my plants, we are surrounded by possibilities. So when I turn to her, intent on finding out what Paul wrote in his letter, I feel a strange calm settle over me. I'm still concerned, but I'm less plagued with worry and more focused on my next move. In here, I feel more certain that I can deal with this obstacle and maybe even benefit from it.

I reach down and tug off a leaf of apple mint. Handing it to Madison, I watch as she brings it to her nose, inhaling deeply. I wait for the calm to overtake her in the way that only the scent of fresh mint can do. "Better?" I ask, already knowing the answer.

A hint of a smile hits her lips, and her eyes find mine. She's ready to talk now.

"Tell me more about the letter, Madison."

She pulls in a deep breath and lets it out slowly. "He didn't come home last night. But"—she casts her gaze to the ground—"that's nothing unusual for Paul. I guess you could say, he has a pretty active extracurricular love life." She chuckles humorlessly. "I went to bed early, hoping he might wake me up when he got home, but instead, I woke up to an envelope on his pillow this morning." Her bottom lip begins to quiver and she brings the mint leaf back up to her nose, taking a moment to find her calm. "Before I even opened it, I knew what was inside. He's always threatened to leave me, but I never thought he'd actually do it. It's why I looked the other way when he came home smelling of cheap perfume or when I emptied his pockets while doing the laundry and found a receipt from Victoria's Secret. Lord knows he's never shopped there for me." She rolls her eyes in disgust. "The thing is, Jeanette, I had something these women didn't have." She thumbs the ring on her left hand, spinning it on her finger. "I was the one he came home to. I was the one he woke up next to. I had his last name. I had him. And that's all gone. Now I have nothing."

I'm having some trouble wrapping my head around this new development. Was Paul really planning to leave her? And what are the chances that he'd do it now? I need to read this letter.

I grab her hands in mine. "No, not nothing, Madison. You have me. You have my family. But most importantly, you have you." I'm not sure what exactly Paul wrote, but whatever it was, she seems very convinced that he's gone. This wasn't how I planned it, but the outcome is still the same. I look into her eyes, willing her to see what this could mean for her. "Listen, I can't pretend to know everything that goes on behind closed doors. And that goes for the ones in my own house. I can only hope my children are being safe when they shut themselves in their rooms. The same way I've hoped that you were safe when you were in your house alone with Paul. But you weren't, were you?" She dips her eyes, but doesn't speak. I'm overstepping, but sometimes, when the moment is right, you have to seize it. "I'll say this, if Paul couldn't see your worth, then it's his loss, not yours. He doesn't deserve you. And as your friend, I need to say, it's time you put yourself first."

She smiles sadly. "You're my friend. You have to say things like that."

I shake my head. "You're right. I am your friend, but come on, Madison. I know you haven't known me very long, but do I seem like the type of person who would feed you lies?" Okay, I'm exactly that type of person, but she doesn't know that. And besides, the lies I tell her are for her own good. I'm only trying to help her.

She sighs. "No, you're right. I know you are, it's just...I keep picturing him with this *mystery* woman. And I can't stop wondering what she has that I don't."

Wait—he mentioned another woman? Did he write about me? A tingle runs down my spine. "What mystery woman?"

"Paul said he had met someone who 'changed the game.'" She curls her peace sign fingers, signifying a direct quote. "He wanted me to know he wasn't looking for her. She just 'walked into his life and knocked him on his ass.' Apparently, she's exactly his type." Madison speaks through clenched teeth, mimicking the words with her hands raging into fists.

This revelation stuns me. Paul called me his type right before I plunged a needle into his neck. I'm overwhelmed with the need to see the letter with my own eyes. "Madison? Do you happen to have the letter on you? I'd like to read it, if you don't mind. I think I could help you break it down so you could see that all of this is Paul's fault and not yours."

She shakes her head. "Oh no, I crumbled it up and shoved it into a drawer. I can't bear to see it." Dammit. I want to scream at her. Who shows up at someone's house distraught over a letter and then doesn't even bring the letter with them? But that's not fair. She's upset, and in that state, people often act rashly. I should be happy she came here first.

I pat her arm. "It's okay. Listen, you've been through a lot. Why don't you head home and lie down? I'll be by later to check on you. Okay?"

She bobs her head and wraps her arms around me. "Thank you, Jeanette. You're a true friend." I swallow hard around the lump in my throat. A true friend who killed her husband. A true friend her husband may have been planning to leave her for.

Madison tiptoes out of the garden, silently closing the gate behind her. I need to figure out my next move. I take a deep breath and watch her walk toward the side gate. When she's out of sight, I turn my attention back to the plants growing around me. My eyes flit over the tomatoes, broccoli, and peppers. It's when my gaze reaches the kale, that I notice a patch of hairy bittercress sprouting out of the dirt. "Excuse me," I call out to the weed as I crouch down beside it. "Just what do you think you're doing squatting in my garden? You, sir, are not welcome here." I wrap my hand around the base and pluck it from the earth, smoothing the dirt back around the kale. It's been a long time since a weed has found its way into my garden. I'm usually so on top of tending to my plants, weeds never stand a chance. I guess I've been preoccupied lately. I stand, clutching the intruder in my hand. Surveying the space, I don't see any more weeds. In here, order has been restored.

I open my palm and flick the tiny white flowers on the rosette of leaves. Weeds are often like this, masquerading as something beautiful in the hopes that they'll be left alone. And if they are, they will spread, choking every good thing in their path. So we do what's necessary—we snuff them out, cutting them off at the quick. That's exactly what I did with Paul and the others who came before him. I should be happy about Paul's letter; after all, he handed me the perfect explanation for his sudden absence. But standing here, in my garden, my happy place, I feel like there are weeds everywhere. Threatening just below the surface, and if I'm not careful, they'll overtake everything I've worked so hard for.

WYATT'S AT THE ISLAND, sitting on the same stool Madison occupied earlier. He's thumbing through Instagram with one hand and shoveling Lucky Charms into his mouth with the other. He doesn't look up as I stroll in through the door.

"You're up early."

"Yep." Back to one-word answers, I see. It takes everything in me to refrain from groaning.

"So, how was golfing last night?"

He raises a brow in a silent answer.

"That good, huh?"

He huffs. "It was the *most* fun," he says dully. "I mean, who doesn't love playing third wheel on a date with their sister and her possibly psychotic boyfriend?"

I sidle up beside him and plop down on a neighboring stool. "I know it wasn't your idea of a good time, but it meant a lot to me, if that helps at all."

"It doesn't," he deadpans, but the edge of his mouth lifts.

I give his arm a playful shove, causing him to slosh milk onto the counter. "Now, Jeanette, what have I told you about horsing around at the table?" He repeats the words I said to him when he and Gertie were little. We both laugh.

Shaking my head, I walk over to the sink and wet a paper towel. As I wipe up the spill, I prod him for more information. "Did you learn anything interesting from your time with Reed?"

He shrugs. "Nothing I didn't already know."

"Meaning?"

"Meaning, either the guy is a master at pretending or he really does care about Gertie. Either way, she's buying what he's selling. And I don't think any of us will be able to change her mind." He locks eyes with me, and I can see how much he cares about his sister. And he's right. Young love just may be one of the strongest kinds of love. When you're a teenager, you aren't as focused on the future or the past. You only care about the here and now. And right now, Reed is Gertie's whole world. That kind of devotion is borderline obsessive. It's also often short-lived. I'm not going to worry about it, for now.

My mind drifts to Paul. If he left a letter for Madison, did he leave one for Reed, too?

"Mom, are you okay? You look a little pale."

I wave my hand. "It's nothing. I haven't eaten breakfast yet. Hey, Wyatt, is your sister in her room?"

"No, she left with Reed a few minutes ago."

"Wait, she did?" He was here and I missed him! "How did he seem?"

Wyatt's face scrunches. "He *seemed* like an asshole, but what else is new?" He laughs.

I sigh loudly. "Wyatt, this really isn't a time for jokes."

"Sorry." He shrugs. "I guess I wasn't really paying attention." He's staring at his cereal like it may hold the meaning of life. I'm taking this out on him, but it's not his fault. It breaks my heart to think I've driven another wedge in our relationship. I feel like I'm juggling and I have so many balls up in the air right now. But desperate as I am to read Madison's letter and to find out if Reed got one, too, I need to remember what I'm doing all of this for. My cardinal rule is *those I care about must be protected at all costs*. And right now, the person my son needs protection from is me.

"Did I ever tell you about your grandma?" That gets his attention quick.

"No, you never talk about her. All I know is she left when you were young and then your dad died not too long after that."

"That's all true, but I think it's time I told you about how things were *before* she left. You see, I was once the invisible child, too."

His forehead wrinkles, but I shake my head. "You're definitely not invisible, Wyatt, but I also know you can't pretend that you haven't felt that way sometimes. I see so much of myself in you when I was your age, and it makes me feel so ashamed."

"I don't understand."

"Well, no, you wouldn't because I've kept so much of my childhood locked up tight. So tight, I can barely find the key.

Your dad doesn't even know much about what my life was like before I met him. You know, you hear all the time about how childhood trauma can be damaging to a person's mental growth. These days it seems like everyone blames anything that ever happens to them on the abuse they suffered as a child. I don't mean to make light of that. So many people have suffered greatly in their formative years, and that most definitely comes with a steep price. Our early years are where we form lasting emotional habits. We learn to depend on others, or maybe we learn we can only depend on ourselves. We learn how to balance happiness with crippling disappointment. We learn what love looks like, or instead, what it means to truly feel hatred. But perhaps the most important thing of all, we learn what kind of person we want to become. And we do this by compiling a list of traits from every person we encounter who holds any sort of value to us. We take from their good and we take from their bad and then we mesh it together to form our own perfect ideal. I doubt any of us intends to take on the traits that brought us suffering, but, kiddo, it's inevitable. And I know that sounds ominous. How can we be expected to look forward to a future righting the wrongs that were done to us if we're only going to absorb those wrongs and inflict them onto someone else? But here's what I've discovered. There is hope. Because even though, at times I've found myself treating you the same way my mother treated me, I'm able to recognize that and I'm able to redirect my behavior."

I can almost hear the questions poised on his lips. I let out a breath and push on. "I grew up knowing I was unwanted. I know a lot of kids feel that way at some point during their childhood, but I truly was. It wasn't a feeling I had. It wasn't just a notion or a worry. It was a cold hard fact. Because as soon as I was old enough to understand language, I was told how much of a burden I was. My mother would huff loudly every time I asked her to help me tie my shoes. She'd roll her eyes when I was hungry or mutter under her breath if I forgot to wipe my toothpaste out of the sink. I once overheard her tell my father that I was a noose around her neck." Wyatt's eyes widen, but he remains mute. "And then, one day, she stopped talking to me altogether. I thought it might be better that way, but it was worse. When she acted put out by me, at least she was acknowledging my presence. Once she decided I was invisible, I almost believed I really was and was surprised whenever anyone noticed me." I rest my hand on his shoulder. "I know I haven't treated you as harshly as my mother treated me, but I also know, at times, my behavior wasn't far off from hers. And Wyatt, that hurts me more than anything my mother ever did to me. Because I know better. I've already been through this. I know what that side is like, and I never want to be the cause of anyone feeling the way I felt when I was a child. For that, I am truly sorry, but I don't expect forgiveness. Not yet. Not when I haven't earned it.

"When you were maybe three or four, we were reading one of our favorite books, *The Spotted Puppy.* It's a sweet story about a little dog who gets into all sorts of trouble while his mother just watches. She never intervenes except to say, 'Life is full of hard lessons.' She says those words over and over each time the puppy finds himself in a predicament. And then, at the end of the book, he says those very same words to his mom when she has a disagreement with a porcupine over a bone. We read that book so many times, I lost count, but on that day as I turned the last page, I heard your soft sniffles. You were sitting on my lap and I remember you used your sleeve to wipe your nose. Even though you were so young, you still tried to conceal the emotion from me. I asked you why you were crying and you looked up at me with those big brown eyes of yours and said, 'Mama, didn't the mommy dog have someone to help her the way the spotted puppy had his mommy?' I asked you what you meant, and I'll never forget the words that came out of your mouth. 'The mommy dog

188 · LAYNE DEEMER

tells the puppy life is full of hard lessons, but I don't think anyone told her that when she was little. She's lucky she has her puppy to remind her.' I remember sitting there completely stunned because you managed to sum up my parenting with one sentence. Life *is* full of hard lessons, and when I was younger, I had no one to guide me. It's the fire behind everything I've done for you and your sister. But sometimes, I get smoke in my eyes and I get off track, so I need a little reminder." I lock eyes with him, holding his stare hostage. "Never let me off the hook, Wyatt. Parents are supposed to teach their kids all of life's lessons, but sometimes it's the kids who do the teaching."

He watches me in a way that lets me know he's heard every word I said. Then he abruptly stands, sliding in his stool and walking his bowl to the sink. He scoops up his backpack and looks back over his shoulder at me. "I need to get to school. I'm walking today."

"Let me drive you."

He holds up his hand. "No, that's okay. I'd rather walk."

I nod, too overcome to speak.

Just as he rounds the corner to leave, he doubles back, dropping his backpack along the way. He pulls me into a firm hug and whispers, "You are nothing like your mom."

I close my eyes, savoring the words as I grip him tightly to me.

He pulls back and angles his head toward the door.

"Go on, you don't want to be late." I reach up and ruffle his hair, and just this once, he allows it. With his hair all mussed, he looks more like that little boy who used to sit on my lap. I may have repeated some mistakes, but when I look at him, I know I did something right.

Chapter Twenty-One

BIRDS OF A FEATHER

ONE OF THE MOST PIVOTAL MOMENTS IN MY LIFE HAPPENED ON A random Tuesday in mid-September, when the leaves had just started to turn and there was a chill in the air that even the afternoon sun couldn't touch. I was seventeen and had just started my junior year. We lived in a neighborhood much like this one, and my school was only a ten-minute walk from our house. I was on my way home. The sun was beginning its decent; the long days of summer already a distant memory. I remember the way my shadow moved on the sidewalk, swaying slowly as I trudged along. I was in no hurry to get home. For me, my house was just a roof and walls; a place to sleep and nothing more.

When I reached the front door, I paused. I always did. I had to give myself a mental pep talk before I went inside, preparing myself for my father's scorn and my mother's apathy. But on this day, when I pushed open the door, I was met with silence. An almost eerie calm came over me as I moved through each room of the house. My father always made his presence known. I was always told to keep my volume at a minimum, but that rule never applied to him. I lost so many years under his controlling thumb. But on that afternoon, I heard no telltale signs of activity from him. When I tiptoed down the dark upstairs hallway, every door was open except for the one leading to my parents' bedroom. On any other day, I would've ignored it and continued on to my household chores. But for some reason, I felt compelled to open the door. It was as if I knew I was meant to make the discovery.

The gold knob was shiny and smooth and slid easily in my hand as I turned it. I pushed the door open, and the first thing I saw was my mother's arm draped over the side of the bed. Her hand dangled a few inches from the carpet. I assumed she was sleeping, but when I looked at her face, I found her eyes open wide. They were staring into space, like she was lost in thought. Before that day, I had never seen a deceased person, but I didn't need a doctor's confirmation to know that my mother was dead. When a person dies, their essence leaves their body and all that remains is an empty vessel. You can see evidence of that emptiness in the way their body slumps, not unlike a dummy or how their gaze is fixed and uninterrupted by blinking. My mother had all of those symptoms, and as I moved toward her, cutting off her line of sight, it was as if she were finally looking at me. Given my mother's history of negligence, it's almost crudely comical that the day she would finally see me, she'd do so with dead eyes. There was a folded piece of paper crumpled up next to an empty bottle of Vicodin on her nightstand. I saw my name scrawled on the front. When I peeled it open, the first thing I noticed was the inconsistent writing on the page. The ink was faded to the point of being almost illegible at parts. She couldn't even be bothered to find a working pen to use in her suicide note. I wasn't worth the effort. On the page, she had only written six words. "I'm sorry. I tried my best." For my entire childhood, I was inconsequential, and the only time she gave me a second thought was to make me a reason to kill herself.

There are bad mothers and then there's mine. The day she left should've been horrific. As her daughter, I should've mourned her, but you can't mourn something you've never had. When she died, I felt more free than I had in a very long time. A parent is supposed to protect their child. But both of mine failed. I lived in a constant state of fear because of my father and my mother never once stood up for me So, when I backed out of her room that day, I was only thinking one thing. One down. One to go.

I OPEN the door to my house with a feeling of defeat settling on my shoulders. I just spent most of the morning canvasing the neighborhood in search of Paul's truck. It wasn't easy, walking around like I'm out for a stroll when really I'm on a frantic search. I looked everywhere I could think of, but I came up empty-handed. As unnerving as it is to not know where his truck is parked, at least I know from my search that it isn't anywhere near my house. I'm not going to completely give up trying to find it, but for now, I think I'll put a pin in it and shift my focus back to Madison's letter.

"No fucking way is this shit real!" The shouting catches me off guard. I thought I was home alone, but the sound is coming from Gertie's bedroom. I race up the stairs.

Her door is closed, but I don't bother knocking. Reed's incestuous yelling is echoing throughout the house. I twist the knob and give the door a hard shove. It careens back and smacks into the drywall. I'm overwhelmed with sudden memories, but when I look down at my hands, I'm not holding *The Polar Express*. I close my eyes briefly and count to three. When I open them, Reed is flailing his arms. A folded piece of paper waves wildly in the air. Gertie is seated on the bed with her hands out in front of him. She's speaking in a

192 • LAYNE DEEMER

calming tone, but it's clearly not helping. Neither one of them has even noticed me.

"Excuse me. What the hell is going on in here?"

Both sets of eyes are on me. Gertie looks shocked to see me while Reed looks more annoyed that I had the audacity to interrupt.

"Mom. Um, I'm sorry. I know how you feel about shouting. It's just—"

"It's just my father apparently abandoned me." Reed spits out the words like they're venom he's attempting to expel from his system.

"Hold on, let's back up a second. It's not even noon. Why aren't the two of you in school?" My eyes flip back and forth between them.

Gertie speaks first. "I know how this looks. We were on our way to school when Reed realized he left his History notebook at home. So, we turned around and when we got there, we found a letter on the nightstand by Reed's bed. It was from his dad."

There's so much to process in this moment. I don't even know what to tackle first. Reed and Gertie skipped school. That's not behavior I ever would've expected from my daughter and we're going to have to talk about it. But right now my attention is more focused on the reason for their truancy—Paul wrote Reed a letter, too.

"Reed?" I make my voice soft and almost meek. "Is that the letter you're holding?" I haven't been able to get my hands on Madison's, and to be this close to another piece of the puzzle is almost too much. I have to ball my hands into fists at my side to keep from ripping the paper out of his hand.

He dips his head harshly.

"Mind if I see it?"

"Sure. Why not? Everyone may as well read the bullshit on that page." He hands it over freely. "Take notice of the perfect penmanship. Wait, you can't. Because it's typed." He rakes a rough hand through his hair. "He couldn't even be bothered to write his last 'fuck you.'"

With a sad nod, I look down at the wrinkled paper in my hands. He's right. The letter, if you could even call it that, consists of two short paragraphs, typed and doubled spaced. The only ink is at the bottom where he's signed *Dad*.

Reed—

It's been good to know you, son. You're a good kid and a hard worker. I think you'll be just fine in life as long as you don't do anything to fuck it up.

I think it's time for me to move on. You probably won't understand and that's all right. I don't need that from you or anyone. I just need you to know that I'm doing what I need to do for me. And when the time comes for you someday, you should do what you need to do for you. You may not get it now, but trust me, son, it'll all make sense, eventually.

Dad

What an odd thing to write to your child. The tone is ominous, and the words don't say much of anything. But I definitely get the sense that Paul was intending to leave and not come back. Despite the strange presentation, I have to admit, it sounds like Paul. It's the right amount of concern mixed with "who gives a shit." It's exactly what I would expect from him.

I look over my shoulder at Reed. His hands are shoved deep into his pockets and he's looking at the carpet like he might want to burrow into it. It wasn't that long ago that I was just like him, holding a note not unlike this one. He's reactionary and he needs to get his anger under control, but he's still just a kid who feels alone in a world where no one wants him. And now I've played a part in making that worse. I know taking Reed's only parent away makes me seem like a villain. This decision is not without repercussions. And all of the agonizing I put myself through before I made my decision doesn't change the fact that with one plunge of a needle, I made him an orphan.

I cross the room and put a comforting hand on his shoulder. He looks up at me, and I see a war waging behind his eyes. He's hurt and struggling to come to terms with the hand he's just been dealt. "Reed, I can't pretend to understand why your dad wrote this." I drop the paper onto Gertie's bed. "But even though I don't know the meaning behind it, I do know what you're feeling."

He rolls his eyes. "Come on. Everyone always likes to pretend they know what someone else is going through, but they don't. You have no idea what I'm feeling."

"I know because my mom left a letter like that for me." Off to my right, I hear Gertie gasp. "You feel discarded, pushed aside like you never meant anything to him, right?"

He nods and I continue, "I felt the same way and you know, maybe we're right. Maybe we didn't mean anything, or if we did, it wasn't enough. But that's on them, Reed. No matter how awful it seems, they made those choices. The mistake is theirs. It's not our fault. And we don't have to pay for their mistakes. Do you hear me? You did nothing wrong and you don't need him."

I can see his jaw working back and forth as he studies me for a moment. He doesn't say anything at first. For a few quiet seconds, we just stare at each other and an understanding passes between us.

"I'm sure you and Madison have a lot to discuss right now. You may already know this, but she got a letter, too. Have you had a chance to talk to her?" I wonder if Reed has already read her letter.

"Talk?" He belts out an angry laugh. "Yeah, I tried that. She told me she was too *overwhelmed* right now to deal with anything else and maybe it would be better if I went back to live with my grandma full time."

My eyes dart over to Gertie. "Is this true?"

She bites at her lip and nods. I don't understand. I know that Reed and Madison weren't close, but I thought that would change with Paul out of the picture. I need to get a handle on this situation. It feels like it's getting away from me. I look over at Reed. He's almost a man, but the way he's standing there—bent over, shuffling his feet, looking defeated—he looks more like a little boy. He needs someone to lean on.

I smile at him and say the only words I can offer. "Well, you're always welcome here. I hope you'll join us for dinner."

He shoves his hands deep into his pockets. "Thanks."

I think I've given Madison enough time to collect herself. I need to read her letter and maybe while I'm there, I can talk some sense into her about Reed. "I could use some fresh air. I'm going out a walk and when I get home, I'll start dinner, okay."

"Sounds good, Mom. Thanks." Gertie smiles at me.

As I step out into the hallway, Reed's voice stops me. "You look like her, you know?"

I turn slowly until I'm facing him. "Who?"

"My mom."

Chapter Twenty-Two

YOUR GUESS IS AS GOOD AS MINE

THE AFTERNOON SUN BLAZES HOT ON MY BACK AS I AMBLE ALONG the sidewalk. I'm beginning to feel like I'm in the middle of a war zone with the bombs that keep getting dropped on me, left and right.

I look like Stacy? Is that why Paul thought it was *interesting* that Madison invited me into their home? That must be why he said I was his type and yet, Madison told me he didn't reciprocate Stacy's feelings. Did he keep that from her? And why didn't Madison ever mention the resemblance?

She and I have a lot to discuss. I have a long list of questions and she's the only one with the answers. I'm on my way to collect them.

I notice Bob trimming his hedge when I walk past. "Beautiful day, isn't it, Bob?" I make it a point to keep my feet moving in the hopes that he won't stop me with idle chitchat. Of course, I have a better chance of being struck by lightning without a cloud in the sky.

"Sure is," he calls from behind the greenery. "Say, don't suppose you know anything about where the husband ran off to in such a hurry last night?"

I stop walking and pivot on my heels to find Bob peering

at me from between the branches. His beady, judging eyes assess me like I'm holding the puzzle piece he's been looking for. I can't let him see that his comment disarmed me. "I'm not sure I know what you're talking about."

He snickers. "Oh, I forget sometimes that I'm the one with the front-row seat."

A front-row seat to what? What is he not telling me? "I'm afraid you're talking in riddles again, Bob."

"Jeanette, you're a funny bunny," he quips. "But you must know who I'm talking about." He slides his eyes over to the Munch's Cape Cod.

"I don't know what it is you thought you saw, but surely, I wouldn't know anything about it." I'm pretty sure I know *everything* about it, but I'll never let him know that.

He raises a brow. "Come on, you and I both know you make it a point to know *everything* about anything in this neighborhood."

I bristle at his words, even though there's a mountain of truth to them. "I wouldn't go that far. I care about the people who live here and I just want Whispering Woods to be a safe place."

He smirks. My last shred of patience is on the verge of snapping, but I take a calming breath and keep my voice even when I speak. "You said you saw Madison's husband leaving in a hurry." I need him to stay on track so I can determine if he saw anything incriminating.

He angles his shears and snips off more branches. "Those two sure know how to make a spectacle of themselves. At first, as you know, there was the glass breaking fiasco. And then, of course, there was the shouting match in the driveway last week." So, Bob saw that, too. It shouldn't surprise me. He's been known to shove his curtain aside and blatantly stand in front of the window munching on popcorn like the neighborhood is performing just for his enjoyment.

"And get this, last night, what's his name comes running

out of the house like he's being chased. Then, he hops in his truck and takes off, burning rubber. Left tire tracks over there in the road." He points in front of Paul's driveway, and I see the faint tread marks on the asphalt.

This story is strange, but maybe Bob saw Paul leaving on his way to my house. I already know he parked his truck somewhere secret and as disgusting as it makes me feel, he was probably in a hurry to meet me, which would account for his erratic driving. I just have one question and if Bob answers it the way I think he will, I can be on my way.

"Huh, that is a little odd, but maybe he had somewhere to be and he was running late. What time was this, Bob?" My tone suggests a hint of disinterest. I don't want him to get suspicious, even though I'm desperate for his answer.

"Hmm, let's see," he says, drumming his fingers on his leg. "It was just after my shower. I was getting ready to watch *The Handmaid's Tale*—have you seen that?" I shake my head. "Jeanette! You have to watch it! It's so disturbing. I think you'd love it. Anyway, that would've been close to ten."

My stomach drops and a wave of nausea washes over me. It isn't possible that Bob saw Paul leave at ten. Not when he was at my house at seven thirty and on his way to being compost by nine. My thoughts are a blur as I mentally take myself through the events of that evening. I never checked Paul's pulse after I administered the phenobarbital, but there's no way he could've survived such a huge dose. Is there? No. He couldn't have, and even if he did, how would he have gotten out of my compost bin? It was sealed shut. There's no way out from the inside. The only way the door could've been opened is if someone had turned the crank on the outside. And I would've known if someone had broken into my shed because my alarm system would've alerted me. Except...I was preoccupied in the shower with Frank. I could've missed the notification.

A loud screech pulls our attention up to the sky just as a

hawk flies overhead. It angles its body, soaring in a circle before swooping down to pluck a chipmunk out of the Thorn's yard across the street. It holds the rodent tightly in its clutches as it hoists itself back up into the air. We both watch with rapt attention as it glides through the air far off into the distance until it's nothing but a speck in the sky.

Bob slaps his knee. "Well, I'll be a monkey's uncle! That was something, wasn't it?" I look over expecting to find him gaping at the sky, but instead I'm met with the eyes of a man who knows more than he's letting on. "Just goes to show, there are always predators waiting for the right moment to strike. Guess you can't be too careful, can you, Jeanette?"

I smile like my whole world isn't spinning out of control. "Especially if you're a chipmunk. Well, I should be going. Enjoy your day!"

"You, too."

I walk away, fighting the urge to run.

"Uh, Jeanette?" Bob calls after me.

"Hmm?" I answer, never stilling my feet.

"Their house is that way." I look over my shoulder to find him pointing at Madison's house.

I nod rapidly. "Mm-hmm, I know, but I just remembered I borrowed a book from Madison last week and I want to return it. I left it inside on the dining room table."

He chuckles to himself and keeps on trimming his shrub.

I pick up my pace slightly, desperate to get home. I told Bob I left Madison's book on the dining room table so I can't just breeze through the side gate and back to my shed like I want to. I have to go in through the front door and walk through the house. When I'm inside the foyer, I pause and listen for voices upstairs. All I hear is a low hum of music and the sound of Gertie's laughter. Looks like Reed calmed down a bit since I left. I'm glad, but I don't have time to appreciate it. Now, thanks to Bob's information, I have to run outside and double-check my compost bin, making sure Paul hasn't somehow escaped.

I rush toward the kitchen door and fling it open. Peering around the corner, I make sure Bob hasn't moved to his backyard. I can't risk having him see me bolt to my shed like a crazy person. Once the coast is clear, I do just that. The lock appears secure and nothing looks out of the ordinary. Still, I waste no time keying in the code and shoving the door open.

The steel structure in the corner looks just as it did when I left it last night. I push the shed door closed behind me and creep across the floor. This is insane. There's no way Paul survived the shot I gave him, much less managed to open the bin from the inside and free himself. And yet, here I am, slowly inching toward it like I'm in a horror movie and I'm about to peel open a shower curtain to reveal the murderer.

When my hands land on either side of the crank, they're visibly shaking. I never peeked inside of the bin when Ty or Henry were composting. The process takes thirty days, and I was content just letting it happen. There was no need to check on things. But now I don't have a choice. I have to make sure that Paul is still in here and not outside somewhere ready to strike.

The sweat from my palms makes my hands slide as I give the wheel a turn. I hear the internal lock disengage as the seal opens and with a quick tug, the door flings open. The first thing I'm hit with is the indescribable odor. The temperature inside this bin is sweltering, which speeds up the decomposition process. There's no mistaking the smell of death, but even if there was any doubt, it's gone the minute my eyes land on the decaying arm peeking out from under the wood pellets I layered on top of the body. Paul's wing tattoo stares at me, making me question everything that's happened since I woke up this morning.

Did Paul write those letters? Or was it someone else? Someone who also took off in his truck late last night.

Right now, I'm only certain of one thing. Paul is dead and he's been that way since I left him last night.

"CAN'T I at least get you some water?"

Madison hasn't stopped fretting over me from the moment I walked in the door. She's desperate to bring me food and drink when all I really want are answers. If I didn't know any better, I might think she's stalling. I let out a relented sigh. "Okay, Madison, sure. I'll take some water."

I've barely gotten the words out and she's dashing about the kitchen, filling a cup with crushed ice and water from the fridge dispenser. When her back is turned, I slip Paul's phone out of my pocket and set it on the seat of the chair next to me. It's pushed in against the table, obscuring the phone from view. She won't see it unless she pulls out the chair or hears it vibrate. I turned it on before I knocked on the door and put it on silent mode. Once the glass is in front of me and I've thanked her, I immediately launch into question mode, skipping right over pleasantries. "I don't really know how to say this so I'm just going to ask, why didn't you tell me I looked like Stacy?"

Her eyes widen. "Who told you that?"

"Reed. He's at my house with my daughter right now."

She nods solemnly. "You do look like her. It's the reason I wasn't very friendly the first day we met. The physical similarities are almost uncanny. Your hair is the same color and length, and your eyes are the same shade of green. Even your nose has the slight lift at the end the same way hers does. Did, I mean." She pauses, clasping her hands together and resting them on her lap. "It was like seeing a ghost."

I squint at her slightly, as though that might give me more insight. I'm sure it was alarming to have someone show up at her house looking exactly like her husband's dead ex-lover, but I still think it's strange that she never told me. Especially since she told me the history between Paul and Stacy. That would've been the perfect time to include how much I look like her.

I give her a minute to add more to her story, but she never does. "Okay, well, as I mentioned, Reed is with Gertie and he's really upset, Madison. He told me you thought he should move back in with his grandma, but don't you think it might help to have him here? The two of you are hurting over the same thing. Shared grief can really bring people together."

She starts shaking her head before I even finish what I'm saying. "No, I can't deal with one more thing right now. I feel bad for Reed, but I have enough on my plate as it is."

I cock my head. "Because of Paul leaving or...is there more?"

She looks off to the side, fixing her gaze on the wall above my shoulder. "What more could there be?"

Her eyelashes are clumped together with dried tears and her eyes are ringed with a deep shade of purple. Her skin looks gaunt and her hair, which is normally sleek and shiny, is matted and wiry. She looks exhausted and utterly devastated. I feel a little guilty for berating her. Maybe she never told me I looked like Stacy because she didn't want to be reminded of it. We were becoming friends, and it's possible she just didn't want to jeopardize that by making me feel awkward. And seeing her in this state, I think sending Reed back to live with his grandma might be for the best.

I reach across the table and rest my hand on her arm. "You're going to be okay, you know?"

She nods, but she doesn't look at me.

"Madison?" Turning her head slowly, her eyes slide to mine. "You're going to be okay. I promise."

She smiles. It's small and almost undetectable, but it's real.

"I spoke to the police today." She tosses out the words like she's telling me she had tomato soup for lunch.

I suck in a breath so fast, I almost choke. "You did?"

"Mm-hmm. After I left your house, I came home and called Paul's mom, Amelia. I wanted to find out if she had heard from him. She hadn't, but with everything that's happened with Reed over the years, their relationship is a little strained so it's not really a surprise. Still, I was worried because even though Paul left me a letter, what if something happened to him?"

When I swallow, it feels like there's broken glass in my throat. "You think something happened to him?"

She shakes her head. "No. I mean, I guess I don't, but I didn't want to take any chances. The officer I spoke to said people usually don't file a missing persons report until at least twenty-four hours has passed and since his truck is gone and I have a note from him explaining that he was leaving, they weren't in any hurry to help me."

I let out a slow exhale. She said Paul's truck was gone; that means she thinks he left in it. I've already ruled out Paul as the one who drove off last night. If it wasn't him and it wasn't Madison, who was it? Could Reed have taken it? Or is there someone else—a mystery person that I don't know? I need more information. "Maybe there are clues in the letter he left. You know, I'm sure you were thorough when you read it, but you were also very emotional. Suppose you missed something? I'd be happy to take a look at it for you."

"There's nothing in that letter that I didn't already know, and if Paul wanted me to find him, I would."

She stands, shoving her chair back so that the legs screech on the linoleum. She grabs my glass of water and strides over to the sink, dumping the entire contents down the drain. I never drank a drop. Her hands splay out on the sink and her back heaves with labored breaths. "For so long, I've never known what to think or how to feel." Her voice is low—so low that I find myself leaning forward just to hear her. "I was always told those things. And you know what happens when someone is dependent on someone else to tell them how to act? All intuition leaves them. They become a hollow void of nothingness, unable to call any shots simply because they can't remember how. That was me. I lived that barren life for way too long. I may not have had the guts to physically leave Paul, but mentally? Mentally I left him a long time ago." She turns to face me, crossing her arms over her chest. "Jeanette, you're an intuitive woman. You can't tell me you didn't notice what was going on." She holds her hands to the sky and twirls in a circle.

I nod, feeling less of a friend than when I first walked in here. "I had my suspicions." I had more than that, but I have no way to explain myself.

"I've spent—no, wasted—way too much of my life trying to figure out what's going on inside of that man's head. And now he has me fretting over him and he left me! He. Left. Me. I have a lot to work though, but I think the first step is letting go of this hold he's had over me." Her eyes are glassy with unshed tears, and when they land on mine, I feel the weight of everything she's been through. "What do you say, Jeanette? Will you help me?"

I smile at her. "Absolutely."

She reaches for the cabinet above her head and pulls out two wineglasses, plunking them onto the kitchen island. She selects a bottle of wine from the back of the fridge and pops the cork, filling both glasses to the brim. When she hands one to me, she gives a small half shrug. "Water isn't the right beverage for this moment. What is it they say? It's five o'clock somewhere!" She giggles and I join her.

Holding up her glass, she declares, "To finding your own way."

"Here, here," I respond. We both clink our glasses and toss back the wine.

"HOLY SHIT, Jeanette! I don't know what's gotten into you, but I hope whatever it is, it's here to stay. That was incredible."

I chuckle softly. "Well, I'm glad you enjoyed yourself."

"Enjoyed myself? Lady, you rocked my fucking world!"

I roll off of Frank and adjust my nightgown, pulling it down until the hem is below my knees. Staring up at the ceiling, I replay the events of the last two days. Paul is composting inside my shed and Madison is free from his abuse. I managed to slay the dragon, but instead of celebrating like a warrior coming back from battle, I'm filled with unrest.

When I left Madison, I was feeling a sense of pride with how she was handling everything. She's still grieving the loss, but she's also fed up with being controlled. I rode that high all the way home, and it lasted through dinner and into the evening. When we came upstairs to get ready for bed, all it took was one look from Frank and I attacked him.

But now, as I lie here in the afterglow, unease is beginning to creep in. I covered a lot of ground today, but I never managed to read the letter Paul left for Madison. She breezed right over my offer to take a look at it and dove into a diatribe on finding independence. I'm happy that she's putting herself first for once. It's exactly the outcome I had hoped for, but…I still want to read what Paul wrote and I also need to figure out who was behind the wheel of his truck last night. I feel like I'm dancing in circles around the truth. It's right here, and yet I don't see it.

Reed took me up on my offer and joined us for dinner tonight. I know he and I got off on the wrong foot, but I'm beginning to think that may have had more to do with me looking like his mom. I made homemade macaroni and cheese for dinner and while we were eating, he mentioned that Stacy wasn't the best cook, but she used to make him mac and cheese out of a box. Even though he smiled when he spoke, there was a hint of sadness in his voice. I asked him a few questions about her, but he couldn't really answer them. He told me she wasn't around very much. She used his grandma's address, but rarely slept there. He and I have more in common than I thought.

Technically, he's still a "person of interest" in the mystery of Paul's missing truck. I can't rule him out completely, but he seems too distraught over his dad leaving to have secretly stolen his truck. It just doesn't make sense. The more I think about it, the more I'm convinced there's another person involved somehow.

Frank folds his arms behind his head like a makeshift pillow. "Listen, I don't want to jinx what happened, but you know it's Wednesday, right?"

Yes, Frank, I'm aware, but you see I killed our neighbor and now I've learned that his truck is missing and he's left mysterious letters in his wake that are causing me to overthink everything. I needed a distraction.

Those thoughts swirl in my head, and I latch on to the last one. "I thought we could both use a break from the monotony." My head lolls on the pillow until I'm facing my husband. There's a mischievous glint in his eye. "I'm going to regret this, aren't I?"

He shrugs. "Depends on how you look at it, I guess. Unexpected surprises can be fun." He hoists himself onto all fours and hovers over me, looking ready to pounce.

"Sometimes." *Other times they're a spoke in the wheel, causing enough of an imbalance to throw your entire plan off its tracks.* As Frank lowers himself onto me, I push all of those thoughts aside. Tomorrow, I'll find Madison's letter and hopefully learn more about who drove off in Paul's truck. For now, I'll embrace the distraction.

Chapter Twenty-Three

ADDING INSULT TO INJURY

I STROLL UP THE FRONT WALKWAY JUST IN TIME TO SEE MADISON pulling the door shut. She lifts the strap up onto her shoulder and turns around, startling slightly when she sees me. "Jeanette! It's so nice to see you. I'm sorry; I'm just on my way out."

Oh, fudge. This doesn't bode well for me getting my hands on that letter. "That's too bad. I made a chocolate sheet cake for dessert last night and I was hoping you and I could sit down with some forks and finish it off."

She giggles and starts walking toward her car. "That sounds amazing, but can I take a rain check? IKEA is having a sale on shelving today and I want to go get some for the house and maybe a new chair for the living room and some plants, too."

My eyebrows lift in surprise. "Wow, it sounds like you're ready to make this house a home. Good for you! I was wondering why you had such little furniture and no decorations. A few new homey touches will be nice."

Her hand freezes on the door handle and she looks back at me over her shoulder. "I guess the place does look pretty barren. I never really noticed it before. Paul was always saying we didn't need 'stuff' to be happy, but now I think it's more that he never wanted to make a home with me. It's easier to leave when there's nothing to lose." Her eyes fall to her feet.

I pat her shoulder. "Hey, where's that fire I saw in you yesterday, huh? I know you're hurting, but it's time to put yourself first. Going furniture shopping is a great start."

She smiles. "You're a good friend. Thanks, Jeanette."

"Anytime." I wink.

She settles into the driver's seat and closes the door behind her. I can't believe I'm going to have to wait even longer to read the letter. I shift the SnapLid cake carrier in my hands and an idea hits me. Leaning over, I knock on the car window. Madison lowers it and peers out. "What's up?"

I smile sheepishly. "So, weird question, but…do you think I could go inside your house and drop this off?" I lift the carrier up in front of me. "It's just, if I take it home with me, Wyatt and his friends will end up eating it and I would really rather share it with you."

She glances at her front door and then back at me. "It's not locked," she whispers. "Go ahead inside. You can set it on the counter. I'll call you when I get home. Maybe we can have a furniture building party."

"It's a deal."

Once her car is out of sight, I waste no time briskly walking toward her front door. She was right. It isn't locked. I'm going to have to talk to her about that. Whispering Woods is safe, but not enough to keep your door unlocked. For now, though, I'm glad for my good fortune.

I can't believe how easy this was. After Madison was so quick to dismiss Paul's letter yesterday, I had assumed I'd have my work cut out for me if I wanted to read it. Instead, I barely have to work at all.

It's a strange feeling to be in someone else's home without them there. You notice things you hadn't before. It's easier to study every detail when you aren't under the watchful eye of the homeowner. For instance, the dust ruffle along the bottom of the living room sofa is torn on the left corner. It's only a slight tear, but it causes the fabric to droop and touch the carpet. It's barely noticeable, but being in here alone with the freedom to look around, it's the first thing I see when I walk into the room. My gaze falls along the back of the sofa and down the arm, settling on the empty end table. The last time I was here, I saw signs of Reed, but not this time. There are no abandoned soda cans. No sneakers by the door.

The living room and dining room are still fairly empty, but Madison is working on fixing that. I'm happy she's feeling comfortable enough to put down some roots here. I like having her around.

I stride into the kitchen and leave the cake on the counter. Now it's time to find the letter. When she was in my garden the other day, Madison said she crumpled it up and shoved it in a drawer. I think she was probably referring to one in her bedroom.

I stroll down the hallway like I own the place. I'm not used to this level of comfort in a house that isn't mine, but I'm not an intruder. Madison invited me in. I'm pushing the limits of that invitation, but relatively speaking, I've done nothing wrong. I'm just a concerned neighbor looking out for her friend.

The sight of Madison's bedroom pulls a sad sigh out of me. It's still the same stark, loveless room. These walls are suffocating me, and I don't even live here.

I give my head a shake, tamping down the emotion that threatens to distract me. This isn't the time for that. I'm alone now, but who knows how long before Madison returns home. And when she does, I shouldn't still be in her house, and I definitely shouldn't be snooping in her bedroom.

I scan the room and move hastily toward the table on Madison's side of the bed. Last time I looked inside, I found a bevy of pens. I tug open the drawer and they're still here, along with the notepad, but it's no longer blank. At first, I'm not sure what it is I'm seeing. It looks like a series of letters written over and over. There's a capital D repeated again and again, each time the style changes slightly. I stare at the handwriting, following the letters al the way down to the last one. I've seen a D just like this before. It was scrawled at the bottom of Reed's note. The only word written in ink. Dad.

My breathing becomes shaky and my heart rate increases. I feel a sheen of sweat begin to build at the base of my neck. Did Madison write Reed's letter? She must have. Why else would she be practicing Paul's handwriting?

I let the notepad fall back into the drawer with a *thunk* and I shove it closed so hard the lamp on the table shakes. I turn my head back and forth, unsure what to do next. If Madison wrote Reed's letter, that would mean Paul had nothing to do with it. Does that mean he never wrote one for her either?

My eyes land on the dresser where I hid the camera. If there is a letter, maybe it's in there, stashed under clothing. I yank open the top drawer and find bras and underwear, all neatly folded and arranged by color. There's a bin inside to help keep everything separated. A few pairs of socks line one side, and I see some nylons along the back still in their package. When I reach underneath them, my fingers catch on something metal. I tug it out and hold it up in front of me. My fingertips graze the embossed letters *GTYIUP*. Paul's license plate. Why does Madison have this? My head feels heavy and there's a pounding behind my ears. In a matter of minutes I've found the answers I was looking for, but now that I have them, I don't know what to do.

"Well, look what you found." I jump at the sound of Madison's voice. She's standing in the doorway, a casual hand resting on her hip.

I hold up the plate so the letters face her. "This is Paul's license plate."

"Uh-huh," she nods.

"What is it doing in your dresser?"

"I'll tell you, but first come with me. This conversation deserves a proper beverage." She strolls down the hallway, never once looking over her shoulder. She seems so at ease. So relaxed.

I trail a few steps behind her, unsure of what exactly is happening. She doesn't appear upset or surprised in any way. It's as if she was expecting me to find the plate, like she was hoping I would.

She traipses into the kitchen and opens the fridge, propping the door with her hip. "Let's see." She drums her fingers on her chin. "Ahh, perfect." She wraps her hand around the neck of a bottle. "How about a rosé?" She's talking like we're just two friends getting ready to spend an afternoon gossiping over wine. An hour ago, that might've been the appropriate scenario, but after my recent discoveries, it feels more like we're strangers. It's as if I'm stumbling over a mountain of obstacles while Madison blows right through the middle with two glasses in one hand and a bottle of wine in the other. "It's so nice outside. Why don't we take this party out onto the deck?"

I don't know about her, but I've never been to a party quite like this. I'm still gripping the license plate in my hands when I follow her onto the deck. We sit opposite each other and Madison fills our glasses. "So," she says with a clap of her hands, "I know you must have a million questions in that pretty little head of yours. Go ahead. Ask away."

I study her for a moment, trying to decipher what kind of game she's playing. I don't know what her angle is. She isn't angry. On the contrary, she seems excited, like it's her birthday and I'm about to give her the present she's always wanted. I decide to start with the obvious. Tapping the metal plate, I say, "Why was this hidden in your dresser drawer?"

"I bet if you think about it, you already know the answer." She eyes me pointedly.

I have an idea, but I wanted her to explain it away. I don't like where my mind is going. "Bob told me he saw Paul drive off in his truck the night he left." I let the words dangle like an ellipsis.

"Hmm." She rests her elbow on the table and cradles her chin in her hand. "Is that so? And he's sure it was Paul that he saw?"

I already know it wasn't Paul. I cringe when I remember how I confirmed that. Bob thought it was him, but it was dark at ten and Bob's also been known to drink a few wine coolers before bed. I considered the possibility that it was Reed, but that didn't seem very likely, either. "It was you."

She touches her index finger to her nose and points at me. "See? I knew you'd figure it out. But the question is, why?"

I shake my head. It's as if I'm trying to solve a math equation with apples and toothpicks. Nothing is adding up.

"Oh, come on, Jeanette! Don't give up that easy! I'll give you a hint. If you want people to *think* your husband left you, you can't very well leave his truck parked in your driveway, now can you?"

Her words cause my stomach to lurch. "I know you wrote Reed's letter. I thought maybe you wrote it because Paul never left one for him and you felt sorry for him. But that's not true, is it? You said he wrote one for you, but that's just what you wanted everyone to believe." I let out a deep sigh. "You made it up."

Her head bobs up and down enthusiastically. She actually looks thrilled to be having this conversation. "Not to brag, but I *was* pretty proud of myself. I thought Reed might question why his dad would type out a letter, but it ended up working out in my favor. It's just one more way his father let him down. And with me being the distraught wife, no one would ever have to see my letter. But you just wouldn't give up." She wags her finger at me.

"Wait a minute, didn't you say the police saw the letter?"

She cocks her head and doesn't say a word.

I close my eyes and exhale. "You never called them."

She clasps her hands on her lap, a broad smile on her face. "Of course, I didn't"

"I don't understand. Why would you want everyone to think Paul left? And if he didn't leave you, then where is he?" There's no way she could know where he is.

She frowns at me. "Come on, Jeanette. This is me you're talking to. You can drop the act." She leans in. "I know everything."

It's like she's trying to get me to slip up. But I don't know how she'd ever suspect me. Unless…did Paul mention me to her? Did he plant the seeds of doubt before I shoved him in my bin? "I'm afraid I'm not following. What is there to know, Madison?"

She leans forward, placing both palms flat on the table. "Let me be abundantly clear. You're a woman who cares deeply for her family. I saw it that day you came over here to talk about Reed. You protect the people you love, and I know how you've managed to do that. Which reminds me. How's your new batch of compost coming along?"

Chapter Twenty-Four

IGNORANCE IS BLISS

You know that moment when you've been caught red-handed? A bullet ridden body is bleeding out on the ground in front of you and you're still gripping the smoking gun. That's exactly how I find myself now. Madison has just outed me, and if I weren't so surprised, I'd congratulate her on the eloquent way she was able to gain the upper hand.

"I can see by the rounded *O* of your mouth that you're a little short on words at the moment, so let me say this. I'm not going to tell anyone. That was never part of my plan."

She stands and begins a slow walk around the deck.

"When we first moved here, I thought it was the fresh start we needed. See, I lied when I said Paul never loved Stacy. I know now that she's the only woman he's ever loved. I think the only reason he and I started dating was because he knew it wouldn't work out with her. The two of them were like a stick of dynamite and a match. Their relationship was always burning hot." She glances at me sideways. "And I don't mean in the bedroom, although from the little I've heard, I've gathered it was pretty explosive." She rolls her eyes. "Anyway, Stacy had a temper and it often led to huge blowup arguments—the kind where the police are called by concerned neighbors. It wasn't a good situation. And for Paul, it took Reed to figure that out. I told you the truth about them. No one would ever think of giving Paul an award for being a good dad. He wasn't even a mediocre one. But he wanted that to change, and that's when he met me. That day at the gas station…it changed my life. He saved me and when I heard about all he had gone through with Stacy, well, I wanted to save him, too."

She sighs, looking out into the expansive backyard. "But you can't save someone who doesn't even know you're there. He would be with me in body, but with her in every other way. I tried so many things to make him notice me, and nothing seemed to work. Then one day, I was cutting up lettuce for our salad and the knife slipped, gauging me in center of my palm." She holds up her left hand and I see a faint, pale scar about a half inch long. "That sure got his attention!" She cackles. "He went overboard, driving me to urgent care and holding my uninjured hand the entire time. I didn't even need stitches. But it got me thinking…if a tiny cut could make Paul react that way, what would he do if I started hurting myself on purpose? So, I tried it out during one of our heart-to-hearts about Stacy. She was always trying to meddle in our lives—texting Paul in the middle of the night, using concern for Reed as a way to manipulate him. Whenever I tried to point it out to him, he always defended her. This particular time, she had called him to say she couldn't find her car keys and she needed him to drive her to work. It was right in the middle of a candlelit dinner that I had made for the two of us and he just stood right up and reached for his keys, hellbent on coming to her aide once again. I was desperate, so I reached for my fork and jabbed it into my forearm. Not super deep, or anything. It barely punctured the skin, but it was enough to make Paul throw down his keys and come rushing over to me. All thoughts of Stacy were gone. He never even called her back to tell her he wasn't coming. She blew up his phone that night, but he put it on silent and never left my side. After that, it became my go-to method." She looks back at me and shrugs. "I know how this sounds. I'm sure you must think I'm pathetic, but love can make you do crazy things. And I loved Paul. I still do."

I'm sitting on a metal chair out here on Madison's deck, but after what she just confessed, I barely register my surroundings. Everything I've done up to this point has been out of concern for her wellbeing and now she's saying the bruises I saw were from her own hand. But wait a minute, I *saw* Paul hit Madison. Didn't I? I close my eyes and rifle through my memory. The video was clear and so was the audio, but it's that moment right before Madison hit the ground that I keep replaying in my mind. Paul was standing in front of her with his back to the camera. The view was blocked and I never saw the actual moment when fist made contact with skin. She was standing and then she wasn't and he immediately crouched down to console her, the same way she just told me he would whenever she would self-harm.

She spins around to face me and lets her hands rest on the wood rail behind her. "I can see the look on your face," she continues. "I know you thought Paul was hurting me. Don't be so hard on yourself. You believed it because I wanted you to. But I'm getting ahead of myself." She holds up her hand. "Let me back up. Before we moved here, I thought my routine was working. I'd get hurt and Paul would come running. I knew it was ridiculous, but I didn't care. And then a few years ago, he didn't come home from work and he wasn't answering his phone. I tried not to panic, but my mind immediately went to Stacy. I told you she was living with his mom for a while, but by this point, she had moved into a little one-bedroom apartment not very far from our condo. So when dinnertime rolled around and I still hadn't heard from him, I got in my car and drove over to her building." She lowers her arms and clenches her fists at her sides. "His fucking truck was parked in the lot. The son of a bitch wasn't even trying to sneak around. I drove across the street and into a space at a Chinese restaurant and I just sat in my car, staring at Stacy's door. About an hour later, he emerged, but it's what happened next that changed everything." She grits her teeth. "Stacy came running out of her door wearing nothing but a silk robe. Paul turned around and she jumped on him, wrapping her bony legs around his waist. She started kissing him and I waited, Jeanette. I waited for him to push her off of him. But it never happened. Instead, he grabbed onto her and kissed her back. My heart broke as I sat behind the wheel of my car—the same car he helped me pump gas into the day we met."

It's an odd feeling to pity someone who lied to you, but that's exactly how I feel right now. I can't reconcile all that Madison has done and yet, I can't feel sorry for Paul, either. He may not have hurt her physically, but he still ruined her. That much is clear. But I still don't know how she found out about my compost bin and the way she spoke about it, leads me to believe she knows Paul is in there right now. I have so many questions, but I don't think I'm going to have to ask a single one. She's on a roll and showing no signs of stopping.

"Something snapped inside of me that night. It didn't matter that I was his wife; it was obvious to me that he would always choose her. So, I did what I had to do. I eliminated the problem."

My eyes widen at her casual confession. "I thought you said Stacy died in a car accident?"

"She did, only it wasn't quite an accident. See, my dad was a mechanic. I used to hang around his shop when he'd be working on cars and I learned a thing or two. As it turns out, it's not the easiest to compromise a car's brakes, but if you plant a bug in the electrical connection, it can work in your favor. So that's what I did and, well, you know the rest of that story."

I must be in shock because I can't form any coherent thoughts. My mind is swirling with all of this information and I don't know what to do with it. Madison killed Stacy. If I consider my code, I can't really blame her. After all, Stacy was a threat to her and Paul's happiness. She didn't have a choice. But didn't she get what she wanted after that? It doesn't make sense for her to have done everything she could to hold on to Paul only to let him go. What am I missing?

"After Stacy died, Paul changed. He was angry and dismissive, and he drank a lot. I hoped I could give up my side gig of hurting myself, but it was still the only thing that managed to get his attention. And then Reed had that incident at his school, and suddenly Paul wanted to be this unsung hero for his son. He said we needed to move so Reed could use our address. He didn't mention anything about Reed actually staying with us, so I went along with the idea. As you know, Reed and I are not close, but when Paul started talking about us buying a house, I saw it as a new beginning. Our old condo came furnished so when we moved, we had to start over, but I was so excited about that. I mean, how perfect was it that we could fill this home with whatever we wanted and finally make a life for ourselves?" She sighs. "And then I met you and that's when I knew I was holding onto a dream that would never come true."

My face scrunches. "Why, because I looked like Stacy?"

"Yes! That's exactly why!" She stomps her foot and I lean back in my chair. "That day, when you knocked on my door, I couldn't believe it. What are the fucking chances that I would get rid of Stacy and then move to a new town where I lived two doors down from her look alike? I mean, someone must really hate me to sabotage my life like this."

"But, Madison, I'm not her." I press my hand to my sternum. "I'm married. Happily. I'm not a threat."

She shakes her head. "I can see how you'd think that. But unfortunately, just because you didn't act the part didn't make you any less of a threat. I wanted to hate you. I tried, but you made it impossible. You were so nice and helpful and I thought, maybe I was overreacting because like you said, you weren't Stacy. So I decided you would be the ultimate test. Once Paul met you, I would watch his reaction and then I would know for sure if we had survived the worst." Her eyes cast down and her throat bobs with a slow swallow. "I don't have to tell you what happened next. You were there. But Jeanette, when I saw the way he looked at you, that was it for me. I was done. Maybe he didn't control me the way I let you think he did, but he still controlled my emotions with his disinterest. I was never enough for him and I was blind to it. But that day in my kitchen, when he found you in our house, my eyes were finally wide open. It was as if he thought I brought you to him as a gift." She groans in disgust. "He didn't even bother to hide his attraction, either. In fact, he flaunted it. You're all he talked about. He was obsessed with you. So I started thinking about how I could get out of this. And before you even suggest it, I'm just gonna say, leaving him was not an option. Because even though I was done with this, I would never be done with him. Either he was with me or he was with no one. It was all or nothing." She's gesticulating wildly, marching around in circles as she describes the way she formulated her plan. "I didn't know what to do at first, but I noticed you were very attentive to my bruises so I used them to my advantage. I needed an ally and what better person to be that for me than the one who started the ball rolling in the first place. And when you hid that camera in my bedroom, I knew you were more than just a concerned friend."

I suck in a breath. "You *knew* about that?"

She nods, a triumphant smile on her face. "The old lady who lived here before us had security cameras installed all over the house. She wanted extra protection because she lived alone. We talked about removing them after we bought the place, but never got around to it. You were gone so long looking for your ring that day; I was curious. After I watched the footage, I erased it and then that night, I made sure to give the performance of a lifetime. Paul and I were arguing about you so it wasn't very hard."

I rest my forehead on my palm. "I never knew Mrs. Heart had cameras."

She chuckles. "Well, that's pretty obvious. And then you gave me that tour of your garden and I knew I was right to keep you in my corner."

What is she talking about? "I was just trying to show you how peaceful it is to grow something of your own. What more could you have possibly taken from that?"

"Oh, Jeanette, who needs a stainless steel bin that large if they're just composting banana peels? As soon as I saw it, I knew there was way more to it than just regular compost. When I got home, I hopped on Google and a couple of clicks later I was reading about a place in Washington that composts people instead of burying or cremating them. Your bin looks eerily similar to the ones they use. And then I started thinking about that man who disappeared around the time we first moved here. No one seems to know where he is. It got me thinking, maybe there was some connection, but you're good at covering your tracks." She shakes her head, a sly smile playing on her lips. "You know, Bob next door is quite a talker. I met him not long after we moved here, and he managed to cover a lot of ground in one conversation. He mentioned you; said you had lived here for five years and before that you lived somewhere called Littleton. It was one of those random facts that just stuck in my head. You know how that can happen? A seemingly small detail just stays lodged in your mind and you wish you could just let it go because when are you ever going to need it? But this one time, it came in handy. I looked up your name and that town. And it turns out, you were pretty active there. You ran a neighborhood gardening club and from there, I was able to learn your former address. You probably shouldn't include personal details like that on PDF fliers, you know? Everything online is permanent." She eyes me with something resembling concern. "Funny thing, not too long before you moved, some guy named Ty Westing went missing. The article I found said that he was believed to have relocated to Thailand, but no matter how hard I searched online, I couldn't find any more information on Ty." She taps her index finger on her chin. "It was like a game of connect the dots. Ty goes missing and Henry goes missing and the one thing linking the two is you. You and your garden."

I don't bother denying anything. There's no use. "You were so sure you knew what I'd do if I thought Paul was hurting you. But what if you were wrong about me?"

She nods. "I considered that and I decided to take my chances. I'd let you believe he was abusive, and I wouldn't stand in his way when he made a move on you. I hoped you would take care of him so I wouldn't have to, but the truth of the matter is, I wanted him gone and if I was wrong and you weren't who I thought you were, I would've done it myself. It was just less messy this way."

"Hmm," I muse. There's so much to digest. "But you got rid of Paul's truck that night and showed up at my house early the next morning all distraught about the letter. How did you know I went through with it?"

"Well, let's just say you're not the only one who's good at sneaking around." She giggles. "After Paul left, I waited for a bit and then went out for a little walk. I carried your empty container like I was on my way to return it, and when I reached the gate, I peeked in through the holes at the top and saw Paul follow you into the shed. Call it intuition, but I just knew you wouldn't let him get out of there alive. Then I pretended to get a phone call, in case anyone was watching, and I walked back to my house acting like the person on the other line needed me for something." She grins wide. "I was so proud of myself for the way I played it off."

I bite at my lip. This is the oddest conversation I've ever had. Madison has figured everything out, but she isn't behaving like a threat. I'm not sure what my next move is. "So, what now?"

She smiles warmly. "Now, we just sit back and enjoy the fruits of our labor. Or should I say, vegetables?" She laughs. "Which reminds me, I was thinking maybe you could help me finally start my garden. The compost will be ready in a few weeks. If it's okay with you, I'd like to use some."

Can it really be this easy? She's talking about gardening and using my compost, like it isn't the remains of her husband. I give my head a shake. "This is a lot to digest. I think I need a minute."

"Of course." She nods. "I unloaded a lot on you. It's only natural that you need some time, but Jeanette, just think about how great this could be. You and I are so much alike. We've been keeping secrets and that gets exhausting, but we wouldn't have to do that with each other. It's all out in the open. When we're together, we could just be who we are. Think about how freeing that would be."

She's not wrong. It would be nice to have someone in my corner. Someone I wouldn't have to pretend around. She knows the worst about me and she isn't running away. I stand and walk over to stand next to her. I stare out into her yard and point at the upper right corner. "Still thinking about that spot for your garden?"

She grins. "Mm-hmm. It's perfect." She claps her hands together. "Ooh, this is gonna be fun! So, we should probably put our heads together and decide how we're going to take care of Reed."

My arms break out in goose bumps. "What do you mean, take care of Reed?"

"Jeanette, he's a loose end. We can't have that."

I shake my head. "No, Reed's okay. He's just a kid who's been dealt a rough hand, but he's living with his grandma and working through his issues. He won't be a problem."

"Oh, come on." She scoffs. "You can't honestly believe that."

I turn to face her, crossing my arms in front of me. "I do, and there's no reason you shouldn't either."

She rolls her eyes. "So this is how it's gonna be? I know I encouraged you to be okay with Reed hanging around Gertie, but that was only so you would see how wrong he is for her. I was just trying to force your hand. And now you've gone and developed some kind of soft spot for him. Well, I guess if I want something done, I'll have to do it myself. But make no mistake, your daughter has gotten pretty cozy with Reed and if she gets caught up in the crossfire, well, don't say I didn't warn you."

My blood turns to stone. "Is that a threat?"

"No, it's not a threat, per se. I'm just stating the obvious."

I push off of the rail and feel it bend from the force. "This was a mistake."

"Ha! The only mistake here is you suddenly gaining a conscience."

I sulk toward her. "This has nothing to do with my conscience. I have a code and I intend to follow it. Reed is not a problem. He's not causing harm to anyone I love. He's just trying to find his own way in life. No thanks to his father or to you, for that matter."

"Oh, Jeanette," she tsks. "I think I gave you the wrong impression here. I don't really care at all about your code. It doesn't matter how you justify what you do. You're a murderer. You *are* aware of that, right?" She rests a hand on her hip. "And what would happen if, say, Frank became aware of it, too? Or your kids? How would they react if they knew their dear mommy was turning their neighbors into compost?"

She's beyond reason. My mind races to try to form a plan. She said Reed was a loose end, but he isn't. She is. And now she's tossing out threats like they're hand grenades.

She blows out an exasperated breath. "And here I thought you were strong. Wow, did I ever misjudge you. You're so weak you'd probably blow over if the wind hit you just right." She tosses her head back and laughs.

My father laughed at me like that once. It was the last sound he made before his heart gave out. Sure, I didn't cause the heart attack, but I knew he was in danger of having one and I still didn't back down. Not long after my mother killed herself, I confronted him. I told him I was through listening to his rules. Just like Madison, he called me weak, and just like her, he was wrong. I wanted to see him cower like a frightened animal and when he finally clutched his hand to his chest, I saw the terror in his eyes when he realized how wrong he'd been about me. Dead wrong.

I know it's Madison in front of me, but when I narrow my eyes, I see my father. I take a step forward, and she steps back. "Did you really expect me to just go along with you?" Another step. "You underestimated me." Another step. "I follow my rules and *only* mine." Another step. "I have no use for you." This is the part where my father clutched his heart, but it doesn't happen now. I squint, and he morphs before my eyes. Madison is back. Her mouth rounds in terror. Her eyes are impossibly wide. With my last step forward, she retreats until her back pushes against the rail. I can hear the popping and splitting as the wood strains behind her. There are several feet between us, but she's behaving as if I'm right up against her. I leer at her, and it's just enough to send her body back with a jolt. The board snaps. Her arms flap wildly as she tries to stop the momentum, but it's no use. She loses her footing, tumbling off the deck. I know the moment she hits the ground. There's a *thud* that comes when her body makes contact with the earth. It sounds heavy, like an unabridged dictionary dropping onto a table in a quiet library. I can feel the sound from the inside, out. I hesitate for a second, afraid to look over the edge. I'm not sure if the fear is that I'll find her dead or alive.

I inch my way forward until I'm standing in front of the spot where a wooden beam once was. Splintered wood litters the deck at my feet. I place a hand on the fractured board, but then I think better of it. At best, I'll get another splinter. At worst, I'll join Madison on the ground below. I crouch down and gradually lean forward until I'm peering down at the yard. Madison's body lies sprawled out on the grass. Her right arm is extended above her head and her left is draped loosely at her waist. Her legs are splayed out in front of her like she's simply resting. And maybe if she had just fallen on grass, she *would* be resting; blacked out from the fall, but still alive. Only that's not what happened. Below the Munch's deck, there are cement pavers that form a little walkway leading up to the walkout basement door. Madison's head managed to land smack in the middle of one. Her neck is bent at an unnatural angle and her wide eyes are unwavering. Blood begins to pool from the back of her head. It slowly coats the paver and begins spilling out over the side where it seeps into the soil.

I slide back onto my bottom and sit in stillness, waiting for my breathing to even out. I just killed my only friend. She gave me no choice, but that thought does little to fill the void I feel deep in my chest. I didn't want it to end this way. But this is what I get for blurring the edges of my cardinal rule. I cared for Madison too much, too fast. I won't make that mistake again.

With my eyes fixed on her, I reach into my pocket and pull out my phone.

"Nine-one-one. What's your emergency?"

I clear my throat. "There's been an accident."

Chapter Twenty-Five

A TASTE OF YOUR OWN MEDICINE

Three and a half weeks later

I GIVE THE CRANK A FINAL TURN AND LEAN IN CLOSE. "NOT much longer now, Paul." I thought I'd feel more excited to be so close to having a new batch of compost. It's how I felt when I first loaded Paul's body inside the bin. But now, after so much has happened, I just want to get it over with.

It's been a hectic few weeks in Whispering Woods. Everyone was so shocked when Madison fell to her death, but no one was more shocked than me. At least, that's what I had them believe. She and I were friends enjoying a glass of wine on her deck. Imagine my surprise when she leaned back on a board that was too old to withstand the pressure. I tried to get to her in time, but it was no use. I've been drowning in casseroles and flower deliveries from concerned neighbors ever since.

Paul's name has come up several times. The police have been trying to reach him, but since he left his phone at his house, they've come up empty-handed. Reed's letter wasn't much help either and when they asked about Madison's, I told them she said it made her too upset so she tore it up and threw it away. They still haven't been able to locate Paul's truck, either. Madison never told me what she did with it, but I have no doubt it'll never be found. And as far as the license plate goes, I slipped it inside the dish with the cake before the police arrived. In all the excitement, no one even noticed me leaving with it. I later used Frank's handheld torch to disfigure it, making it completely illegible. It's important to me to keep up the narrative that Paul willingly left Madison. If she would suddenly become a suspect of foul play, it would create a huge mess that I don't care to deal with. It's better this way.

The house is still vacant, but if they can't find Paul soon, then the mortgage will foreclose. It's just as well. It'll be nice to have new neighbors again.

When I stroll into the kitchen, I find Wyatt at the stove. He's tearing open a packet of cheese powder and dumping it onto buttered noodles. We've been spending more time together lately. Tonight he told me he wanted to make dinner. He said, "I think it's time you take a break, Mom. You do enough around here." No joke, I nearly fainted. It feels good to be appreciated. I'm not sure I deserve it, but I also won't argue.

"Smells good in here!" I call out. Wyatt looks over his shoulder, smiling sheepishly. The hair that usually falls in front of his eyes is gone, recently shorn and neatly styled. It's on the tip of my tongue to compliment his haircut, but I keep it to myself. "You keep stirring. I'll go get the table ready." He has plates and silverware stacked on the island. Instead of my fine china, he's chosen paper plates. I hesitate for a second, feeling a momentary urge to replace them with my good dishes. But then, I look over at my son standing at the stove preparing dinner. It's a sight I never thought I would see. He's in charge of food tonight so if he feels like paper over china is a better choice, then who am I to argue? I scoop them up and push through the bi-swing door.

As I dole out a plate and silverware to each place setting, I think about the small, sad table in Madison's dining room. Even when we've had our differences, this table has always been filled with love. I doubt that's ever been the case at the Munch's. And now it sits alone in an empty house.

As I lay out the last napkin, I hear the *ding dong* of the doorbell. That must be Reed. He's still living with his grandma, but he's been joining us for dinner at least once a week. I've been keeping an eye on him; not because I don't trust him. Aside from being leery of any boy dating my daughter, I've let go of the reservations I had about Reed. I feel more of a kinship with him now. We have a lot in common and I've come to see him as part of our family. It's important to me that he's safe, and with Madison gone, I think he finally is.

I breeze out of the dining room toward the foyer, but Gertie has already beaten me to it. She greets Reed with a kiss, but he notices me and graciously keeps it PG rated. They walk hand in hand with Gertie tugging Reed up the stairs. "Dinner will be ready soon, you too."

My daughter gives me a toothy grin. "We'll be right down."

I know she's going up there to give him a proper hello. I should probably put a stop to it, but eh, how much can they really accomplish in a couple of minutes? As if on cue, Frank sidles up behind me, draping his arms around my waist and pulling my back to his front. "There's my girl," he murmurs in my ear.

I lean back against him, inhaling the woodsy scent of his aftershave. "Did you just come from the kitchen?"

"Mm-hmm." I feel his chin brush against my shoulder as he nods.

"How's it looking? Is Wyatt almost ready?"

He pulls back slightly and tilts his head to look down at me. "Almost, but tell me. How in the world did you convince him to make dinner? He can't even be convinced to clean the toothpaste out of the sink after he brushes his teeth."

"Elementary, my dear husband." I chuckle, recalling Wyatt saying the same to me not so long ago.

His chest vibrates with laughter and he releases me, only to spin me around so that I'm facing him. "Have you seen Gertie? She should probably help her brother carry everything to the table." He glides the back of his hand down the side of my face.

I catch his hand in mine, holding it still on my cheek. "She just ran upstairs with Reed?"

"Wait, Reed's here?"

"Yep. He just arrived right before you found me."

He glances over my shoulder at the staircase and his forehead wrinkles. "And they're upstairs right now in Gertie's room, alone?" When I nod, he adds, "Do you think that's a good idea?"

His fatherly need to protect his daughter warms my heart. I smile at him. "Frank, it's only a few minutes."

"How many minutes?"

I glance down at my watch and shrug. "I don't know. Maybe seven or eight?"

He rests his hands on my shoulders like he's trying to hold me steady. Or maybe he's trying to keep himself from falling over. "Jeanette," he whisper-yells. "A lot can happen in seven minutes. Remember the other night? You and me? In the closet?" My face flushes with the memory and he clocks it. "And that was only six minutes."

I shake my head, but maybe he's right. I should probably call Gertie back downstairs while there's still time. It's at that moment I hear the bottom stair creak as she and Reed walk up behind Frank.

I grin, feeling a little relieved to see them. "There you are. I was just about to come get you. Do you think you could help your brother finish making dinner?"

Gertie nods. "Sure, we can do that." Frank and I watch them push through the door into the kitchen, giving each other a side-eye glance when they're out of sight.

"I guess we should probably set some ground rules, especially if that boy continues spending so much time here."

I brush my hands down the front of his T-shirt. "Yes, I suppose we should, but why don't we wait until after dinner. I don't want to do anything to spoil this momentous occasion. I mean, Wyatt *cooked* dinner!"

An incredulous expression fills his face. "Do you think it's going to snow tonight?"

I giggle. "Frank, it's June."

"Yes, I know, but honey, Wyatt made dinner. *Wyatt.*"

I give his arm a playful smack. "You're the worst. Go sit down."

We take our seats and within a few minutes, Gertie and Reed emerge carrying salad and a basket of bread. They set everything on the table and sit down. I look at the two of them and then back at the door. "Where's Wyatt?"

"Oh, he's busy preparing his grand entrance." She rolls her eyes and bites at her lip to hold back a smile.

Just then, the door flings open and Wyatt bursts out. The opening notes of Beyoncé's "Crazy in Love" blare from his back pocket where he's stashed his phone. He holds the edges of a silver bowl filled to the brim with macaroni and cheese and dances around the table. Just as Beyoncé gets to the "Oh-oh, oh-oh" part of the song, he pretends to set it down between Reed and Gertie only to lift it up again. He sashays over to Frank and sets it in front of him, but nope. He picks it up and then his eyes find mine. We're all in hysterics at the spectacle he's making. He zigzags his neck back and forth as he dances his way toward me and then he sets the bowl right in front of me. I assume he's only going to lift it up again, but he doesn't. Instead, he reaches his hand into his back pocket and silences the music. He looks down at me and smiles. "Tonight, you get to go first, Mom."

My eyes well up at his incredible gesture. I grab his arm and give it a squeeze. "Thank you," I whisper. He nods and takes a seat next to me.

Dinner is perfect. I'm surrounded by everyone I care about and all of the threats are gone. It feels like everything is exactly as it should be.

Conversation ebbs and flows as we share bits and pieces about our day. Summer break is in full swing so most of the kids' stories involve the community pool. Frank is excited about a new allergy medication and as for me, well, it's peak garden season so my days are all pretty exciting.

"Oh, Mrs. Singleton," Reed calls from my right. "I saw Mr. Stuart outside earlier when I was walking up the front path."

"Yes." I nod. "He's been working pretty hard on his yard this year."

Reed laughs. "He was working on that shrub again. You know, the one by his walkway? He told me he's trying to make it look like a swan. It's like he thinks he's Edward Scissorhands or something. It looks more like a blob with a beak, if you ask me."

I chuckle. "I guess it's good he's trying, at least."

"That's true." He nods. "So, listen, he wanted to know if I had heard from my dad and I said no. Then he asked if I ever talked to you about it."

My arms erupt in goose bumps and I fight to suppress a shiver. "Talk to me about your dad?"

"Well, that's the thing. At first I thought he meant I should talk to you for like, you know, moral support, or something. But then he said he thought my dad stopped over here a few days before he left and maybe you might know something." He studies me for a moment and then shakes his head. "It's weird, right? I mean, I told him you would've told me if you knew something."

My mind races to play catch up. I glance around the table, but Gertie and Wyatt are ribbing Frank for the way he says "GIF." They aren't listening to Reed and my conversation.

I lean in toward him, keeping my voice low, not enough to arouse suspicion but enough that the rest of my family won't overhear what I'm saying. "Yes, I definitely would. Bob is right; your dad was here, but that was just to take a look at the roof on my shed where I had a leak. I'm afraid he didn't say much of anything, except that I might need a few shingles replaced." I give him a sad smile and lift my shoulder in a half shrug.

He nods, looking a little disappointed. "That's what I thought. It's fine. It's not like I want to find him, anyway."

"Reed, I know what it's like to mourn a relationship you never really had. Everything you're feeling is completely normal. And I know we're not your family by nature, but we can be your family by choice." I pat his forearm.

He smiles warmly. "Thanks."

"What are you two talking about over there?" Gertie asks.

"I was just telling Reed that nothing is more important than family. And if you don't like the one you're given, well then you can go out and find a new one. Isn't that right, Reed?" I wink.

"Well, I'll drink to that!" Frank raises his cup of ice water and we all clink our glasses.

The conversation morphs into other topics, and I sit back like a spectator watching from the sidelines. To look at me, you'd think I was relaxed and enjoying a fun family dinner, but behind my eyes a storm is brewing.

What exactly was Bob trying to prove by planting seeds of doubt in Reed's mind? It sounds like he was trying to catch me in a lie, but he should know, a fly will never trap a spider. It's always the other way around.

It's time I paid Bob another visit. I think it's going to be a good summer for compost.

Afterword

The idea for this book popped into my head one night when I was having trouble falling asleep. The main character presented herself and demanded to be given real estate inside my brain. She would not be ignored. I *had* to tell her story. And the timing couldn't be more perfect since we had just entered the beginning of quarantine. Writing this book saved my sanity these past few months and gave me something to look forward to.

When I really started delving into the subject matter, I wondered if it was even possible to compost a human body. A quick Google search confirmed that it most definitely is and it's actually a viable way in which a person can honor a deceased loved one in a highly sustainable way. I found the entire process fascinating. If you'd like to read more about it, visit Recompose online.

Acknowledgments

Adam—You are an endless stream of support and I am eternally grateful.

Stella & Jasper—I wrote this entire book while the two of you were home. Thank you for gifting me with time.

Angela—You got a dedication. What more do you want from me? Haha! Thank you for pushing me to write this book and for helping me get all of the gardening stuff just right. This book had your name all over it the minute I had the idea.

Marissa—Thank you for *always* saying exactly what I need to hear at the exact moment I need to hear it. I am so lucky to have you in my corner.

Traci—This book completely transformed thanks to your incredible insight.

Marla—Thank you for getting through this so quickly and for helping me spot the mistakes when my eyes were too bleary to notice

Murphy—You're amazing. That is all.

My family, friends, fellow authors, bloggers, & readers—Thank you is not enough, but I'll say it anyway. I am so in awe of the support I receive. I feel unworthy and I will never take it for granted.

About the Author

Layne Deemer aims to push boundaries with her writing. Her stories deconstruct the ordinary until it becomes something else entirely.

She has a degree in Communications with a minor in English and has worked in the fields of public relations, marketing, and advertising, but writing has always been her true passion. When she isn't writing, she's reading. Her wish list of books will take her a lifetime to get through.

She resides in Pennsylvania with her husband, Adam, their two kids, Stella and Jasper, and their bulldog, Archie.

Other Books by Layne:
Frayed
Life Forgotten

Printed in the USA
CPSIA information can be obtained
at www.ICGtesting.com
LVHW041914060424
776630LV00006B/709

9 781088 149942